CRITICS. PRAISE COLBY HODGE!

TWIST

"Hodge's latest is a whip-smart rollercoaster ride with a tortured hero and a kick-ass heroine I loved and a unique world you won't soon forget. I couldn't put it down."

—Bestselling author Susan Squires

"Fast-paced, gripping, haunting and sexy, Colby Hodge rocks your world with *Twist*. It's a story of choices, it's a story of no-way-out except the one thing you don't want to do, but must. And it's a story of the redemptive power of love. It's one terrific read."

—RITA award-winning author Linnea Sinclair

"A heroine with a black belt in danger! *Twist* rockets its way through enough twists and turns to satisfy any fan of action-adventure romance. Romantic thrills, sexy chills, and a fascinating new take on the paranormal genre!"

—*USA Today* bestselling author Alyssa Day

STAR SHADOWS

"The action is intense and fans will thrill as pieces continue to fall into place."

—*RT BOOKreviews*

Star Shadows "casts a fabulous spell over the reader."

—Fresh Fiction

SHOOTING STAR

"This action-packed story picks up after the events of Hodge's previous novel, *Stargazer*...Hodge is definitely on a roll, and it is a great pleasure to revisit her thrilling world. Entertainment galore!"

—*RT BOOKreviews*

"*Shooting Star* is an exciting tale featuring high-tech adventure and showcasing a fun side with the author's humor...Ms. Hodge has created an exciting new world of good and evil with characters I want to hear more about."

—Romance Reviews Today

W9-COI-916

THE TOUCH OF DOCTOR MAD

"Physical comfort is a precious thing," he said. "You're the first person to give it to me in one hundred years."

I didn't know what to say. I'd only done what I'd wanted, gave him what I felt he needed. I'd offered comfort. It was the most natural thing in the world.

"Abbey…" His voice trailed off as his hands freed themselves from my shirt and his fingers caressed my back. I felt that touch down to my core. Heat coiled inside me. It bubbled and twisted and spread from the center of my body to follow the trail of his hand, which moved gently up my spine.

"Abbey," he said again. I turned toward him as he lifted his head from my shoulder.

"Abbey," he whispered as I looked into his eyes.

They were blue. Very blue. For a moment I'd been afraid they'd be glowing with red fire. Instead, I saw something more dangerous. Dangerous, yet so very very tempting.

Our lips met. The heat that came with his touch exploded with his kiss. I wanted to feel him, to touch him, but I was afraid that when we touched I would ignite and burn like a supernova.

There were worse ways to go.

Other *Love Spell* books by Colby Hodge:

STAR SHADOWS
SHOOTING STAR
STARGAZER

COLBY HODGE

TWIST

LOVE SPELL NEW YORK CITY

LOVE SPELL®

February 2008

Published by

Dorchester Publishing Co., Inc.
200 Madison Avenue
New York, NY 10016

ISBN 10: 0-505-52748-0
ISBN 13: 978-0-505-52748-6

The name "Love Spell" and its logo are trademarks of Dorchester Publishing Co., Inc.

Printed in the United States of America.

10 9 8 7 6 5 4 3 2 1

Visit us on the web at www.dorchesterpub.com.

TWIST

TWIST

PROLOGUE

Would I make it?

My feet pounded on the pavement, splashing through the puddles that remained from last night's rain. Was it just last night that it rained? It seemed as if years had passed. They *had* passed. Still, the things they held were yet to occur.

Think about it later. Just run.

I had to get there on time. I just had to. I refused to think about what I'd do if I didn't.

My hand tightened on the hilt of my katana as I ran. The scabbard was laced against my thigh. I didn't even feel it; it had become so much a part of me in the time just past.

When I started martial arts training, I'd never even considered the possibility that I would use the weapons to actually kill anyone. It turned out to be one of those funny twists of fate. It was just something that happened.

My original life plan was to be an architect. Just like my dad. But in another one of those funny life twists he was killed in a freak accident. The last words he spoke to me were, "We've got all the time in the world." Then he stepped off the curb and got hit by a speeding car.

Like I said: funny twists of fate. And here I was, caught up in another.

One more block. Luckily I was used to running. I ran every morning with my dog, Charlie—or used to. Lately my running consisted of "for my life" instead of exercise. How many mornings had it been since we ran? Two, as far as Charlie was concerned. More for me.

Don't think about it.

I saw the lights from Java Joe's up ahead.

Shane had told me it happened when he left. When he got tired of waiting for me. How long had he waited?

The door opened, and my heart skipped a beat as the light bounced off golden blond hair and he stuck his hands in his pockets and moved down the sidewalk.

"Shane!" I yelled as I tried to run faster. She would be waiting for him, just past the coffee shop in the alleyway.

He didn't hear me. He kept walking, and then he disappeared. He was in the alley. Shane had told me it happened in the alley. I gripped the katana in both hands as I reached Joe's and raced on by. When I reached the alley I skidded to a stop.

"Hey, Lucy," I called out. My heart pounded wildly in my chest; I took a deep breath and willed it into submission. If I made a wrong move, Shane would be lost to me forever.

Lucinda turned. Her bright red hair settled on her shoulders, and she looked down her aristocratic nose at me. Behind her Shane stood as if hypnotized, his bright blue eyes staring off into the night as if he were waiting for something. If he only knew what fate this woman planned for him.

"How do you . . . ?" Lucinda stopped suddenly, and looked me over appraisingly. "You know," she said. "You did it. You opened the gate."

"I did," I said. I held the katana firmly in my right hand and stood balanced on the soles of my feet, my legs slightly apart. Ready . . . waiting . . . willing to do whatever was needed.

"I think I'll keep him anyway," she said with a flip of her hair. "It will be fun to watch him fight his nature."

"He's *mine*," I said. "You told me yourself. He will always be mine, no matter what you do to him."

"How about if I kill him?" she said.

I twisted the blade of my katana so that light from the streetlamp was reflected into Lucy's face. It also must have awakened Shane from whatever trance she'd put him in; he blinked and looked over Lucinda's shoulder at me.

"What's going on?" he asked. "What are you doing?" He looked in shock at the katana, which was so much a part of me now that I barely noticed I was holding it.

"Lucy and I have some unfinished business," I said.

"You told me you didn't know her," Shane said accusingly. My heart lurched at his tone, at the strangeness he felt around me. I would fix that. I had to fix that, or I might as well have stayed where I was.

"Oh, Lucy and I go way back," I said. "Don't we?"

"Do we?" she asked.

"About a hundred years, give or take a few."

"I'm out of here," Shane said.

He took a step and Lucinda slammed him against the wall. With one hand closed around his throat, she lifted him in the air so that his feet dangled over the ground. She kept her eyes on me; even when Shane grabbed her wrist and kicked her in the side, she barely flinched.

"Put him down, Lucy," I said.

"Make me," she replied.

I looked at Shane, whose face was full of confusion.

He was desperately gasping for breath. I had to make sure he stayed. If he ran I would lose him forever. So I said the only thing that made any sense at all in the madness that my life had become.

"Ninjas are way cooler than pirates."

ONE

The night before

"Canceled due to flooding." I looked at the sign on the door of my American Karate class and then peered through the bars that protected the storefront from break-ins to see if anyone was inside. The lights from the street reflected off a huge puddle on the floor and I caught the shimmering reflection of the ceremonial sword collection that hung on the wall. What I really wanted was to punch my fist through the door. Why hadn't someone called me? I was supposed to test for my black belt this Saturday. I needed to practice. More than anything, I hated wasting my time. I had my days scheduled down to the minute.

I pulled my cell phone from my pocket so I could rant at Master Thomas for making me come out in the pouring rain for no reason, and quickly realized why no one had called me. My battery was dead and I'd totally forgotten to pick up a new charger since my old one had been accidentally cut in two.

Okay, so my totally bad day was turning into a totally sucky evening. But I refused to give in. I'd make good use of my time. I had a project at home just waiting for me and I could get a new charger in the morning. It's not like I was expecting any calls.

I pulled my dad's old baseball cap down over my eyes and started down the rainswept sidewalk toward Java Joe's. My shoes were soon soaked, though I navigated around all the puddles, and so was I. I positively steamed when I finally made it to the coffee shop and staggered inside, my backpack streaming water.

"Abbey!" the owner said as I wrung the moisture out of my ponytail. "Nice night for a walk?"

"Yeah, Joe," I said. "Right." I grabbed a napkin and wiped the water from my face while he grinned at me. He was gloating. He lived right over the shop; I still had two blocks to go before I got to my place.

"So, how was your day?" he asked as he fixed my usual apple chai.

"Like the weather," I replied. "It sucked."

"Come on, it couldn't have been *that* bad," he pushed. "What happened?"

"What didn't happen?" I said. The chai felt nice and warm in my hands, and I took a moment to inhale the aroma before I took a drink. "Remember the project I was working on for my design class?"

"Contemporary Cottage?"

"Yeah. My drawings got soaked this morning. The end came off my tube and they fell out when I was getting on the El."

"Ouch."

"Then the bank called and said the title search they did on the property somehow didn't mesh, and now they're *doubtful*"—I held my hands up and made quotes when I said it—"about financing the property. It's weird because everything was cool when I signed the papers but suddenly they're backtracking on me."

"But you've already been there a month," Joe said.

"Exactly," I agreed. "I've already sunk a fortune into the place. If the bank withdraws the loan I'm screwed. I've maxed out my credit card waiting on them to get their ducks in a row. If they take back this loan my credit will be ruined forever, along with my life."

Banks aren't happy about giving loans to college students. They think we're bad risks. Luckily, my dad left a small insurance policy in my name, something his second wife was unable to get her greasy paws on, and I'd kept it back for collateral.

"Maybe it's the ghosts trying to get rid of you," Joe suggested. A couple dashed inside from the rain, and he turned to serve them.

"Yeah," I muttered. "If only." I took another sip of my chai while Joe finished.

Screwed. That just about covered it. I'd had my eye on this place for over three years. It had taken me three flips to finally be able to afford it. I just knew that the place had great potential, and the fact that it had sat empty for more than fifty years didn't bother me. For some strange reason I was drawn to the house, like we were meant to be together. The bank had to come through; they just had to. Who knew if I'd ever get this chance again? Whoever it was who'd suddenly turned up with some old claim on the property had had plenty of time to claim it before I came along.

I flip houses to pay my tuition. It's kind of risky, but I love it. I find a place that needs some love and attention, put lots of sweat equity into it and then sell for a profit. As long as the place has a sound structure, or "good bones" as I call it, I'm willing to take the chance.

The house I was currently working on had quite a reputation in the historical neighborhood where I found most of my potential flips. I didn't care that it was supposedly inhabited by ghosts. The ghosts were welcome to stay, especially if they wanted to help me hang drywall.

No, I didn't care about the problems. All I cared about was that it could turn a huge profit, even if it did take a lot of work and was "special." I didn't have time to form attachments to anyplace. I had to keep moving, keep flipping, and with luck keep paying for college. I was used to moving. My dad and I had never stayed in one place too long. Being in college had kept me planted here in one place longer than I'd ever lived anywhere in my life.

Between classes during the day, preparing my portfolio in hopes of getting an internship at a reputable architectural firm, and my martial arts hobby, there just wasn't time for banking disasters.

"So, how are the ghosts?" Joe asked when the couple he'd been serving found a corner table for some serious eye-gazing.

"No ghosts," I said. "Not a sign of them. Not unless you count some weird whirring sound."

"Whirring sound?"

"Yeah, kind of like when you turn your bike upside down and spin the wheel real fast, then just sit back and let it wind down. . . ." Okay, so I admit it. I'd been a weird kid. I was always trying to figure out how things worked, spinning wheels and twisting bolts. You know, breaking things down.

Joe laughed. "Can't say that I've ever done that, Abbs. But I get what you're talking about."

I sighed as he turned to start cleaning up a table, and prepared for the last part of my soggy trek home. "So, I'll see you in the morning?" I said. I came in every day for breakfast.

Joe shook his head. "Not me. I'm going snowboarding. Leaving tonight. It might be raining here, but it's snowing in the mountains. My sister's covering for me."

"Lucky," I said. I headed for the door. Joe caught me before I reached it.

"Be careful out there," he said, serious for once. "They found another body today."

"Another?" I asked. A shiver slipped down my spine. There were a lot of homeless people in the neighborhood, and someone was gruesomely murdering them. At first it had been once a month or so that a body turned up, but lately it had gotten to be every week. This would make two in one week.

"I'll watch out," I said, then dashed out the door and crashed into a guy who was on his way in. He was strong. He didn't give much when I hit him, and I staggered back as he caught my arm.

So much for me watching out.

I caught a glimpse of his soaking wet golden blond hair and bright blue eyes as we did the which-side-are-you-going-to-take dance, and my heart did a little flip in my chest. I knew him.

"Sorry," we both said at the same time. He gave me a nice grin as he found the door and then froze.

"Hey, I've seen you on the El," he said.

"Er, yeah," I replied. "I ride it to class every morning." Then I fell silent. I am so bad at small talk.

"And I ride it home from work every morning," he said.

So, we had something in common besides the El. We both suck at small talk. And we both eat at Joe's. I kind of shrugged and gave him the *small world, what a coincidence* smile. I didn't want to admit that I'd been covertly lusting after him every morning on my way to class. There was no time in my life for a guy, even if he was a major Paul Walker–type hottie. Besides, I was standing in the rain. My shoes were soaked and my backpack seemed heavier, as if it was full of water. I really wasn't at my best.

"So . . . I guess I'll see you in the morning," he said.

"Yeah," I replied. "See ya."

"Hey, Doc!" Joe called out as he went in. I took a quick glance through the window. So, the hunky El guy was a doctor? That was interesting.

I took off down the sidewalk at a quick jog. The rain didn't seem so bad at the moment. Apparently Doctor Hunk had noticed me, too. Maybe I should make some time in my life for a guy.

Speaking of guys, my favorite guy Charlie was waiting for me at the door. Charlie is my pound puppy. He's a huge retriever mix who happens to be a great snuggler on cold and rainy nights.

"Hey, Charlie!" I said as I walked in. "No walks tonight," I added. Luckily for Charlie, the first thing I'd installed in the new place was a pet door. He had full access to the tiny backyard, which was surrounded by a ten-foot-high brick wall.

Charlie wagged his tail at my announcement, while holding an old running shoe of mine in his mouth. You could call Charlie a lot of things, but stupid isn't one of them. He didn't want to go out any more than I did. I did feel a bit guilty, though, about his recent lack of exercise. We'd missed our run this morning and our walk last night. It seemed like it had been raining forever.

"I tell you what, Charlie. We'll spend Sunday afternoon at the park." His tail swished and thumped against the wall of the foyer. I never had to worry about cobwebs with his Dustbuster of a tail around.

I threw my backpack and hat into the corner, kicked off my shoes and hooked my raincoat and hoodie over the banister. Charlie and I both padded into what would someday be a beautiful kitchen but was at the current moment a disaster zone. I fixed myself a bowl of cereal and opened a can of food for Charlie, which he swallowed in one bite; then we both went into the gutted room that was supposed to be the parlor.

I've got great vision. I can see what a project will look like when it's done before I even swing a hammer, and I was aching to get a good look at the fireplace that I knew was lurking behind the bricks some idiot had placed about four feet from the side wall in this room. Like I'd guessed, the house had great bones, and it also had some of the most gorgeous woodwork I've ever seen. I just knew there was an antique mantel hiding behind the brick wall; there was a chimney going up the side of the house, and a fireplace directly above this room that was also bricked in.

Charlie went to the wall and whined. Ever since we'd moved in he'd been as fascinated with the wall as I. The worn carpet was shredded where he tried to dig through the floor to get behind the wall. I also had a sneaking suspicion that the weird sound I kept hearing was coming from behind the wall.

Charlie scraped at the floor with his paws and gave me an expectant look.

"I know, boy," I said. "Tonight is the night." I put on my safety goggles, work boots and gloves, and picked up the sledgehammer that sat in the corner. "Tonight we're going to find out what the big mystery is."

Time does not fly when you're swinging a sledgehammer. But at least there was some satisfaction in watching the bricks and mortar come down. My arms ached after a while, so I put the sledge aside and used a crowbar to pry the bricks loose. I made good progress until I ran into a beam that ran from floor to ceiling. The top third of the wall that I'd torn down concealed another brick wall that ran straight back to the exterior wall.

"What the . . . ?" My contemplation of the insanity of the person who'd built the wall was interrupted by Charlie suddenly going berserk. He ran to the foyer, barking and growling as if we were suddenly under attack.

I gave my heart a second to resume its normal rhythm, then went after him with my crowbar firmly in hand. Charlie stood at the door with his hackles raised and gave out a low growl that made me feel protected but also scared beyond words. I peered through the leaded glass. Thoughts of serial killers crossed my mind.

All I saw was rain pounding against the pavement in the small glowing circle of the streetlamp. Just to make sure, I turned on the porchlight. Charlie gave another low growl and then a huff of disgust.

"All gone, boy?" I asked.

Charlie snuffled around the doorjamb, then walked into the kitchen. I heard his sloppy lapping from his water bowl and gave a sigh of relief.

I checked my watch, surprised to find it was almost eleven. I walked back into the parlor and looked at the mess on the floor. I really needed to clean it up before things got out of hand.

Then I heard the noise: a soft whir that lasted several seconds, followed by a *click click click*.

It was louder. And it had definitely come from behind the wall.

Charlie heard it, too. He gave out a sharp bark and went back to digging a hole in the carpet.

"Move," I said. At this rate he'd be down to the wood beneath, and the less sanding I had to do, the happier I would be.

I stuck my crowbar in between the beam and the

brick and pushed. I'm not sure if I was stronger than I realized or the wall was loose, but I heard a loud creak and, before I could move, a huge section of brick and mortar fell toward me. I jumped back and threw my arm up as I tripped over the mess on the floor. A sharp pain shot up my left arm.

I lay on the ground, muttering. As the dust cleared, I took a quick inventory of all my parts while Charlie did the same. He stuck his nose in my face and nudged away my mask.

"I'm okay," I said. But really I wasn't. I grabbed my arm and realized it was soaked with blood. I pulled up my sleeve and found a long, deep gash that went from my wrist to my elbow. The crowbar lay next to me and blood dripped from the end.

I needed stitches. But more importantly, I needed to stop the bleeding. There was already a big puddle on the floor and the side of my jeans was stained red.

I stood, grabbed my hoodie from the post and wrapped it around my arm. Using the sleeves as a tourniquet, I dug into my coat pocket for my cell phone.

Dead. I'd forgotten it was dead. I looked at the two halves of cord that I'd left lying on the kitchen table. My charger was a victim of one of my projects.

Charlie looked at me with some concern showing in his brown eyes. He gave me a little whine and nudged my leg. I needed to do something before I bled to death. The only option I had was walking the four blocks to the hospital. I had a good chance of bleeding to death either way, but at least by walking I had a chance of hailing a cab or finding a policeman.

Stuffing my wrapped arm into the sleeve of my coat, I grabbed my keys and wallet and took off into the rain.

TWO

Bad times make you realize how alone you really are. Even if my phone had been charged there was no one for me to call. Sure, I had several acquaintances from school and martial arts, but none of them were go-to friends. I guess I could have called Joe, but he was out of town. I really didn't know any of the neighbors; they were all either senior citizens who had lived there forever or young families who couldn't afford anything in the suburbs. There was no one I imagined would drop everything on a rainy night to take me to the emergency room.

My life was pretty sad, really. If not for Charlie I would be totally alone. It was my own fault. I had no time for friends, no time for socializing. My life was full of work, school and exercise. How pathetic was that? It wasn't fun to think about.

I looked up and saw the lighted cross on top of Sacred Heart Hospital. It wasn't far. Just a few blocks up and one over.

The streets were deserted. The news had said there were supposed to be more frequent patrols by the city police, but you couldn't prove it by me. My arm throbbed, and I would have given anything to see a police car drive by. Instead, all I saw was darkness. That's when I realized the streetlights were out.

Between my house and the hospital, the neighborhood changed from homes with lawns to row houses. Most were dark except for a few upper-story windows. Strange. The light in front of my place was burning, but the rest . . . there was nothing.

Most people would be asleep now, I supposed, warm and dry in their beds. I myself wished I was snuggling with Charlie while we watched the weather report on TV and hoped for sunshine. I heard an ambulance go by and realized it was one block over, on the street behind my house. If I'd gone out the back I probably could have flagged it down.

I quickened my pace. I felt kind of spooked and kind of nauseated, like I wanted to throw up. I was so cold, but my arm felt warm and sticky. I wondered how bad the bleeding was but didn't dare look. The last thing I needed was to pass out in the middle of the street.

I kept my eyes on the cross and concentrated on putting one foot in front of the other. The skin prickled on the back of my neck, and I suddenly had the weird feeling that someone was watching me. I stopped and turned to look back. I caught a glimpse of something, a dark shadow that moved into the alley between a row of houses.

"Get a grip," I told myself. But just to be safe I crossed to the other side of the street. I could no longer see the lights of Sacred Heart but knew I only had a block to go before I could cut over to the back entrance.

Then I heard a noise. It sounded like something metallic rubbing against brick, like maybe someone was climbing on one of the fire escapes. I was totally spooked. I turned and saw the shadow again. It looked as if something or someone was floating to the ground.

Whoever lived in the end house must have heard it, too. A porch light came on and revealed what appeared to be a woman dressed in a long black coat standing in the street. We stared at each other for a moment—a moment that to me seemed to last forever. It was strange; I couldn't look away. She was just an outline in the light but she held me captivated in a strange, bizarre, sickening way.

Then she vanished. I know she moved, but it was so quick, so graceful that I missed it.

I myself turned and ran. And it was purely instinct to do so. I had no idea why she spooked me; she just did.

It was hard to run in my steel-toed boots. More so because I couldn't use my arm. My heart rate was up and my arm throbbed with my pulse. I knew I should stop; I was losing a lot of blood.

But I couldn't. I knew the woman, whoever she was, was following me. I couldn't hear her. I couldn't see her. I just sensed her.

The pumping of my blood pounded in my ears until I lost all sense of time and place. All I knew was that I needed to reach the lights that shone brightly ahead of me as I turned the corner.

I don't know how I got there. I couldn't tell you that I ran through the alley that led to the emergency entrance behind the hospital; all I know is that I saw an ambulance pull in, saw a man in scrubs waiting to meet it, and that I staggered into the light with blood trailing down my arm.

"Help me," I gasped as the lights around me swirled into a rhythm with the flashing red of the ambulance.

"I've got you," a gentle voice said. I slid into a pair of strong, welcoming arms as the lights grew dim.

When I came to, I was in a bed in the emergency room. I felt something tugging on my arm and quickly realized that my sleeve was being cut away.

"Check her all over," a voice commanded. "She's covered in blood."

"Dr. Maddox," a voice called out. "We need you."

"Start an IV and get a match on her blood. She's going to need a transfusion. We also need X-rays. Tell them a portable is fine."

"It's just my arm," I said. "Just my arm." I had a quick vision of all my clothes being cut away.

"She's awake," a woman's voice said.

The light shining above the table blinded me. I turned my head and saw a man standing with his hand on the door as if he were ready to walk away. I blinked and wondered if I was dreaming as the handsome face came into focus. Bright blue eyes studied me intently, and he smiled.

"Hey," he said in a soft voice. "Java Joe's?"

"Yeah," I said. It was the guy I'd crashed into. "You're the doctor." Obviously. He wore a pair of blue scrubs and had a stethoscope hanging over his shoulder.

"Yes, I am." His smile was nice. Reassuring. Calming. "Do you know who you are?" This guy had great bedside manner.

"Abbey Shore," I said. "957 Halifax," I added. "And it's Thursday, April—"

"Dr. Maddox!" a voice called out again, interrupting my list.

"I gotta go," he said. "But I'll be back. That arm is going to need stitches."

"Yeah," I said. "That's what I thought."

"Lucky you," the nurse said with a smile when he left. "You passed out right in his arms."

I felt my face flush as she went to work cleaning the blood from my arm. "I did?"

"Yep." She smiled at me. "He carried you in, himself."

"Too bad I missed it," I complained. Being carried into an ER by a handsome doctor was definitely high on my fantasy list. Though I didn't know if I'd give an arm for it.

I heard a loud crash from the treatment room across from me. The nurse glanced up, then said to me, "You definitely need stitches. Too bad no one from plastics is here."

"Is it that bad?" I asked. I looked at my arm. The gash was long and jagged, and whatever she was wiping with stung.

"You're going to have a scar," she said. "But Shane's pretty good with a needle, so you'll be fine. The important thing is to make sure no ligaments or tendons are damaged." She stuck some gauze on my arm. "Is there anyone we can call for you? We didn't find any emergency numbers in your wallet." She inserted a needle in my good arm and attached a saline drip.

I shook my head. "There's no one," I said.

There was another loud crash. Through the windows I saw Dr. Maddox along with three or four other people dressed in scrubs working on a patient. They seemed to be frantic, and I wondered what was going on.

"What happened over there?" I asked.

"Another victim," the nurse said with a shake of her head. "There's a killer on the loose. That's why we're so short-staffed tonight. It's freaking people out."

"They never disclose on the news how the people die. Just that they're mostly homeless," I said.

The nurse looked over her shoulder at the group working across the hall.

"You live pretty close?" she asked.

"Yeah."

"You walked here?"

"Yeah," I said. "The battery was dead on my phone."

"Well, don't do it anymore," she said. "Whoever is doing this is bad. Real bad. *Psycho.*"

"What is it?" I asked.

"It's like they've been stabbed in the heart," she said in a hushed voice. "But no one can figure out what kind of weapon is used. And while there's blood loss, that's not really the cause of death. It's more like they're . . . deflated."

I gave her a doubtful look, but the nurse was totally serious. She was scaring me.

"The guy they're working on now got away somehow before he was finished off. He's lost a lot of blood but is still alive. They're trying to stabilize him so he can identify the killer, but I'm not sure if he's going to make it."

"Where did they find him?" I asked.

"High Street." The nurse shook her head. "The way they come in here . . . I've never seen anything like it," she said in a whisper.

I suddenly felt very sick. High Street ran right behind my house. Chances were pretty good that the ambulance I'd heard when I was on my way in was picking up this guy.

And Charlie had pitched a fit. Could it be that the person responsible for all the killings had stirred him up? Had he or she been right outside my house? I had a vision of the woman on the street and my stomach rebelled.

"I'm going to throw up," I said.

The nurse grabbed a plastic dish and turned me onto my side as I yakked up cereal and apple chai. She wiped my mouth when I was done and helped me lie back down on the table.

"Susan!" The call came from across the hall. "Susan, we need you!"

"Will you be okay for a minute?" the nurse asked me.

I nodded, though I wasn't really sure. The light seemed to be getting dim, and I felt kind of woozy. She filled a long stainless bowl with a brown liquid and placed it next to me in the bed. She laid my arm in it, gave me a reassuring pat and took off.

I'm not sure how long I lay there. I know I was kind of fading in and out. I opened my eyes and a woman was in the room. I wondered how long she had been there, as I had not heard her come in. Her skin was as pale as paper, and her hair the brightest red I've ever seen. It was long and flowed around her shoulders in waves. I'd kill to have hair like that instead of my own straight-as-a-stick brown hair that I usually wore in a ponytail.

Her eyes were a really strange shade of blue. Almost violet. Like there was a red light shining behind them. They were hard to read. Impenetrable.

She was dressed in black leather from head to toe, including a long black coat like the one Trinity wears in *The Matrix*. They must have put some sort of painkiller in the IV; that's the only way I can explain what happened next—I laughed. The idea of someone out in the pouring rain dressed in black leather was totally ludicrous.

"What do you find so amusing?" she asked. Her voice surprised me. It sounded very cultured, and definitely out of place in this neighborhood.

I bit back my giggles. "Um, are you looking for some-one?" I asked.

She sneered at me. I don't think anyone has ever ac-tually sneered at me before, unless you count my dad's second wife. The one who left me penniless.

My amusement fled. I was hurt, practically bereft of all medical help, and some weird chick in black leather was sneering at me.

"I'm pretty sure you're in the wrong room," I said. I suddenly felt very cold and exposed. If only Nurse Su-san had given me one of those warmed blankets before she left.

The redhead walked to the table and looked at my arm, which was still soaking in the brown liquid. The light from above was in my eyes, which made it difficult for me to focus on her. She stared at my arm. Then, for a quick moment, I could have sworn she hissed. It was so strange and so bizarre that I wasn't even sure it hap-pened. Maybe I was just dreaming.

The door opened, and she turned so quickly that I missed seeing her move. I caught her face from another angle and a sense of déjà vu washed over me.

"You," I said. "You followed me here." She was the woman I'd seen on the street. She had to be. What were the chances that two women in black leather were out in the neighborhood on the same night?

"Can I help you?" Dr. Maddox strolled into the room. His blond hair was wet and spiked like he'd just rubbed a towel through it. He was wearing green scrubs now in-stead of the blue.

The woman stared at him for a moment. Actually, star-ing is a mild word for what she did. She looked him up one side and down the other, as if taking inventory of all his parts. I knew the look. I'd been doing it covertly for weeks.

"Are you a friend of Ms. Shore's?" Dr. Maddox asked. He looked at me and I shook my head.

The woman moved toward Dr. Maddox. I can't say that she walked, because it's more like she glided. It was totally strange and weird. Or else I was really tripping on meds.

She extended her index finger and touched his name badge. "Dr. Maddox," she practically purred. Then she lay her hand on his chest over his heart. "Dr. Shane Maddox."

Shane looked at her as if he was in a trance.

"I will surely remember your name if I am ever in need of . . . medical assistance."

Then she left.

Shane blinked, shook his head and then watched for a moment as she glided out of the room. "Do you know her?" he asked me incredulously.

"Nope," I said. "I just opened my eyes and she was here."

"It must be the full moon," he said. "Even when it rains it brings out the weirdos."

"And obviously I'm some sort of weirdo magnet," I said.

He grinned and shook his head, then looked down at my arm. "So, tell me, Ms. Shore. How did you manage to slice your arm open?"

"Abbey," I corrected. *Ms. Shore* reminded me too painfully of my father's second wife. "It involved a brick wall and a crowbar," I said. "The crowbar won."

"We'd better get you a tetanus shot, too," he said. "Has X-ray been down?"

"Not that I know of," I said. "I have to admit I kind of dozed off."

He shined his little flashlight in my eyes. "Did you hit your head?"

"No. At least I don't think so." I reached for the back of my head to feel for lumps, and my fingers ran into Shane's, who had tried to do the same thing.

"Let me do the doctoring," he said. His eyes met mine, and my heart gave a little flip. I don't think I've ever seen eyes so blue.

"So what happened to the other patient?" I asked as his fingers massaged my scalp.

"He didn't make it."

"Sorry."

"It happens," he said. "We do the best we can and trust God to take care of the rest." He finished examining my head and picked up my arm.

"Get X-ray down here," he said as Nurse Susan came in. "And get a match on her blood," he repeated.

"I'm A-negative," I said.

"A-neg," he called over his shoulder, and Susan popped out into the hall.

"Have you seen a lot of the victims?" I asked.

He was silent a moment. "More than my fair share. I work nights, and that's when most of them come in. The killer seems to be centered in this neighborhood."

"Yeah," I said. "It's kind of creepy."

"It also means that you shouldn't be walking the streets at night by yourself," he said.

"I hear you found me," I remarked. I felt my face flush. "And carried me in."

"It was more like *you* found *me*," he said. "You came flying into the ambulance bay and fainted."

"I guess I got spooked on the way here. I think someone was following me." Someone wearing black leather. Like the woman who'd just left. But why?

"Why didn't you call 911?"

"My cell phone was dead. No land line."

"No family?"

"Just me," I said. "And Charlie."

"Charlie?"

"My dog."

"For a minute there I thought I might be jealous," he said with a grin.

A warm surge burst from the top of my head down to my toes. Dr. Shane Maddox was flirting with me! I was drenched with rain, my sleeve was cut off, I was pretty sure what wasn't wet was covered with dust, and a hot doctor was flirting with me. If I had known that slicing my arm open with a crowbar was all it took, I would have done it a long time ago.

"Tell me about the crowbar and the bricks," he said. "Starting with why."

"I flip houses," I explained. "The one I'm working on has this stupid brick wall right in the middle of the parlor, and I decided it needed to go."

"Really?" he asked. "I wonder why they built that."

"I don't know. All I know is it's coming down."

"In big chunks?"

"Unfortunately," I said. I knew he was distracting me from my arm, which he was poking and prodding.

"Wait a minute. Halifax. Are you flipping the haunted house?"

The X-ray tech came in with a portable machine, along with Nurse Susan, who carried a bag of blood. They busied themselves around me while Shane stepped back out of X-ray danger.

"Yeah," I said. I kept my eyes on him while the tech moved my arm around. "Though I've yet to see any ghosts.

There's a weird noise that I keep hearing, but that's about it. Do you live around here?"

"No," he said. "My dad grew up in this neighborhood. His aunt, my great-aunt, still lives in the old family home over on Stanley. You might know her. She's the crazy cat lady."

I had to laugh. "Me and Charlie run by her house every morning," I said. "I think the cats lie in wait for him."

Shane laughed too. "The attack cats?" He shook his head. "She doesn't need protection with those animals, that's for sure. I have dinner with her every Thursday before I come in. I usually stop at Joe's and pick up something sweet for dessert. I'm surprised I haven't seen you there before yesterday."

"I have a class on Thursdays. It was canceled last night."

He nodded. I wondered if it was strange to the other people in the room that we were talking as if no one else existed. We might have been chatting over coffee instead of having my arm twisted and turned and poked and prodded in examination; except for the tetanus shot, I was oblivious to everything that was done.

"So, do you think Charlie will be okay for the night?" he asked.

I wondered if the flip my heart did would show up on any of the equipment that filled the room. I'd read books where stuff like this was supposed to happen, but until this very moment I did not believe it was possible. I was falling fast and hard for Dr. Shane Maddox. And what exactly was he inviting me to do?

"He'll be fine," I said. "He's got food, water, a pet door and full access to all the shoes in my closet."

Shane's touch on my arm was gentle as he gave me a

shot, numbing the flesh so he could stitch it up. I watched his face as he concentrated fully on what he was doing. Nurse Susan had covered me with a blanket, and I felt warm and drowsy even though I was surrounded by sterile instruments and stainless steel.

Shane checked the IV when he was done wrapping my arm. "Just rest for a while," he said with a reassuring squeeze of my shoulder. "My shift will be over in a couple of hours and I'll walk you home."

Ah, well, that sounded perfect. "Doctor's orders?" I asked drowsily.

"Doctor's orders," he agreed with a smile.

I watched as he went into the hall to talk to some cops that were waiting. With Doctor Hunky and the police, at least I wouldn't have to worry about getting murdered on my way home. And maybe I'd have some happy dreams.

THREE

Not only did Shane walk me home the next morning, when we got to my door he asked me to meet him for coffee that night—if I was feeling up to it. I greeted Charlie with a big grin on my face as Shane waved from the edge of the sidewalk. The rain had stopped, and even though it was cloudy it looked as though the sun would eventually peek out.

"I got a date tonight, big guy!" I giggled as I rubbed his ears. Charlie sniffed me all over and gave a disgusted *whuff* when he finished his thorough exam of the bandage on my arm.

I knew there was no way I had enough energy to run, but Charlie had been cooped up for way too long, so I grabbed his leash and we walked down to Joe's. I bought a coffee and a bagel and we went back home with Charlie checking out every puddle on the way. He whined and tugged on the leash as if he wanted to go toward High Street right as we got to our intersection, but I wouldn't let him. My arm was throbbing again and I wanted nothing more than to take a pain pill and fall into bed. Too bad I had a class and errands to run.

By the time I got home from that, I was again so tired

I could barely keep my eyes open. Charlie was still hoping for a run but there was no way I could manage.

"Tomorrow is Saturday," I reminded him, rubbing his ears. "I promise we'll spend the afternoon in the park."

Charlie gave me the sad eye, but I ignored him. Even the thought of climbing the stairs to go to bed was daunting. I looked at the mess in the parlor. I was going to have a busy weekend.

I staggered up the stairs and crawled into bed. I was asleep before Charlie settled in beside me.

It was nearly dark when I woke. Between the pain meds and sheer exhaustion, I'd slept like the dead. I looked at the clock and saw I had an hour to get ready for my date with Shane.

After showering, I dressed in jeans and a black sweater. I let my hair hang loose around my shoulders and put on some purple eye shadow because all the magazines said it would complement my brown eyes. I put on my boots with the two-inch heels since Shane was tall. I figured he was a bit over six feet. As I turned Charlie out back for some exercise, I went into the kitchen to open a can of food.

Shane had said he'd come to the house, but I'd told him I'd meet him at Joe's. I didn't want him to think I was clingy, and figured the walk between my house and the coffee joint was safe enough. Besides, what with all the renovations, there was no place here for us to sit and talk except for my bed, and I was so not a do-it-on-the-first-date type. Actually, I was more of a hardly-ever-do-it type. Not because I'm a prude, but because I hadn't dated that much—and hardly anyone more than a few times.

Still, I made an attempt to make sure the kitchen looked decent.

I put on my leather jacket and was on the way to let Charlie in when I heard the noise again. *Whirrrr* . . . *click* . . . *click* . . . *click.*

It was louder. More pronounced. As I walked into the parlor I heard it again. There was something behind the wall. I briefly wondered why I hadn't come immediately back here to check it out.

I had a big spotlight that I used for work, and I turned it on. Stepping closer to the opening I'd made in the wall, I shined it inside. The light reflected off a smooth surface. Strange. Was it a mirror? I stuck my hand out and touched smooth glass. I turned the light a bit and realized I was looking at what only could be described as a giant aquarium. It went from floor to ceiling and was nearly four feet wide. That explained the twelve-foot beam in the basement: this much water was heavy.

But why? Why was there a giant water tank behind an added brick wall in the parlor of my house?

Whirr . . . *click* . . . *click* . . . *click.*

I shone my light into the water. There was something inside, a shiny object sitting on a narrow pedestal of some sort. This thing kept getting weirder and weirder. I heard Charlie's nails on wood.

"Stay," I commanded. I didn't want him walking through the mess that still covered the parlor floor. He whined but obeyed. I heard his *whuff* of disgust and a groan as he lay down.

Whirr . . . *click* . . . *click* . . . *click.*

The thing inside the tank was moving. I felt a chill go down my spine. What was it?

I got closer to the glass. So close that my cheek lay against the cool pane. I could see it then: about a foot high, something like an hourglass. Except, it was spinning sideways like a top. That was the noise. It spun and made the whirring sound, then slowed down with the *click, click, click.*

I moved the spotlight. I wanted to see if there was anything in the darkness on the other side.

The cord was stuck. As I knew it had plenty of length, I jerked on it. Unfortunately, as I yanked the cord forward I lurched off balance. The metal of the light rapped down hard against the glass, and I heard a splintering. Before I could move, the glass shattered and water washed over me. It hit me with such force that I was thrown back against the wall. I managed to stay on my feet but got soaked. The smell of peroxide made my eyes water.

"Damn it!" I exploded. I knew my clothes were probably ruined, and now a mess covered the floor. "Son of a—"

Charlie's barking interrupted.

"Charlie! Stay!"

I needed to change. I checked my watch. Luckily, it was waterproof. I had five minutes to change and get to Joe's. I didn't want to leave the mess, but it wasn't as if it was going anywhere.

Whirrr . . . click . . . click . . . click.

I picked my way through the puddles and broken glass, and was now able to step inside the frame of the aquarium. The thing that stood on the pedestal slowed to a stop. I touched it with the tip of my finger. I pushed on the side of the hourglass-like object, and it turned.

Click.

Strange. I pushed again. Harder. *Click. Click. Click. Click.*

The thing suddenly started spinning clockwise. As it spun, I felt my body pulled into a bright light that came out of the column. It was as if time stopped. I heard

Charlie barking. My hands, then my arms dissolved, molecule by molecule, and were pulled into the light. I opened my mouth to scream but no sound came forth. I saw it all happening; I felt the pull as I was sucked into a hole. For an instant all light turned to darkness, and then I rematerialized.

"What the hell?" a voice exclaimed.

To say that what happened next was surreal would be an understatement. When I think back, it's hard to believe that I survived.

I found myself face-to-face with two men. They were lounging in a set of chairs on either side of the column. They both jumped to their feet as I stumbled forward, trying to recover from the shock of whatever it was that had happened to me. One of them grabbed my arm, then screamed in agony. I heard a sizzling sound, and smelled burned flesh. He held his hands up in front of his face, and in the dim light I saw that they were horribly burned.

"Acid!" His face was contorted with pain. "She's soaked with it!"

I fell back and away, crashed into a table as the other man approached me cautiously, slowly. The one who'd grabbed me held his hands as if in great pain.

"When did you come from?" the second man asked.

My mind whirled as I tried to focus on what had happened to me. Then realization struck. This was still my house. I recognized the molding around the ceiling and the shape of the room and placement of the windows. But it was different now. Elegant. The way I'd imagined it in my mind. But, who were these men? And why was I instinctively terrified of them?

Of course, having a man in agony because he'd touched my "acid-covered" wet clothes was bizarre enough, even without my overwhelming feeling of being out of place.

Was I dreaming? Could that explain why the surroundings were so familiar? Was this all an hallucination?

"Get her," said the man with the burned hands.

"I'm not touching her," the other growled. "Get her yourself."

They looked at each other and grinned maliciously. Then their faces changed. Their eyes turned bright red, and their faces took on a predatory look—the kind the mad axe-murderers of my dreams usually wore. I shook my head in denial.

"Who are you?" I asked, but I already know the answer. They were without a doubt the bad guys, and I was in a lot of trouble.

I took off. Bolting from the room, I found the front door. I felt one of the men behind me, breathing down my neck. As I made it outside he grabbed at my coat . . . and shrieked.

Acid.

They couldn't touch me without pain, but that didn't mean I should stick around. Eventually it would dry, whatever this stuff was that hurt them but not me. I took off as fast as I could toward Joe's, where I knew there would be light and safety.

"Let her go," I heard one of my pursuers call out. "She'll run out of gas and we can track her."

Track me? I wondered.

The streets were bright, but I soon realized it was the waxing moon that lit my way instead of any electric lights. My feet knew the path but everything felt disjointed, as if I were on an alien planet. The world seemed different. Even the moon. Hadn't it been full last night?

Debris littered the street. The nearby homes seemed deserted, and as I reached Joe's block I realized that the storefronts were either boarded up or the glass was shattered. I skidded panting to a stop and saw a burnt-out shell where the coffee shop used to be. I put my hands on my knees and sucked in great gulps of air. My adrenaline rush was about to kill me.

What was happening? If this was a nightmare, then I really wanted to wake up. My arm throbbed from exertion and my blood felt sluggish from the meds I'd taken.

Call 911.

I pulled my phone from my pocket, punched in the numbers and got dead air. I looked at the phone, which I'd plugged in with the new cord. I had power, but no bars.

What was happening?

"Where arrrrrrre yooooou?" I heard the singsong call from behind me. The two men were indeed on my trail. They sounded like they were playing hide-and-seek instead of something more deadly. Were they trying to kill me? I decided not to stick around and find out.

"Safe place," I muttered. "I need a safe place."

Sacred Heart. The hospital.

I couldn't go back the way I came, so I dashed down an alley toward High Street. From there it was a six-block straight shot to the hospital. I would have to go past the back of my house, but that was a risk I'd have to take; I didn't know where else to go.

The alley rose before me like a long tunnel. As I ran into the darkness, the moonlight gave way to long shadows from the buildings, and there was no end in sight. I soon found out why. The alley was blocked off. I crashed into a crate and fell against a solid wall, landing on my arm with a sickening crunch. I lay on the ground and fought the nausea that washed over me. My arm throbbed, and I had a sinking feeling I'd ripped some stitches.

"God help me," I whispered.

"Down here!" I heard.

I had to move. I scrambled to my feet and climbed onto the crate. Moonlight washed over the top of a wall a couple of feet higher than my head. I heard footsteps and the two men giving what they clearly felt were persuasive calls behind me.

I jumped, and just managed to grab the top of the wall with my hands. I felt splinters grind into my palms but I held on and planted my feet. I needed leverage, so bracing one leg against the brick of the building, I pushed up.

"She's going over," one called.

"She'll never make it," the other answered.

I *would*. Years of swinging a sledgehammer helped. I possessed a great deal of upper body strength, and was able to pull myself up and over.

I hung for a few moments on the other side, then dropped. I landed on something hard, and pitched forward. I braced my fall with my arms as I slid and crashed against boxes, crates, what felt like a bicycle and an old refrigerator, then finally landed with a thud on the pavement, beneath the rusted-out body of a car that was wedged up against the wall. My arm was bleeding. I felt the warm stickiness once again, and managed to find my feet even though my hip was numb from the crash. I stumbled forward and looked back at the barrier I'd just come over. It didn't seem as if the men were following me, but I couldn't take the chance. I staggered off toward Sacred Heart.

I hadn't gone more than a dozen steps when I suddenly found myself surrounded by a ragtag group of men and women wearing an odd assortment of weapons. "Dust her," one of them said, as I slowly raised my arms in surrender.

"She's not one of them," another said. "Look at how much she's bleeding. And it's red."

I was totally confused. What color was blood supposed to be if not red? I didn't know who or what they were talking about, but if they were going to dust somebody I preferred it not be me. I decided to go with not being "one of them," whoever "they" were.

"I'm not," I agreed. "Two men were after me."

"Well, she's not one of us either," a woman said. It was as if I hadn't said a word.

"She came over the wall," another spoke up. "She knew this was safe ground."

Safe ground? What was wrong with these people?

"I need to get to the hospital," I said. I also wanted to call the cops, but wasn't sure if I should mention it to this group. I held out my arm so they would once again notice the "red" blood seeping down my hand.

"We'll take her to Doc," one said. "We can figure out what to do with her after he takes a look."

They surrounded me, and one nudged me in a direction away from Sacred Heart. Everything looked so strange that I could have been wrong, and since I didn't seem to have a choice in the matter I went along.

I looked up to see if I could find the lighted cross on top of the hospital building, but there was nothing beyond the glowing moon. There were no such lights that I could see anywhere; the buildings were dark, drab, and desolate. The street was littered with trash and broken glass that trailed to the huge pile of junk that I'd fallen on when I came over the barrier.

"What's going on?" I asked.

"Shut up," a man barked, and jabbed a crossbow in my back.

"Watch it!" I snapped. This was getting to be too much.

"You watch it, girly," he snapped back.

"Girly?" I said incredulously. I got another jab and felt my temper flare at the treatment. This guy was definitely on a power trip. He also seemed to be especially cranky, and I wondered if I was the reason. I noticed that the rest seemed to defer to him as we trudged along. If he was in charge, then I was still in trouble, and for what reasons I could not begin to imagine. I felt as if I'd been asleep for a long time and woken up to find the world I knew gone, changed . . . or again, was I just having a rather bizarre and graphically real nightmare? The pain in my arm said no. This was real.

We turned off of High Street and onto Stanley. The sign was still there, although it was bent at a strange angle. An old-fashioned lantern hung from the sign.

As we moved on, I noticed that what used to be nice lawns were now overgrown with trees and shrubbery, and the fine old houses stood in hollow disrepair. Some of the windows gave off the soft glow of candlelight. I blinked, trying to make sense of my surroundings. This was my neighborhood. I ran this street every morning with Charlie. We liked it because of the trees that lined the sidewalks.

For some strange reason, the "Time Warp" song from *The Rocky Horror Picture Show* funneled into my mind. This was some strange dream. When I woke up and met Shane for coffee I'd have to have a talk with him about the meds he gave me.

Our group made its way between the junked cars and

old appliances that littered the street. Ahead I saw a patch of light and realized as we came closer that it was a bonfire with ten or twelve people gathered around. A boy of mixed heritage who seemed around ten or so years old ran up to us. A cat followed and bumped against his legs as he fired questions at the group.

"Who is she?" he asked. "Where did you catch her?" He kept on: "Is she a tick?"

A tick? What did he mean by that? Was I being insulted on top of everything else?

The changed faces of the two men who'd chased me from my house swirled into my mind as the boy chattered at the group, asking a million questions.

A tick? What did ticks have to do with anything? Was I on some kind of acid trip? Ticks? Had the entire neighborhood gone to hell?

"Could someone explain to me what's going on?" I asked.

"Quiet," barked the man who seemed to be the leader. He was older—late forties I guessed—and gave off an *I'm in complete control* kind of vibe. We turned up a paved path. The house at the end looked vaguely familiar. The windows were lit with a welcoming glow, and the wide front porch sported cats who lounged on the rails, the steps, and on a ragtag collection of chairs.

"Crazy cat lady's house?" I asked in disbelief.

"Nope," the boy said. "Doctor Mad's house."

"Doctor Mad?"

"Don't worry," the boy said. "He's not really mad. Just pissed off most of the time."

"Shut up, Trent." The man who'd done most of the poking shoved me through the front door. He and one of the women followed.

The house was surprisingly clean compared to the

disaster area we'd come through. We stood in a foyer that arched overhead, with a curved staircase and rooms off either side. The wood of the floor and the banister was beat up, and its finish was long gone, but evidently someone took steps to keep things tidy.

Candles stuck in sconces lined the walls and gave off a bright welcoming light, and the smell of cooking food wafted from the back. A cat washed its face on an antique bench with padded upholstery that had faded into a nondescript gray. Another cat wended its way down the staircase and sat at the bottom, looking up at the three of us with obvious interest.

I was shivering. I don't know if it was from the cold, the fact that I was still wet, or the fear. Or maybe it was just the fact that my adrenaline rush was gone. All I know is that I was trembling from head to toe and wanted nothing more than to crawl into a bed, pull the covers over my head and wake up with Charlie snuggled beside me.

"This way," the man said, and led me into the room off to the left.

It looked like a doctor's office. A stainless-steel table rose in the middle of the room, and cabinets lined the wall, packed with what seemed to be medical supplies. The space was well lit, too, with a blazing chandelier with real candles right over the table.

"Hey, Doc?" our group leader called out.

"Coming," a voice said.

A door opened beside the fireplace, and to my immense relief Shane Maddox walked out.

I couldn't help myself. Even though we'd just met, I felt such relief at seeing him that I threw myself into his arms. I heard a hiss and he gave a yelp. The next thing I knew I was flying across the room. I landed against the wall and slid to the floor, staring up at him in disbelief.

"Acid," he spat out in disgust. He was dressed in jeans and a well-worn T-shirt, and they steamed where I had touched him. The side of his face looked red, and he gingerly touched it. "I'm not hurt, it didn't break the skin," he said. My escorts leveled their crossbows at me.

"Do you think they sent her as an assassin?" the grouchy man asked as he jerked me to my feet.

"We better find out," the man said, and he hauled me to my feet.

"Wait!" I cried. I had reached my limit with the man-handling and the prodding and the bullying. "Shane." I took a step toward him and immediately had the points of two crossbow bolts aimed at my face. I shoved one out of the way impatiently but it came right back.

"Don't you know who I am?" I asked.

Shane held up a hand to stop his friends, and they both stepped back as he walked up to me. His bright blue eyes searched my face, and I felt the same sense of disquiet that had come over me when the woman in black leather stared at me in the ER.

Wait. His hair . . . it was different. Longer. Impossibly longer. Before, it was close-cropped and spiked. Now it curled behind his ears and a lock fell over his forehead. How had that happened in one day? Or had the meds from last night really messed up my memory?

He shook his head and gave a bitter laugh.

"Yeah," he said. "I know you. You're the one responsible for all this." He waved his arm to encompass the room. "Take her out and dust her," he said.

FOUR

"No!" I yelled. "Wait." I jerked my arm away from the man who grabbed me as Shane turned away. "What's going on? What are you talking about? Do you make it a habit of picking up girls in the ER and then playing elaborate jokes on them? Or maybe you're so hard up that you slip Ecstasy into their meds so you can have your way with them."

My arm throbbed beneath my jacket. Between the running, the climbing, the falling, hauling and mauling, I was certain that all the stitches were torn. I felt warm sticky blood all over my skin.

"You asked if I know you?" Shane said. The look on his face was incredulous. "Baby, you are all I've thought about for the past hundred years." He picked up a towel from the stainless-steel table and then flung it away. "Every time I close my eyes I see your face and know that you tricked me. That it was all part of a trap. That you and your girlfriend planned *this*."—he sneered the word and waved his hands to encompass the room—"from the beginning." The level of his voice rose until he was shouting.

"My girlfriend?" I shouted back. "What are you talking about?" Had everything and everyone gone crazy? "Are you insane? Or is it just me?"

"Your girlfriend," Shane sneered. "Lucinda."

"You're crazy," I said. "All of you." I waved my arm at the crossbow-wielding pair who watched us as if waiting for a bomb to go off. Blood splashed on the floor and I winced in pain. I don't do well with blood. My head felt woozy and I fought to stay alert.

Shane's bright blue eyes watched the blood that now trailed down my fingertips. He licked his lips, and I once again felt the strange sensation that seemed to be becoming a frequent part of my life. He turned his head away quickly when he realized I was staring at him, and I could have sworn I saw a flash of red in his eyes. Or were the meds causing me to hallucinate?

"Who is Lucinda?" I asked in a somewhat calmer voice. The skin on the back of my neck prickled, and I felt the sudden need for caution. I was also feeling sick to my stomach.

"Don't play innocent with me," Shane said. "You were part of Lucinda's gang long before we met. My only question is where you have been hiding the last one hundred years."

"Why do you keep saying that?" I asked. One hundred years. It was almost like a mantra. He kept throwing it out there. My head started to swim, so I braced an arm on the table. This was not the time to get woozy, although my brain felt differently.

Then a sudden thought occurred to me: if this was some med-induced dream, why did my arm hurt so bad?

The look Shane turned upon me was deadly. Where was the compassion? The openness? The friendliness? How could I have been so wrong about him?

"I keep saying one hundred years because today is a special day." His teeth were clenched and the words forced out between them. "Hell, maybe that's why you're here. To help me celebrate."

He walked up to me and trailed his finger through the blood that dripped down my hand. He lifted it to his lips and licked. "A toast," he said with a malicious grin. "Here's to the hundredth anniversary of my rebirth."

I felt laughter bubble up in my throat. The entire world had gone crazy; I might as well join it.

I looked at the pair holding the crossbows, pretty sure they wanted to kill me. And it was obvious that Shane wanted to kill me, too. As I stared at him he stretched his mouth into a wide grin. Except, it was weird. Bizarre. Totally creepy.

I blinked, but the sight remained. What I'd seen before was true. His eyes were bright red. Glowing. He gave his head a slight toss, and the two with the crossbows moved back and away.

"What are you doing?" I asked as Shane moved toward me.

"I'm going to party," he said. "After all, it is my birthday."

His hand stretched out and grabbed my neck. With one hand he lifted me into the air. I felt my throat close as my hands clawed at his arms. My feet swung freely beneath me.

Then my training kicked in; I hadn't spent all those hours of martial arts workouts just to let some psycho doctor do me in.

A very strong psycho doctor, I might add. It was hard to believe that he could lift me with one hand, but my dangling feet proved it. I kicked him as hard as I could in the balls, and as he crumpled I jabbed the fingers of one hand into his strangely luminous eyes. He loosened his hold, and that was enough for me to work my fingers in and bend his hand away from my neck.

It all happened pretty fast. I fell to the floor at about the same time that Shane hit his knees with his hands cupped over his groin. His eyes, which were once again blue, blinked back tears.

"Are you trying to kill me?" I gasped as air once again made its way through my throat.

"Yes," he said, then made a face. "Next time I'll do it."

"You want us to dust her?" the grouchy man asked.

"No," Shane said. He shook his head, more as if to chase away the pain I'd caused him than to give me a reprieve. He gingerly climbed to his feet and looked down at me as I tried to will my pounding heart back to a normal pace.

"Why are you bleeding?" he asked.

"I think I ripped the stitches open."

"What stitches?"

I rolled my eyes. The man was schizo. "The ones you put in my arm last night."

"Last night?"

Very slowly I got to my feet. I took off my jacket and pushed up the sleeve of my sweater to show him the blood-soaked bandage on my arm.

"The stitches you gave me last night. In the ER at Sacred Heart." I recognized the look he gave me; it was the same one I was giving him. "I passed out in the ambulance bay? You carried me in? There was a murder victim you tried to save?" He kept looking at me like I was insane. "Then you totally made a pass at me and asked me out for coffee. Tonight." I was rambling now. "Except I got totally soaked by this weird hourglass thing in my house and then two guys chased me. Then your friends found me and brought me here."

"Let me see your arm," he said.

It was right in front of him, so I jerked it forward.
Wrong move on my part. It hurt like hell.

He reached out his hand to touch my arm and then
jerked back as if he'd been burned.

"Janet," he said to the nearby woman. "Get Claudia in
here to take these bandages off. I can't touch her."

An awkward silence followed as Janet left to fetch
Claudia. Crossbow man kept his weapon on me. Shane
ignored me until a pretty young woman with dark hair
came back with Janet. He motioned me over to the
table and Claudia used a pair of scissors to cut away the
bandage on my arm. Too much was happening. Everything was just too strange for words. What was wrong
with me?

My stitches were ripped and the sight of my arm
made my stomach turn. It had been a long time since
I'd eaten anything, and I was glad there was nothing in
there to come up.

"This is going to burn," Shane said as he picked up a
bottle. He dumped the contents on my arm and I
screamed as the raw alcohol seeped into my wound.

"Son of a bitch," I yelled. "Are you trying to kill me?"
Stupid question, since technically he *had* just tried to
kill me. "Again?"

I saw his lips quirk into a semi-smile as he turned my
arm beneath the light and ran his finger down the gash.
I shivered as I recalled that he had licked my blood earlier as if it were a delicacy.

"How did you get this?"

"I lost a fight with a crowbar."

His eyes moved to my face and I saw something behind the stare. Something desperate. Or maybe hope-
ful? I was way too wigged out to decipher what
someone else was thinking; I just knew there was a

spark of something behind the bright blue depths of his eyes.

"Because?"

I sighed deeply. My arm throbbed and I wanted nothing more than to close my eyes and make the past twenty-four hours go away. I didn't have room in my life for a psycho, schizoid doctor, no matter how cute he was.

"I flip houses. I live on Halifax. Some idiot put a brick wall in the middle of my parlor and I'm tearing it down. Some bricks fell on me and the crowbar gashed me." I rolled my uninjured arm, hoping he'd pick up the rest of the story.

"I found you in the ambulance bay and carried you in."

"Yes!" I said in victory. "Last night."

Shane walked away from me. He pushed his hands through the hair that fell across his eyes and then turned around to look at me.

"It wasn't last night, Abbey," he said. "It was a hundred years ago."

"Enough already," I snapped. "Enough jokes. Why don't you just stitch me back up and I'll go home?" I looked around the room. "Better yet, let me go to Sacred Heart and I'll get someone else to do it."

"Sacred Heart is gone," he said quietly. "Tell me again how you got here."

"I ran."

"From where?"

"From my house." I mentally added *idiot* to the list of descriptors I was compiling for him. "I told you. Two guys were in my house and they chased me. I ran to Joe's and it looks as if it burned down. I took the alley and climbed over a wall, and that's when your friends found me."

"That is where we found her," Janet agreed.

"How did you get covered with acid?" the man with a crossbow asked.

"Acid?"

"Peroxide," Shane said. "It's a form of acid. To . . . some of us, a dangerous form of it."

My mind spun. Peroxide? Acid? The stuff in the tank.

"The hourglass was inside a tank of what I thought was water. It cracked and soaked me. It must have been peroxide."

"The hourglass?" Janet asked.

"This thing I found behind the wall in my parlor. It was an hourglass. Only, it spun around instead of you flipping it over. It was inside a big tank of water behind a brick wall. I tore down the wall . . . that's when I hurt my arm. Tonight, when I was getting ready for our date . . ." I swallowed as I looked at Shane, who seemed to be listening intently to my story, "I heard a noise from behind the wall and found the tank. It broke . . ."

"And you found yourself here," Shane finished for me. He looked at both Janet and the man, who were looking at me now as if they might let me live. "That could be the answer," he said to his friends. "It must be a time portal."

"A what?" I asked. If I was being *Punk'd*, then it was a pretty elaborate joke. I looked around the room to see if I could find a hidden camera.

"A time portal," Shane repeated. "Abbey, I didn't meet you in the ER last night. I met you a hundred years ago."

"Oh yeah, smart-ass," I said as I gleefully pounced on the hole in his joke. "And how is it you are still alive after a hundred years?"

"Because I'm what you would call a vampire."

FIVE

I burst out laughing again. "Yeah," I said. "Good one. They don't exist."

Shane quirked an eyebrow at me, and in spite of all the weirdness my heart did that strange little flip again. Weird and sexy—my first date since I don't know when, and I picked a real winner.

Or course, I couldn't really consider the bizarre circumstances of this night a date, could I? Not unless I was certifiable. At least I'd fit right in here.

"You're right, Abbey," Shane said. "Vampires really don't exist. Not like most people think. But there is a reason why some people believe they do. There's usually some facts behind every legend."

"Show her, Doc," said the guy with the crossbow. I noticed he was still holding it.

Shane kept his eyes on me and raised his left hand in front of my face. He extended his fingers so that his palm flexed toward me. Then, in the most surreal moment of my life, his palm opened and a hollow bone-like thing with a sharpened point protruded from the center of his hand. He moved his hand down until the protrusion was poised right over my breast, right over my heart.

I felt a heaviness in my chest, and the nurse's warning

from the ER rang in my ears, along with the heavy thumping of my heart.

"I could suck your life from your body before you have time to blink," he said. I looked up at his face and saw that his eyes were bright red.

"I am so screwed," I said. The room started spinning around me.

My head hurt—and that was putting it mildly. I postponed opening my eyes as long as I could, mostly because of the pain but also because I knew I wasn't in my own bed. And if I wasn't in my own bed, then the chances were pretty good that the nightmare I'd experienced was real.

Yeah. Right. I was a hundred years in the future, and the hot guy I was supposed to go out with had some sort of Wolverine-thing growing out of his hand.

I felt three distinct lumps above the threadbare sheets, and something furry against the back of my head. Cats. I was also surrounded by cats.

"Charlie . . ." What had happened to Charlie? How long did he wait for me? An image of my dog sitting in the parlor watching the stupid pedestal hourglass time-twisty portal thing brought tears to my eyes.

As I rubbed the tears away, I opened my eyes to find myself looking into the bright green stare of a gray-striped cat.

"Merow?" he said.

"What is this?" I asked him. "Hemingway's Hell?"

Mr. Gray-stripe stood up, stretched and then proceeded to wash his chest with a scratchy pink tongue. I stole a quick glance to check for six toes or some other inbred discrepancy, but everything seemed normal. If only I was in Key West instead of this unbelievable, bizarre, depressing future world.

My head throbbed. I threw the sheet and worn blanket back and realized that I was naked. Cats rumbled in protest as they hit the floor at my disturbance, and I quickly pulled the sheet back around my body.

"Oh God," I said. "Please tell me I only took drugs and then had wild sex with Shane."

Yes, wanting to be a drug-crazed crack whore was better than everything else that had happened last night.

My hair was wild, my mouth tasted like mud, and my arm, which was bandaged—hey, at least I had something on—throbbed.

"Coffee. I need coffee."

I looked around the room for my clothes. Sunlight filtered through a huge oak tree that grew right outside the window. It appeared to be early evening. How long had I slept? I checked the room for an alarm clock, but there was nothing to say what time it was, what day it was, or what year it was.

"Coffee," I said again. I needed to focus on something.

The paint on the walls looked as if it had at one time been lavender. The room's corners still held a hint of the shade, especially where the sun hit. The bed I sat on was huge, with a large oak headboard with spindles and a broken-down mattress covered with sheets so old that they were practically transparent. The blanket on top looked as if it had seen better days. There were no clothes anywhere that I could see. The only other thing in the room was an old overstuffed chair with flowered upholstery.

There was a closet. Clothes usually stayed in closets. At least, that was my philosophy. The four cats now stationed around the room on the floor seemed to share my logic, remaining silent as they watched my struggle for some semblance of order.

Standing was a task I wasn't sure I could handle. As soon as I straightened, my head exploded with a pounding so intense I was sure I would throw up.

"Coffee." I decided to be strong although my every instinct told me to curl up in a ball and cry. "Now."

I managed to shuffle to the closet door without tripping over the sheet that trailed behind me. When I opened the door I had at least some small victory. My leather jacket and boots were both inside. However, there was a definite lack of jeans, sweater and my only matching set of bra and panties.

At this point, I decided my need for coffee was much greater than my need for modesty. I tightened the sheet around my body as best I could and then picked up its trailing end and flung it over my shoulder.

"Well, at least I'm ready if they happen to be having a toga party," I muttered.

I opened the door to the hallway. The cats joined me in my escape and ran ahead, taking time to greet some of the others that were stationed at various places along my trek.

A huge staircase stood at the end of the hall. I recalled seeing the bottom of one that turned in the same way this one did, when I'd first come into the house. I looked up at the wide molding on the walls and the scarred planks on the floor. Early 1800s architecture. This was a mansion that most likely predated everything else around it, including my home; which I had traced back to the 1920s.

Crazy Cat Lady's house. I'd always wanted to see inside it. Now, here I was wandering around it wearing nothing but a sheet.

I gathered up my makeshift garment and went downstairs with several cats serving as escorts. What do you call it when cats run together? Herds? Packs? Schools? Flocks? All I know is that everywhere I looked there was a cat. Big cats, sleepy cats, fluffy cats, not-so-fluffy cats and a cute little orange kitten that hung on to the tail of my sheet as if it had just caught its last meal.

When I made the landing and turned to go downstairs I saw even more cats. They were everywhere. Some of them looked at me with sleepy contentment. Some of them ignored me. A few came to investigate the tips of my toes that peeked out from beneath my makeshift toga. Good thing I wasn't allergic.

I heard voices, so I followed the sound, which led to the back of the house. I stepped through a wide doorway and into what my experienced eye for architecture said was an addition of a kitchen and den, probably around fifty years old—or make that one hundred and fifty years old if I was indeed in the future.

"Coffee," I reminded myself. If I kept thinking about coffee, then I wouldn't remember how absurd my circumstances were. Or the fact that I might be crazy.

Crossbow-man, the boy Trent and a woman who wasn't Janet or Claudia were sitting around an old table. I looked hopefully toward the bar and counter behind them, but my eyes confirmed what my nose had told me: there was no coffee being brewed. There wasn't even a coffeepot in sight. And seeing the electric stove covered with clay pots of tomatoes and peppers did nothing to give me hope.

"Coffee?" I asked optimistically.

They all looked at me as if I were speaking a foreign language.

"Shane?" I tried.

Crossbow-man looked out the window. The last rays

of the sun cast spectra through a crystal that hung there. I turned my eyes away; the light was killing my head.

"He's still underground," he said.

"Ohhh," I said flippantly. "And he said he wasn't really a vampire." I admit it. I get a bit crabby when I don't get my morning caffeine.

"Trent, why don't you go outside and play?" the woman said. Like the man, she looked to be in her forties. Her light brown hair held the slightest touch of gray, and her hands were worn from years of work. But her brown eyes were kind, and I felt that she at least might feel sorry for my predicament.

"Do I have to?" Trent protested. The woman gave him a gentle shove, and with a scrape of his chair, a rolling of his eyes and a great dramatic sigh he rose and stomped past me.

Fine. I wasn't fit company for a child. But who was without their morning fix? Or make that late afternoon fix. Whatever. I just needed to fix it.

I shuffled past the table, holding up my sheet with one hand while keeping it tight with the other. I opened the door on the fridge and was surprised to find it full of canning jars. There was no milk, no soda, no leftover pizza.

My head was killing me.

"Coke?" I asked hopefully. "Pepsi?" Hell, at this point I'd settle for Mountain Dew. "Anything with caffeine?"

They both looked at me blankly.

"How about my clothes?"

"Berta washed them," Crossbow-man said. "We had to get the acid off so you wouldn't hurt the Doc."

"Thank you," I said. I assumed that the woman sitting at the table was Berta, and I made every effort to be civil even though I was ready to kill for caffeine.

"They should be dry now," she said. "I'll go get them

off the line." Which left me alone with Crossbow-guy, who proceeded to give me the evil eye.

"The Doc said to leave you alone," he said. "But just so you know, I'm watching you."

"Thanks," I said. "I'll keep that in mind." I felt a little more cocky, as there wasn't a crossbow in sight. I began the process of opening cabinet doors. There had to be coffee somewhere. I mean, we were still on Earth, weren't we?

I heard the creak of a door and Shane walked into the kitchen. He cocked an eyebrow at my garb and walked to the window to stare into the twilight. The sun had dipped behind the trees and buildings.

"Been lazing about in your coffin?" I'd moved past cranky and shifted into bitchy.

He walked over and put his hand on my forehead. I pushed it away. He grabbed my jaw in a firm grip and held it while looking into my eyes.

Why did his own have to be so blue . . . and so beautiful? Long dark lashes that any woman would kill for made them look even more blue, if that was possible. These were eyes that you could lose yourself in. Eyes that saw into your soul. Eyes that compelled you.

Yet, I could not help but recall that they were glowing red the last time I saw them.

And that thing growing out of his hand. It couldn't be real, could it? I mean, things like that don't really exist. Maybe he'd just *thought* he could suck life from my body with that whatever it was. But, what was it?

Nurse Susan's words once again rang in my ears, and my head hurt.

Shane grabbed my wrist. "Your pulse is down, which means your blood pressure is down. You're obviously irritable"—I twisted away from his grip—"and restless. I bet your eyes are sensitive to light and you've got a killer headache too."

"Excellent diagnosis, Dr. Maddox," I said. "What's wrong with me?"

"Your body is oversensitive to adenosine. Most of your blood is hanging around your brain." He pecked the top of my skull with a finger, which caused pain to shoot down to my toes. "You're experiencing caffeine withdrawal. I bet you had a cup at Joe's every morning."

"Yes, I did," I growled, and readjusted my sheet. "So, why don't you brew me up a pot and let's make it all go away."

"Sorry." His tone was amused. "There's no coffee anywhere. These guys have never even heard of it. I'd say the last time I even smelled a cup was probably fifty years ago."

"How can there be no coffee?" I asked, incredulous.

"Because there's no trade with coffee-producing nations," he said.

"What?" I spluttered. My head hurt too bad to grasp what he was saying. "Why?"

"Because of the pandemic."

"The pandemic?"

"Remember the bird flu?"

I screwed my eyes shut. "Yes, I remember."

"It hit. It wiped out two-thirds of the earth's population."

"Leaving the rest of us as tick fodder," Crossbow-man spoke up.

I looked at him. He was definitely the life of the party. "Do you have a name?" I asked. Uh-oh. Bitchy hadn't lasted long; I was now in full slap-me-now phase.

"This is Owen," Shane said. "I guess you could say he's our sheriff."

My response was, "I think I'm going to throw up."

SIX

I'm pretty sure I threw up several times over the next three days. The headache that had me begging for death came with a fever caused by the wound in my arm. Both finally abated, and I woke one afternoon to thunder pounding across the sky.

I gave serious thought to nominating Berta for sainthood. The woman didn't even know me but had taken care of me. She'd wiped my brow, helped me stagger to the bathroom, and cleaned up my mess whenever I didn't make the trip.

Shane had been there, too. In the dark of night I remembered him hovering over me. Or maybe that was just nightmares. I put my hand over my heart just to make sure there were no holes in my chest.

I was having a hard time dealing with his whole "Technically I'm not a vampire" shtick. Add to that the idea that I'd traveled one hundred years into the future, and things were even more unfathomable. But I had to admit something weird had happened to me; the world I was in was not one I recognized. So it was either believe the things told to me or hope the institution I went to was a decent one.

I looked at Gray-stripe, who seemed to have adopted

me. His purr rumbled an accompaniment to the thunder. I rubbed between his ears and had an angst-filled moment for Charlie. What happened to him?

"If we're going to hang out together, I'm going to have to know your name," I said. "Do you have one? There are so many of you, how does anyone remember?" I took a good look at the cat as he butted my hand with his head to encourage more rubbing. "Okay, I hereby christen you Jayne. I know it's a girl's name, but I'm a big *Firefly* fan and I think he's cool."

Jayne stood up and gave a long feline stretch, so I figured he was fine with it. He jumped down on the floor and moved to the door as if waiting. I nodded and rose.

At least the future had running water; whoever had primed the pipes had done a great job. I made my way to the hall bathroom with Jayne at my side, shed the old T-shirt that Berta had given me to sleep in, and stepped into an incredibly cold shower that soon had my teeth chattering.

I didn't dare take the bandage from my arm. I didn't want to see it. Still, it felt amazingly pain free and even itched. At least it didn't hurt anymore. Something finally was going my way.

My peroxide-faded jeans slid down my hips when I put them on—that's what three to four days puking and without food will do for you. It was too muggy for my sweater, which looked like it belonged in a rag bag now, so I pulled on a T-shirt from the pile Berta had placed in my room. This one said *Be careful or I'll put you in my novel.*

Yeah, I was so going to write a book about this. Jayne blinked, which I took to mean "As long as I'm in it, I don't care," and we went downstairs, both of us moving on silent feet.

·I was surprised to see Shane sitting at the kitchen table with Berta and Owen.

"Aren't you supposed to fry in the light of day?" I asked.

"Only direct sunlight bothers me," he said, pointing at the window. Rain was falling, and the sky was downright gloomy.

"Why does it hurt you?" I asked. "If you're not really a vampire and all . . ."

"Like I said, there's usually fact behind most legends," he said. "Ultraviolet light—my skin is very sensitive to it."

"Along with peroxide?" I asked.

"That, too."

"Hmmm," I said. "I'll keep that in mind." I ignored the heavy frown that Owen gave me. "Have you tried sunscreen?" I added—just to piss the sheriff off.

"I bet you're hungry," Berta interrupted with a genuine smile. She went outside in her quick and efficient way, trailed by about six cats. I wondered exactly what purpose the kitchen served, since there appeared to be no food preparation ever going on.

"Yeah, I could eat," I agreed, and visions of a medium-rare filet, loaded baked potato and asparagus filled my mind. Or maybe just an extra-large pepperoni pizza.

I got a bowl of tomato soup and a slice of bread. I sat down at the table where Berta placed my meal, and she bustled back outside as soon as she saw me dip the spoon into the bowl. Jayne took up residence on a stool and closed his eyes in kitty contentment. He didn't even blink when Trent wandered in and sat down on a stool next to him.

"We do all our cooking on a stone oven out back," Shane explained. "It's all done with wood fires. There's less chance of the house burning down."

"Makes sense," I said. "So, I'm guessing there's no electricity?"

"Nope," Shane replied. "Most utilities disappeared years ago, sometime after the pandemic."

"Why don't you bring me up to date on what's happened in the past hundred years?" I said. If I was going to write a book, I might as well have all the details.

"Remember the serial killer?" he said.

"Yeah." Of course I remembered. It had been just a few days ago, at least to me.

"She's not what you would call human. She's a Chronolotian."

"What the heck is a Chronolotian?" I asked.

"An alien race," Shane said. The easiest way to explain it is that they are time thieves. They take days from their victims' lives and add them to their own. There are several of them that have been on earth for millennia. The one we know is Lucinda."

"The Queen of the ticks," Owen added.

"Why do you call them ticks?" I asked, trying very hard to not roll my eyes at what Shane was saying.

"Because they suck your life away!" Trent broke in, excited to have something to contribute.

"And it doesn't make them seem so formidable," Shane added, looking grim.

I could see that. A tick could be squashed. A Chronowhatever, on the other hand . . .

"So, this Lucinda person was the serial killer?" I said.

"She *is* the serial killer. She's still here."

I made a face.

"And you know her," Shane added.

"I do?" Now I was totally confused. "How?"

"She's the woman who was in the ER that night."

"The redhead all dressed in leather?"

"Yes."

"No wonder she gave me the creeps. I think she followed me there," I muttered. I took a bite of my bread. It was actually quite good. If only I had some butter . . . "Wait a minute," I said, suddenly realizing something. "When you brought me in here you kept saying I was part of Lucinda's gang and I'd planned something. You said all this was my fault. Why?"

"Because I got changed that night."

"What night?"

"The night you stood me up."

I felt the anger emanating off him, and Shane suddenly stood with a heavy scrape of his chair. The danger was palpable. I saw a flash of red in his eyes; then he turned and walked to the bar. He stood behind it, as if he needed a barrier between us. Trent looked at him with obvious adoration, and I vaguely wondered where the kid was from.

"What happened?" I asked.

"When you didn't arrive, I left. Lucinda was in the alley beside Joe's. I thought it was too much of a coincidence, her being there again, so I went to ask her if she knew what was up with you. That's all I remember until I woke up in her bed the next morning close to death." His voice got quiet. "It was as if everything inside was drained out of me. As if I was all dried up. I needed something . . . anything . . . Lucinda was there waiting. I looked at her and said, 'Please.' She placed her hand over my heart and . . ." He looked down as if he were ashamed.

"Wow," Trent said.

"Trent," Berta said. "Go find someplace else to be."

There was more chair-screeching and foot-scuffing and sullenness as Trent marched dramatically from the room. I was oddly amused to see kids were still the same in the future.

"Don't make promises you can't keep," Owen said to me after Trent had gone. The look on his face was smug. "Like Shane said, this was your fault."

I dropped my spoon in frustration at Owen's open hostility and looked at Shane. He'd said it all so matter-of-factly, as if telling me about some boring job he had to do. But the look in his eyes—it was so sad . . . so lonely . . . so desperate.

"I don't show up because I got sucked into . . ." I looked around the room. "Here."

"Whatever," Shane said. "I guess it was just one of those funny twists of fate." He shrugged and left the room. Owen quickly followed.

"Don't worry about it," Berta patted my arm. "He always gets moody around this time of the month."

I wondered if she could tell the difference with Owen, but decided not to comment since they were a couple. Instead I concentrated on Shane's present mood.

"You mean, like, Chronodude PMS?" I asked. That couldn't be any weirder than everthing else that was going on.

Berta rolled her eyes. "The full moon is coming. It gets hard for him to control his urges. It's his nature. Just like the rest of them."

"Uh . . . what exactly are his urges?" I asked. Berta just patted my arm again. She was the queen of comfort.

Sighing, I went back to my soup. "So tell me, what exactly is the world like now?"

"The world, I don't know so much," she said. "All I know is here. Though, sometimes we hear things when we trade."

"Is there someplace central where people gather? Isn't there any worldwide communication system? What about the Army? The National Guard? The Air Force?"

"We have gatherings," Berta agreed. "We trade for food. Most everything we have is scavenged," she explained.

"So, basically there's been a complete breakdown of society," I said.

"As you and Shane knew it. All I know is this world." She sounded sad.

"The ticks," I said. "What's the story with them? How many of them are there?"

"We're not sure. From what we know, every major population center has both them and us. They don't want to wipe us out because they'd have nothing to feed on. Thus, they let us live and procreate, and they take from us what they need to survive."

"Like cattle," I said, incredulous. "Were the ticks around before the pandemic?"

Berta nodded. "Shane said the tick population exploded right after he was turned. He said no one could figure out where they all came from. They were just suddenly there. Because of them and the fear and disruption of everything, the pandemic hit that much harder. Everything the government tried to do was sabotaged by them."

I felt my headache coming back, and I rubbed my forehead. This was simply too much to absorb.

"So, if the world is all us against them," I asked, "why is Shane with the good guys? If he's a tick now, shouldn't he be running with them?"

"That's something he'll have to tell you," Berta said. "Do you want any more soup?"

I looked at my bowl, which was pretty much empty.

I had a lot to digest, and I figured as weak as my stomach was that perhaps I shouldn't try too much too soon.

"I'm fine," I said. Berta took the bowl to the sink and washed it out. Now I saw the kitchen's function.

I went to the door and looked out over a yard soaked from rain. A stone oven sat under a shelter that ran close to another addition to the back of the house. Several cats snoozed beneath it, and my own feline friend rubbed against my legs. On the left side of the yard was a garage with a caved-in roof and a rusted-out Dodge truck in front of it. I saw the shadowy figures of cats taking shelter beneath.

"Hey, Berta," I asked. "What's with all the cats?"

"They give us warning," she said. "They sense ticks. They're used to Shane, but when another one shows up, they go crazy."

"Really?" I looked down at Jayne, who had joined me in looking through the screen door.

"That's why Owen didn't kill you right off," Berta said. "The cats weren't bothered by you at all."

I knelt down and gave Jayne a thank-you rub. Like I'd said, good thing I'm not allergic.

SEVEN

My body felt sluggish, weak; I wasn't used to being inactive for so long. Between my karate and construction hobbies I was usually doing something, so as the parlor of the house had a large open space in the middle, I went through my stretch routine on an oriental rug that was remarkably free of dust. What I really needed was a good run, but it was raining again and I wasn't sure about the boundaries of safety. I really wasn't sure about anything.

Jayne watched me from his perch on a piano bench as I went through several yoga poses and then dropped into a set of push-ups and ab crunches. The rain set a peaceful mood and somewhere outside wind chimes added enough whimsy to give the feeling that I was listening to a CD of relaxation sounds.

I shook my head. Here I was, longing for make-believe peace.

From the corner of my eye I saw Trent spying on me from the hall. What was up with that kid? Berta and Owen were obviously not his parents, so he must be an orphan. Were there other kids around? I'd seen several adults around the bonfire the first night, and there were Janet and Claudia who could become moms. What exactly was the population of this "herd of tick fodder" as Owen so sweetly put it?

I moved into the first steps of a *kata*. I needed to clear my mind, figure things out, decide what to do—wake up from this really weird dream.

First things first. Clear the mind. I concentrated on the movements, making sure each was fluid and strong as I'd been taught. I let my mind connect with the meanings of each position until I lost track of where and when I was.

"I always said ninjas are way cooler than pirates."

I almost stumbled. "What?"

Shane stood in the doorway, his shoulder propped against it and his arms folded across his chest.

"Ninjas are cooler than pirates," he said again.

I looked around the room in case there was a pirate hanging around. Nope. No pirates; there was just Trent, who had somehow managed to sneak into the room and sit quietly in a corner.

At my questioning look, Shane shook his head. "It's nothing, just . . ." His voice trailed off. "So, are you a ninja or something?" Despite his joke, he seemed sad.

"No," I said. "I take karate lessons. I guess you could say it's my hobby."

"Great hobby," he agreed. "I always wanted to, but there was never time."

"Oh?" I settled onto the floor in a lotus position, and Jayne quickly jumped down and made himself at home in my lap.

"You know, I had other things. Little League, piano lessons, homework—stuff like that."

"Sounds very normal," I said.

He got a faraway look in his eyes. How far back did

one's memory go when you had lived as long as he claimed? How for *could* it go?

"How old are you?" I asked. "Without the entire time warp thing."

"I was twenty-seven when I was turned."

Twenty-seven. And he'd lived one hundred years since.

"How old are you?" he asked.

"Twenty-three. Or am I one hundred and twenty-three? Do the hundred years count if you don't really live them—?"

Before the words were out of my mouth, Shane was across the room and had jerked me to my feet. Jayne went flying as I stood, my shoulders held tight in his grasp. "You seem to think this entire thing is some sort of joke," he growled. His jaw was clenched and I saw a hint of red in his eyes.

Tick or not, no one pushes me around. I shrugged free and stepped away from him. "Excuse me for trying to deal with the situation," I said. "It's not every day I walk through a time portal and find out my date is a chrono-whatever-the-heck-you-are." This going-from-hot-to-cold-in-a-heartbeat thing that he had going on was kind of freaking me out. I turned away and settled into the beginning stance of a *kata*.

"You talk about the past hundred years as if they're a joke . . ." Shane walked over to the piano, where Jayne had once again taken up residence on the bench, and sat down beside him. The cat let out a squeaky meow but stayed put. "But I've lived the past one hundred years." He played a chord, and I recalled he'd mentioned piano lessons. "I've watched people I cared for live and die. Most of them violently."

I recognized the notes from "Stairway To Heaven" as he played an accompaniment to his words. Was he being intentionally ironic?

He continued: "I watched my parents bury a second son, all because I could not explain to them why I wasn't aging, why I couldn't go into the sunshine, why I couldn't eat their food, why every month I . . ."

I stared at the back of his head as his voice trailed off. He was bent over the piano, which sounded remarkably well-tuned. His blond hair swirled around his shoulders carelessly, as if he'd hadn't taken time to comb it. A lock fell forward over his eyes, but that didn't matter; they were closed tightly against the memories he conjured.

"You faked your death?"

He turned to look at me with those bright blue eyes of his, and he brushed his hair back behind his ear. Flip went my heart. Dumb went my brain.

"I 'drowned'," he said in a stark whisper. "They never found my body."

I didn't know what to say. My first instinct was to offer comfort. It had to have been surreal: to fake his death to save his parents the pain of knowing what he'd become. Then, to watch their pain as they buried him. And when they'd died, he couldn't have been there with them.

Bury a second son . . . He'd lost a brother? When? In the pandemic? There were so many questions, so many things that I wanted to know—that I probably would have known had we only had a normal future. If we'd gone out, I could have shared his pain. I never knew my mother, since she died when I was born, but my father . . . Until the day I die I will never forget the sight of his death. I still saw visions of the accident in my dreams.

Yes, these things I could share with Shane. But to do so

now—I was afraid he'd erupt again into scary Shane and shake me like Charlie shaking a particularly vicious shoe.

Just like that, Shane's manner changed and he jumped up to his feet.

"Get dressed," he said. "We're going out."

"Out?" I looked out the window that faced the front of the house. It was late, and the sky was dark with clouds and the rain still pounded. "It's raining," I said. My voice squeaked. No way did I want to go out into Tickworld. It was dark and scary.

Shane laughed. He went to a wardrobe in the hall and pulled free a long black coat. "This will keep you dry," he said, and he flung it at me. "Put your shoes on or come barefoot," he said. "You've got five minutes to decide."

"Where are we going?" I asked.

"Your house," he tossed over his shoulder as he strode from the room. "Consider it our date."

I stood for a moment with my mouth hanging open. Then I heard, "Can you teach me that ninja stuff?" I'd forgotten Trent was there.

My house . . . Was I going home? Could I? Just like Dorothy in *The Wizard of Oz*, could I click some sparkly red shoes together and will myself home?

The time portal. Could it be used both ways?

"Will you teach me?" Trent asked again.

"Um, yeah, sure." The boy stood before me with a big expectant grin on his face; how could I say no? I rubbed the coarse dark curls on top of his head. "Sure, I'd love to teach you how to be a ninja." *If I'm around.*

A big grin filled his face and he ran from the room with a whoop. Jayne laid back his ears and hissed.

"It's been real," I said to the cat as I went to get my shoes. "Or possibly not," I added. Jayne followed, padding up the stairs beside me.

EIGHT

I put the long black coat Shane gave me on over my leather jacket, and gazed into the standing mirror in the corner of the bathroom. I looked like a character in *The Matrix;* all I needed were some really cool dark glasses and Hugo Weaving hissing in my ear. I pulled my hair back from my face with a scrunchie I found in my jeans pocket. No need for makeup even if I had any. *Cosmo* never mentioned whether or not mascara and lip gloss were appropriate when traveling into postapocalyptic Tickworld.

If I could only wake up from this nightmare. Or go back to the dream that was my real world. Vampires, pandemics, time portals . . . And to think, my biggest concern a few days before had been wet homework and bank loans.

Charlie . . .

Mourning my dog wasn't helping things. I might be lonely, but he'd been dead a hundred years. I just hoped that he hadn't died missing me. That someone had taken him in and loved him as much as I.

Jayne meowed, which I translated into "It's time to go," then followed me downstairs to the kitchen.

"Shane said to meet him in the weapons room," Berta

said. She was sitting at the table with Trent, who looked mulish. A huge Bible lay on the table between them. I figured Trent was probably pouting more because he wasn't allowed to come with us. I was also happy to see that faith was still a part of the people's lives. If there were demons on earth, then there had to be angels. It was part of the balance. You couldn't believe in one and not the other. And since ticks seemed to be on the side of the demons . . .

But, what did that make Shane?

I stepped into what had been a laundry room, and followed a hall past a half-bath to a door that stood ajar. Shane was inside, along with Owen and a couple other men. One looked to be in his late twenties, and the other was my age or younger. The younger man looked at me from beneath shaggy brown bangs, and I could tell he was checking me out.

"The rain should keep them inside," Shane said. "Remember, all we want to do is scope out the place, see what's inside."

"If it's the place on Halifax," the youth said, "that's Tick Headquarters."

"Yeah," Owen agreed. "But we want to know why. What makes it so special?" From what we just heard from Abbey . . ."

"We're going to have to get pretty close," the youngster said.

They were loading up with weapons while they talked: crossbows, stakes, knives, guns—the younger guy, a bow and a quiver of arrows.

"This is Jamie," Shane said, indicating the youth, who gave me a sweet smile and a nod. "And Radar," he added, pointing to the other man, who pretended to ignore me. "This is Abbey, our time-traveler."

I made a face at the introduction. Why was every-thing so complicated? Why couldn't I be Abbey, the award-winning architect? Or Abbey, his date for the Hot Doctors Ball? Or both? Anything but relations to time travel and time-sucking predators.

The group's extra weapons were all stored on panels of pegboard that slid out and flipped like the big racks that room-size rugs are sold on at stores. Shane flipped back a panel like he was turning a page in a magazine, and revealed a wall full of swords. I let out a low whistle as Shane pulled down a blade and slid it into a scab-bard that was already attached to his belt beneath the long duster he wore.

"Like it?" he asked, and turned the panel so I could see.

To my amazement, I recognized some of the weapons on the wall. My karate instructor, Master Thomas, had been a total Chuck Norris junkie. The only thing that he loved more than Chuck and all his movies and episodes of *Walker, Texas Ranger,* were Japanese cere-monial swords. He'd had an extensive collection, and he'd taught some of his prize students techniques for handling them.

It just so happened that I was one of his prize stu-dents. I instantly recognized the katana that had been my favorite weapon from class.

"Help yourself," Shane said.

"Yeah, you're going to need one," Owen added.

I grasped the handle of the katana and slid it from its black sheath. Candlelight danced off the blade. The open-mouthed dragon head on the pommel seemed to be smiling at me, as if welcoming back an old friend. I looked carefully at that face and saw the secret Tanto blade still concealed as part of the dragon's snout. I pushed in the eye and the small blade popped up.

Shane arched a brow in surprise as I pushed it back into place.

"You act like you've seen this sword before," Jamie said from beside me. He regarded the blade and the way I handled it with admiration.

"I have," I replied. "Two weeks ago—my time," I added. I didn't want to get into the entire past hundred years discussion again with Shane.

"The only way to kill a tick is to take its head off," Jamie said. "Which makes the blades best." He grinned as he looked at his bow. "But they can be dropped by shots to the heart and then finished off up close." He looked at his friends. "We work as a team." I noticed Shane held a sword, Radar a crossbow, and Owen one of each. They all had knives and guns stuffed into their belts, too.

I slid my new blade home and wrapped the sheath cord around my waist. The sword hung low on my side beneath my coat. The men didn't say a word as I yanked another cord from the wall and strapped the sheath to my lower thigh—If I had to run, I didn't want it banging around and getting in my way.

I looked up to find the men still watching my silent preparations. They all seemed to approve of what I'd done. I felt some satisfaction that my fear didn't show, but I had no guarantees as to how I would act once we were out in the big dark night.

"Stay close," Shane said as we stepped out into the rain.

"The cats are smart enough to stay in," Jamie remarked as he walked by me. I was already shivering, but from fear or cold, I wasn't sure which.

I looked at the four men in their long dark coats. They were all dressed in black overcoats or dusters and dark shirts over jeans. My first thought was that this was the official uniform for any and all bad-asses, but as they faded into the darkness I realized why they dressed this way. You couldn't see them, and their long coats disguised their movements.

"So, it's not just for the look," I observed.

As I stood in the rain, the warm glow of candlelight beckoned me to come back inside. Jayne sat on the windowsill and bobbed his head, as if trying to talk to me through the glass.

"Let's go," Owen hissed from the shadows beyond the trees.

With one last look at Jayne, I followed the men into the darkness.

Radar took the lead. I wondered where he'd gotten his name, since I was pretty sure there weren't any *M*A*S*H* reruns here, but I soon figured it out. He seemed to always know what was coming. He stopped on a corner beneath a lantern hung on a stop sign, and we waited as five new people armed with crossbows moved into view.

I was amazed to see that a couple of cats had followed our group. They weren't happy about the rain, and slunk under the bushes and junked cars that lined the streets.

Owen and James moved up to talk to the newcomers while Shane stayed back with me. We stood under the branches of a maple that was thick with foliage. The rain was nothing more than a thin, cool mist beneath the tree, but it still kept me huddled beneath my coats and wishing for something over my head to keep me dry. The houses set back from the street were lit with candles, each one emanating a welcoming glow.

"It's not a fit night out for man or beast," I said to myself, staring at a cat that pretty much looked the way I felt. Before the night was over, I figured I'd run into both.

"Owen sends out patrols every night," Shane explained. The city is divided between humans and ticks. The wall you came over is the line."

"So, my house is on the tick side?"

"Yes, along with the hospital and most of what used to be the government center."

"Take off the head and the body will crumble," I said, remembering some of Master Thomas's wisdom.

"That was where they struck first," Shane agreed. "Society pretty much went to hell for quite a while until things evened out."

"You mean, when the ticks realized that if they killed all the humans they would starve to death" I suggested.

"Yeah," Shane said. "There was also in-fighting among them. The local tick gangs were battling for superiority."

"Like, tick Mafia families?"

Shane grinned. "Yes. They kept killing each other off until Lucinda's gang came out on top. For a while we were hoping they'd reduce their numbers enough that we could outnumber them."

"Is it pretty much even now?"

Shane nodded. "They let humans reproduce to keep the food chain going. We find the bodies of our people when they feed. And even though we keep dusting them, new ticks keep turning up."

"Could they be from other towns? Berta said you have gatherings." I tried not to think anything about his blasé reference to himself as a human. It seemed normal. He was one of the good guys, wasn't he?

"We don't know where they come from; they just show up. It's always easy to know who the newly turned are. They die in a big way."

I was pretty certain I didn't want to know what that meant. Instead, I asked him something that had been preying on my mind for far too long.

"Are there any more like you out there?" I asked.

"Like me?" he said.

"Ticks aligned with humans."

Shane shook his head. "Not that I know of. I don't go to the gatherings. I guess there could be. I haven't really thought about it."

But his answer only left more questions in my mind. Why didn't he go to gatherings? Couldn't he be of some use since he was a doctor? Surely there were other people out there that needed his help. And he could train others, teach them . . . if he truly wanted to help, then what better way? Then again, maybe being indispensable was what kept him alive. Then another question popped into my mind, one triggered by something he said earlier.

"How *do* you stay alive?"

He didn't answer. Instead, he tugged on my arm so we could join the rest of our small gang.

"No signs," Owen said as we reached him. "I guess, as usual, they're saving it up for the full moon."

"We'll know for sure when we go over the wall," Shane said.

"If this is so dangerous," I asked. "Why are we going?"

"We need to know if what you say is true," he growled. I opened my mouth to protest but he stopped me with an upheld hand. "It might be something we can use against them." He looked at me. "Are you ready?"

Like I had a choice. I gripped the hilt of my katana. "I'm ready."

We took the long way around. We moved under the tracks of the El for a while. The streets were familiar, if distorted, like I was dreaming. Was I? I wished I were. The rain felt real, though, along with the hardness of the sword hilt beneath my palm and the touch of cool air that chilled me to the bone. The night was blacker than any I'd experienced, but my eyes quickly adjusted to the shadows and swirling mass of waving tree branches and overgrown grass that encroached upon the cracked pavement of the streets and sidewalks.

The houses seemed to be crumbling more as we made our way toward my street. No one lived here. This was clearly a no-man's land, a barrier between the humans and the ticks.

I heard the squeak of rats, and occasionally saw the orange glow of cat eyes in burnt-out store fronts. We were close to Joe's, which meant we were close to the barrier.

The men took a minute to confer about where we should cross. Shane seemed to know exactly where my house was, which I thought was kind of strange since he'd only been there once. I suppose he'd had a hundred years after that to revisit the place.

They decided the best strategy was to check out my house from the back, since there was more cover there. I stood huddled in my coat and let them make the decisions. All I could think of was seeing Charlie's bones scattered in the backyard after he starved to death because I abandoned him. I was surprised to see that our two cats were still with us. They padded up to where I stood and looked at me as if I knew what was going on.

We moved on past Joe's. We passed Master Thomas's studio and the small grocery store that had always had fresh flowers out front. What happened to the people I used to know? Joe, Master Thomas, and Mrs. Stein, who'd kept the sidewalks along the shops swept clean and always had a bowl of water for Charlie. Had Master Thomas come to a bad end? The fact that I was wearing one of his prize swords made me think that he had. But I was also sure that he went down swinging. I hoped I could say the same when my time came.

More likely I would piss my pants.

The barrier was just as I remembered: a hastily constructed wall between the buildings, with lots of junk up against it. I hoped I could get over without any trouble. The last thing I wanted to be was weak and girly.

"I'll go first," Shane said. "Wait for my signal." He took off at a run and leapt onto the back of a car without any effort; another leap took him over the wall, and he'd disappeared in a blink of an eye.

Which was what I did. I blinked. Had the rain and darkness distorted my perception?

"Show-off," Owen muttered.

"He does have the moves," Jamie agreed. I saw his teeth flash in the darkness and knew that he was smiling.

Both of the cats bounded up after Shane. Radar was already on the car.

"Must be okay," Jamie said. "The cats aren't spazzing out."

"Do they really let you know when a tick is around?" I asked.

"Oh yeah," he said. "They hate ticks."

"I thought they hated water, too," I said as rain trickled down my collar.

"Not as much as they hate ticks. They'll go after one in a heartbeat."

Radar was now over the wall, and Owen stood on the car as if he was waiting for something. I heard a low whistle.

"That's Shane," Jamie said, and he held out his arm so I could walk ahead of him to the wall.

Oh, great. The thought of Owen heaving my ass over was enough to motivate me. The hood of the car was slick, but I was able to keep my feet in spite of the leather soles of my boots. I felt some satisfaction as I pulled myself over.

That soon gave way to surprise as I dropped into the darkness below and Shane caught me. I hadn't even known he was there; when I'd looked, the ground below was clear except for Radar, who'd taken up position at the end of the alley with the two cats stationed on either side. Yet I dropped into a pair of strong arms and found myself looking into the dark shadows of Shane's rain-slicked face.

Being a tick must give a person super powers, because he didn't even bat an eye as he caught me. And I'm not light. I'm pretty much solid muscle.

"Er," I mumbled. "Thanks."

He didn't say anything. I got the sensation that he was analyzing me, which was strange since it was so dark in the alleyway. Maybe being a tick gave him great night vision. All I know is I had a weird feeling, like I was being stalked. Even though I couldn't see his face, I couldn't tear my eyes away. It was like a flame: you know it's going to burn yet you still want to touch.

If not for Owen and Jamie coming over the wall I'm not sure what would have happened. Or how I would have felt about it.

NINE

We approached my house by the alleyway that ran behind it. The entire block seemed inhabited, but the thick growth of landscaping gone wild kept us hidden as we skulked through the shadows toward the brick wall that enclosed my yard. Radar peered through the tall black iron gate before motioning the rest of us up. The cats sniffed at the bars and hissed.

I was surprised to see that the yard was well-maintained. The shrubs were pruned and there was a nice brick terrace with heavy iron furniture and thick torches placed all around. This would be a great place to spend an evening.

There was also an absence of a dog skeleton, which made me feel somewhat better, even if I still felt pangs for Charlie.

The house was well lit, as if every room was in use. Even the tiny basement windows let out a warm glow.

"Which room had the time portal?" Shane asked in a whisper.

I pointed to the window on the right. The parlor ran front to back in the house, with a kitchen and dining room on the opposite side of the central hall and staircase. Upstairs were three bedrooms and a bath.

What happened to all my stuff? Not that I had much. Were my clothes and makeup and drawings and tools still there? Maybe all neat and tidy in a box in the basement?

"Let's go," Shane said.

"Where?" I asked. Inside? I didn't think so. It was obvious that the place was occupied.

Shane did that uber-hop of his and vaulted onto the top of the wall. The thing was ten feet high, and I stood looking up at him with my mouth hanging open. Jamie held out his cupped hands as Shane lay prone on the wall and reached down with one arm.

Once again, visions of Owen with his hands on my ass motivated me. I placed a foot in Jamie's hands, put my own hands on Jamie's shoulders and used the momentum to pull myself up without any help from Shane. When he saw I was doing well enough on my own, he sat up, swung his leg over the edge and dropped silently behind the dogwood tree that graced a back corner of the yard.

My descent wasn't quite as graceful. The sheath of my sword got tangled in my legs. Shane once again caught me, but this time I quickly turned in his arms and pushed away from his chest. There was no way I wanted to get caught up in his spell again. Especially not when I feared there were at least a hundred more ticks waiting for their own chance to appraise my life expectancy.

Jamie took a post on top of the wall. Owen and Radar did not come over. I could only assume that they were watching from the outside.

Both cats came through the bars of the gate. I wondered if they planned their part of the stakeout, as one of them climbed the dogwood tree and joined Jamie on the wall while the other ran ahead toward the house with its tail straight up. The cats, along with the men, seemed to know where to go and what to do, while I just followed along after Shane and prayed to not become tick fodder.

We crept up to the house. The closer we got, the louder the voices became. Someone was throwing a fit. We heard the sounds of destruction inside at about the same time we reached the window. I winced and kept my head down, while Shane stood bold as brass and looked through the window. The cat that accompanied us huddled beneath the folds of my coat.

"Look," he said.

I rose on tiptoe and slowly stretched until I could see through the window. I heard the cat hiss as it wound around my ankles. I didn't need his warning to tell me what was inside.

Just as I recalled from my appearance here, the room was gorgeous. The deep woodwork glowed in the candlelight, and several pieces of quality antiques and overstuffed chairs were overturned and thrown around the room. A fire roared in the wide fireplace and, just as I'd expected, it was beautiful thick brick and ornate woodwork. The woman from my night in the ER stood in my parlor with her hands on her leather-clad hips and her bright red hair flying. On the floor before her knelt several men and women with their heads bent in submission, while the redhead raged and whirled in anger.

"Lucinda," Shane said, extremely close to my ear. His breath tickled and felt warm against my damp skin.

"Yeah. I figured as much," I replied quietly. "What's got her so pissed?"

Shane shrugged. "She's worked up about something." I felt his mouth widen into a grin.

Lucinda moved forward and, to my amazement,

kicked one of the kneeling men in the mouth. Blood spurted, a deep purplish color, and he fell forward. No one else moved.

"What a bitch," I muttered.

"Is that your time portal?" Shane asked.

My time portal? Any other time and place I would have laughed and made a joke. Oh yeah, sure, my time portal. Where did you find it? I'm always losing the stupid thing. Instead, I looked where Lucinda was standing. The pedestal was there, and on top of it stood the hourglass.

As I watched, the machine started to spin sideways, and I heard the strange whirring noise. One of the minions on the floor raised a shaking arm and pointed. Lucinda turned to look at it. Her face contorted from anger to horror. It was not a pretty sight.

Then she looked directly at the window. The cat at my feet let loose a warbling yowl, and I ducked.

"We better move," Shane said.

We heard Lucinda's shriek. We heard more crashing of furniture, and the pounding of feet.

Shane grabbed my hand and we took off for the wall. I heard the familiar creak of the back door.

"Duck," Shane said. I felt him turn away from me as I instinctively put my head down, and heard a whistling above me. An arrow? I heard a shriek and then what sounded like a muffled explosion. Something wet hit my back, but I didn't take time to see what it was.

"Get them!"

Owen fired his crossbow through the gate as yells to stop accompanied our flight. We weren't going to make it. There was no way we could get over the wall before they caught us, even with the cover.

I saw a cat bolt through the gate. I ran toward the tree,

figuring that if I climbed it Jamie could pull me over. But before I reached the shelter of its branches, I took flight; Shane had picked me up by the waist and pitched me to the top of the wall. I managed to grab hold and pull myself over while Jamie kept firing arrows. The guy was freaking Legolas.

I rolled over the side and landed by Owen, who kept up a steady rain of crossbow bolts through the gate. How long before they ran out?

I drew my sword and held it ready. Not too tight, not too loose, comfortable and familiar in my grip. But could I use it?

Shane landed lightly beside me, his own sword drawn and ready. Jamie appeared behind him, notching another arrow in his bow.

"Time to go," Jamie said, and we took off running down the alley with the cats' raised tails guiding our way.

The alarm had sounded. Lucinda's screams echoed off the houses. As we ran, we heard the slamming of doors and pounding of feet along the alleyway. If Shane had super tick powers, then wouldn't the ones chasing us have them too? What chance did we stand against hundreds of them?

I was about to find out. There were indeed ticks waiting for us at the end of the alley.

Our two cats didn't stop. They launched their bodies full-force at the two male ticks that stood in our way. They sank their claws in the men's faces and knocked them down, nipping at noses and ears.

The cats went flying as the ticks flung them away. But they'd given us a chance.

Shane was the first one forward. He rushed ahead, sword swinging. Two ticks turned to dust before my eyes as he took their heads off.

Behind me, Jamie knelt and fired his bow at those who followed. He struck the leader directly in the heart. I watched in amazement as the female tick staggered a few final steps, purple blood pouring from her mouth. Owen dropped his crossbow and drew his sword. He swung as she staggered by. Her head went flying, and then she—*it*—exploded. Blood and guts went flying everywhere. I gagged.

More ticks kept coming.

"Run!" Shane yelled. He was fighting several now, all unarmed. Except for their blazing red eyes, their super tick powers and their hands that reached like claws for Shane's chest.

"Go!" Jamie yelled to me as he fired again. Owen was in combat also; as ticks fell back and away from Shane, he took advantage and struck with his sword.

The weirdest thing was, how some of the ticks turned to dust but others blew up. It was disgusting. One exploded as I took off across the street, and I felt ick hit me.

Radar had joined the fray. He'd come up from behind on some ticks, and was vigorously hacking away. I turned and watched the four men fight, my sword still gripped in my hand.

Shane was a killing machine. His eyes glowed red and his sword flashed, flinging blood and rain in every direction. The other three seemed to know what they were doing, too, but how long could they last against such odds? I didn't know what to do. Should I keep running?

"Get her!" Three ticks poured out of the alley. "Lucinda said to bring her back alive."

Hell, no. There was no way that was happening. "Shane?" I called as two of the group came toward me. The last stayed back and watched. I guess he thought he was too important to dirty his hands bringing me back alive. Still, I didn't want to go with them. And alive with them didn't seem much better than dead at this point. "*Shane!*"

But Shane was busy. As were Owen, Jamie and Radar. Radar went down with a tick on his back, and I realized there were too many of them. And no one was going to help me.

Could I outrun them? I was doubtful. If they ran like they jumped, then there was no way. And the way Shane moved made me realize that they possessed tremendous speed.

The first tick who approached me was young. Like, high school young. He had long blond hair and kind of reminded me of a musician I'd had a crush on about ten years ago, give or take a hundred.

Or he did until his eyes turned glowy red and he dove toward me.

I swung my katana in a two-handed grip. The sword sliced through the boy tick's arm and into his neck. He fell to the ground and went into convulsions. I looked down as his hand gripped my ankle. His eyes turned a soft blue.

"Help me," he said.

Then he exploded.

I didn't have time to think about it; the other tick was on me and I swung my sword again. This one dissolved into dust as I took its head off.

"That's more like it," I said.

Jamie and Owen had Radar under the arms and dragged him toward me. Shane was covering their retreat, and I ran forward with my sword ready. I took one down who leapt at Shane's back.

"Go," he said. "Get to the wall. They won't come over."

I followed the men. I kept looking over my shoulder to see if we were being followed, and I heard the yowling of a cat up ahead.

"They're trying to cut us off," Owen called back at me.

Jamie and I were now in the lead. The cats stood at a corner, their backs arched and tails twitching as they looked down the street. Owen staggered behind me with Radar as four ticks ran toward us—and these ticks were armed.

I can't really explain what happened next. I guess the best way to describe it is to say my years of karate training took over. All I know is that I charged forward, screaming, my sword in the attack position, and the next thing I knew there was blood and gore all over the place and the four were dead.

It was pouring rain now. I sucked in air as I looked down at the pavement. Water trickled down my neck but it didn't matter; I was soaked through.

"Let's go," Jamie said. He tentatively touched my arm, as if he were afraid I'd swing on him.

"Shane?" I asked. I didn't see him.

"He's coming. We've got to get Radar over the wall."

We ran toward Joe's. I saw Shane coming toward us. His eyes glowed red. The wind and the rain swirled around him, and it looked as if he were flying.

"Like a bat out of hell," I said as he joined us.

He didn't stop. Owen was straddling the wall. Shane lifted Radar in his arms and leapt to the top and then over. Jamie and I scrambled across as best as we could.

"Any trailers?" Owen asked.

"No," Jamie said. The look he gave me was kind of scary. Or maybe he thought *I* was scary.

"Make sure," Owen said. He and Shane took off with

Radar in Shane's arms. I noticed they were trailing blood. But that quickly disappeared as the rain drenched the pavement.

I wiped my hand across my chin and felt something sticky.

"What is it?" I said as I looked at the white thing on my hand.

"Looks like from an eyeball," Jamie said.

"What?" I shook my hand and whatever it was flew off.

"You've got some in your hair," he said.

I touched my hand to my hair, most of which had fallen out of its scrunchie. Sure enough, something trailed away like an egg yolk. It was slimy and sticky.

"Ewww." I went into major freak-out mode. Never mind that I'd just killed several ticks with extreme prejudice; there was something gross in my hair. My entire body shuddered, and I did this hyper dance toward Jamie, who looked at me as if I were totally insane.

"It's sticky!" I shrieked. "Get it out."

"Okay," he said. He dragged his fingers through my hair and flung whatever it was away. "It's gone now."

"Are you sure?" I kept touching my hair. I didn't want to touch anything gross, but then again I wanted to make sure it was gone.

"I'm sure," he said.

We both jumped as we heard a crash, but it was just the cats coming over the wall.

"We'd better go," he said.

"Yeah," I agreed.

As we took off at a run I had to wonder: Why did Lucinda want me?

TEN

"Now I know what 'dying in a big way' means," I said, still creeped out over the gore. "Why do some of them explode?" I asked as we ran toward the house. I felt totally humiliated after my girly meltdown, and thought changing the subject might keep Jamie from having a good laugh over it later with his buds.

Or not.

"Those are new ticks," he said. "Young. They acquire all this power when they're turned and haven't learned how to channel it yet. So when we kill them, they explode."

"Did you know any of them?"

Now I was not only stupid but also heartless. But, he must know them. Wasn't that a fact of life in this time? Humans could be food or they could be turned.

He said, "No. That's the big mystery—where they come from. They just show up."

So, maybe I wasn't so stupid or heartless.

We caught up with Owen. He stood in the street with his hands on his knees, sucking in air. We were in the lighted section, with patrols nearby.

"How's Radar?" Jamie asked.

"Losing it quick," he replied. "We were able to kill the

tick that was sucking on him but . . . Shane patched him up as best he could. He's carrying him now."

I looked at the fresh blood that stained Owen's coat, and I had to wonder: did ticks drink blood like stereotypical vampires? They were supposed to suck the life from you. And Shane did have that weird thing in his hand.

"Tell me about channeling their power," I asked Jamie as the three of us resumed our trot toward the house. "If they've been ticks a while, do they get stronger?"

"Yeah. That's why Shane has all those superpowers," Jamie replied. "He's been channeling it for some time."

"What keeps him from . . . er . . . um . . ."

"Sucking us dry?" Owen contributed.

I nearly stumbled. I had to stop, and Jamie stopped with me as Owen kept on; I heard him chuckling as he disappeared up the street. I leaned against a post that held a lantern, and put my forehead against the cool wet metal.

"He doesn't hurt us, if that's what you're worried about," Jamie said. "He takes care of us. He's a doctor. There aren't any medical schools out there anymore, or hospitals, or clinics or whatever else you're used to having. They're all gone. It's just us versus them, and we've got an advantage because we've got a doctor."

"But how does he survive?"

"He goes off during the full moon," Jamie said. "We don't ask and he doesn't tell. But he wouldn't hurt us."

I grimaced. "Are you sure that some of the bodies you find aren't ones that Shane has fed off?"

"If they are, then that's just the way it is." Jamie was so matter-of-fact about things. "If that's what it takes to keep him alive. He delivers our babies and takes care of us when we're hurt or sick." Jamie pulled up his shirt and pointed a finger to a faded scar on his side. "He took out my appendix when I was twelve," he said. "He's saved my life more times than I can count."

"But why?" I asked. "Why is he helping you? If he has all this power, why isn't he out there using it?"

"That's something you'll have to ask him," Jamie said. "We better go."

We saw a bonfire as we turned the corner. As soon as we got into sight, Claudia, the girl from the first night, detached herself from the crowd and came toward us at a full run. She threw herself at Jamie, who caught her in his arms and picked her up by the waist to swing around.

I get it, he's yours, I thought as I read her body language. Jamie was cute but I wasn't here to pick up guys. Hardly. My luck with Shane certainly hadn't been very good.

"This is Claudia," Jamie said. She gave me the once over and I realized that I probably looked kind of scary. Especially since I held a bloody sword in my hand.

"Yeah, we've met," I said.

At least fighting together had given us a bond. Jamie handed me a rag from his coat pocket and said, "Always keep your blade clean, warrior girl." Nodding, I wiped the gore from my sword before I sheathed it.

"Hi," I said to Claudia when I was done. I took time to pull my hair back into its scrunchie. I didn't think about what I was touching; I was determined to put my wigging-out days behind me after my last meltdown.

"Hi, again," she replied. "I've got to help Shane. But I wanted to make sure you were okay first," she said to Jamie. She gave him a quick kiss and took off for the house.

The mood around the bonfire was somber. I guess the news about Radar spread fast. Close to a hundred people stood around the fire or on the lawn, with more gathered on the porch.

"Hey Abbey," Trent ran up to me as I stepped onto the porch. "Did you squash any ticks?"

I swallowed hard. "Yeah. A few." I needed a drink. In my own time I never touched the stuff, but I could see the need for it now. I needed something to wash away the strange taste in my mouth.

Jayne came out to meet me as Jamie and Claudia moved toward the fire to report on the night's "dustings." He stood on his hind legs and sniffed at the tail of my coat and hissed in disgust.

"Yeah," I said. "I know. I need a shower." I wanted nothing more than to wash all the tick off me, but there were more important things to worry about at the moment. Radar lay on the stainless steel table inside. Shane, Berta and Claudia were there, and I had a flashback to the night I went to the ER. Shane's face held the same look of grim determination. In the corner was Owen, who had his arm around a tearful woman who was obviously pregnant. Did Radar have a wife?

He was stripped down to his jeans, and blood covered his chest and the table. An I.V. hung from a pole, along with a bag of blood that was being pumped into his arm. Shane looked up at me and I saw his eyes were glowing red. Why? Did Radar lying so helpless on the table make him want to feed? Would he be tempted to finish whatever the other tick had started?

Somewhere in the back of my mind the thought that I wasn't being fair to Shane pricked my conscience. But just the thought grossed me out. I pictured an assembly line including everyone from little children to old people, and Shane walking down the line punching holes in their hearts with that thing that grew out of his palm. The sight of his eyes glowing red and the way his hands moved over Radar's chest didn't help much either. Why was he here? Simple. He had it made. He didn't have to compete with the other ticks for food. He could just help himself and blame it on them. He'd had everything handed to him on a silver platter.

Gross.

"I'm losing him," he snapped.

I walked into the room and kept moving until I could see Radar's wound. There was a deep slash across his neck, which Berta kept pressure on. Shane worked on his heart through an incision he'd made with a scalpel. I wanted to turn away but couldn't. It was like watching surgery on TV. I wanted to put my hands over my eyes and watch through my spread fingers.

There was no way Radar could be saved. He needed transfusions, he needed surgery, and he needed a hospital. He needed more than Shane could give him. Yet Shane didn't give up. He attached clamps and tried to stitch up torn vessels.

It was just too much.

"Let him go," Berta said. She reached out to touch Shane's arm but then thought better of it. Instead, she pulled Claudia back from the table. "Let him die in peace," she said.

Shane stopped. He looked down at Radar, who I saw give the slightest nod. Shane looked at Owen and backed away from the table. Radar's wife let out a sob and ran to her husband's side.

I couldn't stand to see any more. I turned to leave, but was stopped by Shane's voice in my ear.

"Like I said," he whispered. "This is all your fault."

I turned to look at him but he was gone.

How could this be my fault?

I stood in the shower and let the cold water wash over me. I'd washed my hair three times and my skin was blue, but I couldn't find the strength to get out of the shower. Why was it my fault Radar was dead?

Lucinda said to bring her back alive . . .

What did the ticks want me for? How did they know who I was? And what was the deal with the hourglass, the time-twister portal, hourglass, whatever that thing was?

This is all your fault.

I didn't get it. One minute Shane was all gallant, catching me and looking at me and talking to me about ninjas and pirates while he played love songs on the piano, the next he was blaming me for all the ills of his life.

"I want to go ho-home," I said to Jayne, who sat on the edge of the tub, safely away from the shower spray, watching me shiver. My teeth were chattering, so I turned off the water and wrapped in a towel.

My jeans had been spared most of the mess because of the long coat I wore. I put them on, along with a cropped pink T-shirt that said *It's Not Easy Being A Princess* in faded, sparkly silver letters. It was reassuring to know that some novelty T-shirts stood the test of time. I wrapped my hair up in a towel and went to my room with Jayne right beside me.

Berta had seen fit to supply me with some of life's necessities. A comb, brush and mirror sat on a small bureau that was now part of my furnishings, along with a toothbrush and some small jars of what I could only assume by the smell were handmade lotion and toothpaste. It wasn't minty fresh but it did the job.

There was also underwear, a supply of T-shirts, a well-worn pair of jeans and flip-flops in the drawers. I hated to think about where the panties came from or who'd worn them last, but it was better than wearing the same pair every day and I wasn't to the point where I'd go commando

I looked out the window as I combed out my hair. The people were in mourning. I saw several groups clustered together. Some were crying, some were hugging and some just looked into the fire with their faces etched with grief. There was no place for me among them. I didn't belong here. This wasn't my time. I was just a visitor. This wasn't my life.

I sat down on the bed, and Jayne butted against my hand.

"I want to go home," I said as I rubbed his striped head.

Could I? If I'd come to the future, why couldn't I go back to the past?

"There's about a hundred or more ticks in my way," I said to Jayne, who gave me an I-don't-care-what-you-do-as-long-as-you-keep-on-rubbing-my-head meow.

Also, how did it work? What guarantee did I have that, if I did manage to get to the time-twister, it would take me back to my own time and place? That it would take me back to Charlie?

It's all your fault . . .

Shane's words haunted me as I curled up on top of the old blanket I'd been given. How could everything be my fault? It hadn't been *my* idea to go to Tick Central tonight.

But as I lay there, rubbing Jayne, the image of Lucinda looking at the time-twister and then at the window where I stood came to me. It was almost as if she'd sensed I was there.

Somehow, I thought maybe it was my fault.

ELEVEN

We need to talk.
        —S

I found the note lying next to me on the bed when I rolled over against the glare of the morning sun. I'd been summoned.

"Thanks for letting me know I had company last night," I said to Jayne's pink-tongued yawn as I threw the paper aside. I took a moment to run a brush through my hair, and stuck it back up in a ponytail since I'd fallen asleep with it wet. I felt like I was going before a grand jury.

The house was strangely silent as Jayne and I padded down the stairs. No Berta, no Trent or Owen, and most of the cats seemed to be gone also.

It was a Disney morning. The birds were twittering in the trees and the sky was a clear bright blue. A soft breeze dried the rain from the leaves and grass. It was a day for picnics and kite-flying. A perfect day to spend in the park with Charlie.

Where was everyone? I went to the kitchen in hopes of at least finding some food, but it, like the rest of the house, was strangely silent and deserted.

The door beneath the staircase stood ajar. Logic, and his appearances in the evening, told me that through this door I would find Shane. My head screamed not to go down there.

"What are you afraid of?" I said, more to myself than Jayne, who peered into the darkness below. "That he'll be laid up in a coffin?"

Jayne gave me a skeptical look before trotting downstairs.

The thought that I'd slain multiple ticks the night before did nothing to give me courage as I cautiously felt my way down the steps into the darkness. It wasn't the thought of facing Shane the tick that scared me; it was wondering what kind of mood he'd be in that had me wigged out.

The last words he'd spoken to me the night before were full of hate, to say the least. What were his plans? Would he throw me out? Is that why everyone was gone? Did they all hate me so much because of Radar that they couldn't stand to be around me?

It was pitch black below. I kept one hand on the banister and another in front of me until my hand touched fabric—a curtain at the bottom of the staircase, I realized as I fumbled for the edge and pulled it back. The fabric was thick and black, likely to keep any accidental sun from shining down the stairs.

A tall white candle sat on top of a huge chest of drawers and cast enough light that I was able to make out the room beyond. Maybe I'd been expecting a coffin. I certainly wasn't expecting what looked like a typical single-guy's studio-type apartment.

The basement was finished with dark paneling. Cherry, was my first guess. The floor was marble tile, and a thick rug anchored a leather sectional sofa. A fluffy white cat was curled up on one end and did nothing more than flick the end of its tail at my interruption.

Jayne went over to say hi with a nose sniff, while I checked out the rest of the room.

The wall by the stairs held a desk with stacks of books and shelves full of three-ring binders. The wall before me held a long table covered with what looked like equipment from a chemistry lab. In the back was a set of stairs that I assumed led to an outside entrance. Beyond was a room sectioned off, and from the pipes running around the ceiling I figured a bath had been built into that corner. On the middle of the far wall stood a huge four-poster bed draped with curtains. The entire room reminded me of something out of Pottery Barn.

"Shane?" I said tentatively, walking toward the bed. What was I doing? A part of me screamed to run away, but another part kept me going. Should I wake him? His note made me think our talking was urgent, but then again, he hadn't bothered to wake me.

Jayne had no doubts. He jumped onto the bed and poked his way through the curtain.

"Shane?" I called out again.

Nothing. I touched the curtain, just enough so I could see through it.

Before I could take a breath I found myself lying flat on the bed with Shane stretched out on top of me. He'd moved so fast there was no way I could defend myself against him. He held my hands pinned flat beside my head and my body . . .

I felt every inch of him. His bare stomach pressed against mine below the hem of my shirt. His thighs covered mine and I felt the skin of his calves as my bare feet looked for some kind of leverage against him. His wide chest rose up over my chin like a wall.

Had he been this cut when we first met? I'd gotten the

impression of a fit bod when I saw him in his scrubs, but my imagination had not conceived anything like this.

Then he very, very, very slowly slid his body down mine, making sure I felt every inch of his movement, until he was exactly at the level where he could look me in the eye.

I could not see his face because of the way we lay on the bed; the light was behind him and all I saw were angles and planes along with the red glow of his eyes. His hair fell forward over his face and gave the impression of a wild animal peering at its prey through cover.

Fear chased through me. He was in tick mode. Would he suck me dry? Was I condemned to be a meal for him as punishment for Radar's death?

It was strange. A shiver ran through my body at the thought: fear and anticipation mixed together.

Now I truly felt every inch of him. Every tantalizing inch. Especially the part that pressed urgently between my thighs.

I was not going to fall under his spell. I was tired of being jerked around.

"Get off me," I said. For added emphasis, I bucked against him.

Big mistake. His thighs slammed around mine and pinned my legs together so I could not move my lower body. He pulled my arms up over my head and held both my wrists with one hand. I was defenseless and vulnerable, and he knew it. My only option was a head butt, and I was certain he could lean away before I could land a blow.

With his free hand, he traced a finger over my face. He touched my forehead, around my eye, down my nose and over my lips. He grinned when I snapped my teeth, and kept on with his fingertip until he reached my left breast, and he flattened his palm against it.

I am so dead, I realized. I wondered if it would hurt. Would the thing in his palm just stab through quickly? How long would it take?

Then, to my utter shock, my nipple peaked against his touch.

Damn it.

Shane looked up at me. Even with the red glow I could tell he was surprised.

I clenched my jaw. "What do you want?" I ground the words out.

"Answers," he responded in kind.

Absofreakinglutely posifreakingtively insane.

"This is your party, not mine," I reminded him. "I didn't ask to come. As a matter of fact, I was brought here by *your* friends."

"Maybe next time I'll just have them leave you out there," he growled.

So not funny.

I tried once more to move him off me; I bucked upward with all my might. In return, Shane ground his hips against me. I felt a clutch deep inside, a sudden impact of lust that made me squeeze my eyes shut so he wouldn't know what my traitorous body was thinking.

"Please get off me," I said quietly. I turned my face away from him in case he was doing some sort of tick trick on my brain. I was glad my legs were pinned. I wanted nothing more than to wrap them around his hips and pull him closer.

I refused to look at him. Even when he tucked his finger under my chin and turned me toward him, I kept my eyes squeezed shut. He moved off me so quickly that I didn't even feel the mattress move. He was just gone. I halfway opened my eyes and watched through my lashes as he jerked a pair of jeans on over his underwear. He shoved his hair back from his face and looked down at me.

I scrambled from the bed as quickly as I could—meaning, without a bit of grace, and I had to grab on to a post as I got tangled up in the curtains. Shane laughed.

"Asshole," I hissed, gathering my dignity and moving over to the table. I pretended to look at its contents while I willed my rebellious insides back to non-lust status.

I heard the flare of a match, and saw the room lighten with the glow of another candle. Shane set it down on the table beside me, and I noticed an old-fashioned microscope in front of me.

Science was not my thing. I'd always been more into math and geometry. Lines and angles, anything to do with building—the thought of dissecting a frog in high school had me running to the restroom with my hand over my mouth to keep from spewing in the hall. Yes, there was a very good reason why I was not in the medical profession. And I'd seen enough blood and gore lately to convince me I was right in not choosing that as a career.

"What's all this?" I asked. I'd taken enough science to recognize the little glass slides that sat all nicely labeled in a tray.

"Research," Shane replied. "I've got to do something to while away the daylight hours."

"What are you researching?"

"My disease."

I turned to look at him. He leaned against the back of the couch with his arms crossed casually over his bare chest. His jeans were low cut, and I had a great view of his chiseled chest, defined abs and serious obliques. He could have been posing for the cover of *People's* Sexiest Demon edition.

I've got to get out of here before I really do something stupid . . .

"You think what you've got is a disease?" I asked.

"What do you think it is?"

I looked at his face. His eyes were normal again, bright blue beneath long lush lashes. Just your average everyday hot doctor hanging out in his pad. McDreamy and McSteamy all rolled into one gorgeous package.

Oh, I was well on the way to McCrazy.

"I don't know." I turned back to his table. "What does all this say?"

Shane moved next to me and lit a kerosene lamp that sat behind the microscope. "My blood has different properties than normal blood," he said as he pulled a slide out of the box. Then he went through a dissertation about blood cells and counts and things I thoroughly did not understand. I tried to follow his reasoning. His digestive system was altered. He no longer required food but did drink liquids to stay hydrated. There had been molecular changes. It all sounded pretty freaky.

When he mentioned ultraviolet light, it finally dawned on me what he was talking about.

"You're trying to find a cure?"

"Yes."

"A cure for being a tick?"

"Something caused it. It was passed on to me through bodily fluids, just like AIDS or hepatitis or even the flu," Shane explained.

I shook my head. "Are you sure it's a disease? To me it seems more like a state of being. Or maybe the presence of a being. Like a demon."

"You think I'm possessed?"

I looked up into his bright blue eyes. "Yes." But knowing there was something evil inside him did nothing to stop my attraction. I wanted to comfort him. To reach out. To touch him. To hold him in my arms, run my fingers through his hair. He seemed so sad. So tired. So very weary.

Or maybe he just needed to feed. The thought gave me mental heebie-jeebies, and I shook my head to chase the vision away.

"I tried praying," Shane said, his eyes still on me. "It didn't work."

I didn't have an answer for that. My own experience with prayer was shaky at best, and usually only came in a time of crisis. Maybe it was time to change the subject.

"Where is everyone?" I asked.

"At the funeral."

"Oh." I was surprised, and almost gave a sigh of relief. Radar's funeral. Of course! Silly me.

Shane looked at me quizzically. "It's not all about you, you know," he said.

"I never claimed it was." But I had been thinking it, damn him. Oops. Too late. He was already damned. And how could he be so vulnerable one minute and such a shit the next?

"It's about to get all about you," he said. His eyes glowed brighter than I'd yet seen them.

TWELVE

"What happened last night?" Shane asked.

"You were there," I replied. Just like that, dangerous Shane was back.

"Yes, I was," he agreed. "So don't play your games with me. I know there's more to you than what you claim."

"What?" I said. "What do you mean?"

"Why does Lucinda want you?"

"I don't know."

"How does the time portal work?"

"I don't know."

"Where did you get your abilities?"

"My what?"

Shane was firing questions at me as if I were under police interrogation. At any minute I expected him to shine a bright light in my eyes and go fetch the "bad" cop. Owen could play the role perfectly.

Instead, Shane hopped up on a table and sat down to look at me, eyes glowing red.

The basement was damp after last night's rain, and I felt the cold creeping into the soles of my bare feet from the tile. I rubbed my arms against the chill that slowly came over me.

Jayne rubbed his cheek against my shins. He was probably hungry. I know I was.

"Well?" Shane asked after a moment of uncomfortable silence.

"I don't know what you're talking about. I don't have any . . . abilities."

"You kicked some major ass last night. That doesn't just happen."

"I've taken American karate for the past four years. I practice two nights a week."

"It takes a lifetime of training every day to fight the way you fought last night. Rambo on his best day couldn't do some of the stuff you did."

"Maybe the fact that I was scared shitless gave me momentum," I guessed. What had I done? I tried to go back over it in my mind, but it was all a blur of swinging sword and exploding guts. "I don't remember exactly what I did. I just know I didn't want to die."

"What about the time-twister?"

"What about it?"

"What was it doing?"

I shrugged. "What it always does?" I crossed my arms in what I knew was a defensive position, but I couldn't help myself. "Why am I suddenly the authority on time-twister function?" I asked.

"Because you're the only person I know who's ever come through it."

"Maybe I'm not. Lucinda seems to be keeping a close eye on the thing. Maybe *she's* using it."

I saw the dawning on his face as soon as I realized what I'd said.

"—*That's where the new ticks come from.*" We both said it at the same time.

"You and Jamie both said that new ticks keep showing

up. Lucinda's going into the past and making ticks. Maybe they're *all* going into the past and making new ticks."

"They can't. Only she can." He paused for a moment and looked down. His face was shadowed, and I couldn't tell if he was reliving the past or thinking about her.

"That would explain a lot of things" he finally continued. "One of the reasons why I always thought you were in league with her was because she lived in your house."

"That freaking bitch," I said. "Why am I her target?"

"That, my sweet, is the million dollar question."

"You're not planning on asking her, are you?" I said nervously.

"There's got to be a reason why she wanted you brought back alive. She's lost a lot of her army trying to get to you. And the way she reacted . . ."

"I've only seen her the one time, Shane," I protested. "In the ER that night."

"Guess we'll have to find out."

"We?" I folded my arms and looked him dead in his glowing eyes. "I'm not going anywhere near her."

Shane laughed again, and I was relieved to see the red fade away and the blue return. "You are a trip, you know it?"

"Me?"

"One second you're slaying ticks and the next you're freaking out because you've got goop in your hair."

"Jamie told you that?"

"Yeah." Shane's grin was wide and infectious. "He told *everyone.*"

"Remind me to kill him when I see him."

As Jayne jumped on the back of the couch and butted my arm with his head, I began feeling a little braver. "There must be something in the water," I said, rubbing rubbed between the cat's ears, "that causes extreme personality dysfunction."

"What do you mean?"

"Take you, for example," I said. "One second you're all sweet and charming, like now, and the next you get those red eyes and scare the crap out of me."

"I scare the crap out of you?" he repeated.

I looked over toward the bed and then back. "Yeah. You do."

He gave a slight smile and pushed his hair out of his face, then nodded. "I guess I have been a little unstable the past few days." He took a moment. "Since you got here, actually. I wonder why that is?"

The look he turned on me was uncomfortable, even if his eyes remained blue. It was as if he were looking inside me—a place I wasn't sure that I wanted him to go.

"Why are you here?" I asked.

"It's my home," Shane said.

"No. Why are you here with the humans? Why aren't you working with the ticks?"

He stared at me, then said, "It's simple. I took an oath."

"An oath? What? Like Superman? To preserve and protect? Or was that Batman?"

"The Hippocratic oath. When I became a doctor."

"Oh. That must have been some oath," I joked.

"I don't make promises lightly, Abbey." His tone was serious, and I realized I'd better put a stop to my snark or else bad Shane would reappear. And I was rather enjoying nice Shane.

"I became a doctor because of a promise . . ." He stopped, as if something pained him. "A promise I made to myself. It's not something I can walk away from."

"But how do you stay alive?" I asked. "Are you ever tempted . . . ?"

The look he turned on me gave me shivers.

"Every damn day."

There was an awkward silence while he turned to his worktable, and I stared down at Jayne who seemed willing to wait until we were done talking.

"You've got superpowers," I said finally. I wasn't being sarcastic. I'd seen him in action.

"Kind of," Shane replied. "It takes a while to figure them out."

"Jamie said the young ticks explode because they've got all this power and they don't know how to channel it."

"Yeah," Shane agreed. "Most of them turn to dust, or explode, but the old ones . . ." His voice trailed off. "You can always tell when you kill a Chronolotian. They die very gracefully."

"What do you mean, an old one?"

"One of the original aliens."

"Are they really aliens—I mean, something from a different planet? That's kind of hard to believe."

"Harder to believe than anything else that's happened to you recently?"

"Well . . ." I half grinned. "Not when you put it that way. So, how do you know all this stuff? What exactly happened to you?"

Uh-oh. Wrong question. Shane slid off the table and stalked toward the bed. He looked down at it for a moment, shoved his hair back from his forehead and then went to his bureau where he pulled a black T-shirt from one of the drawers. I expected to see his eyes all red and glowy again when he finally turned back to look at me, but they weren't. I almost gave a sigh of relief.

"Do you know you're the first person in a hundred years to ask me that?" He pulled the shirt on and moved to the sofa. He sat down next to the white cat as I turned and slid into the opposite corner of the sectional.

"Really?" You would think someone would have been curious.

"Really," he said. He rubbed the bridge of his nose, then his hand dropped and he almost absentmindedly stroked the cat.

"When it first happened," he began. "After Lucinda revived me, I felt invincible. For the first few days it was this unbelievable high—"

"Wait a minute," I interrupted. "Start at the very beginning. Take me through the process. Start in the alley." For some selfish reason I wanted to hear that he had shown up for our date, that he'd been looking forward to it. That maybe we would have had a chance if not for this funny twist of fate.

"The alley . . ." He looked over at me, and I felt the same little skip of my heart from the night in the ER "I waited about forty-five minutes," he began. "I actually thought about coming by and checking on you at your house, then thought maybe I'd give it a day. Walking home, that's when I saw Lucinda in the alley. It was weird—she was just standing there like she was waiting on someone." He rubbed the bridge of his nose again. "After that it's kind of fuzzy until I wake up in bed with her. I could barely breathe, my heart rate was way down, and I felt like my soul was hovering above my body. I remember looking down and seeing a hole in my chest. . . ." His hand moved over the place where he must have been wounded. "I couldn't believe I wasn't bleeding. Instead, it was just black and kind of hollow."

He dropped his hand back to the cat, who stretched and rolled beneath his touch. I watched the cat's movements, hypnotized. If not for fate it might be me enjoying Shane's touch.

"Lucinda was next to me, we were both naked, and I wondered if maybe she'd drugged me or something. But then I realized the wound was just like the ones on the recent homeless victims I'd seen." He quickly jumped up from the couch and paced in front of me. "She just looked at me, and I said 'Please' . . . and then . . . it was like she put more into me than she'd drained out. I was . . . *different*."

"An unbelievable high?"

"Among other things."

I held up my hand. "If you're going to tell me about you and Lucinda having hot sex, then I'd rather not know . . ."

Shane waved a dismissive hand toward me. "She said that she and her friends came to earth several millennia ago. She'd walked the streets of Atlantis. She knew Cleopatra and Aristotle. She was there for all of our history—"

"What about her friends?" I interrupted. "Where are they?"

"I don't know. I'm guessing they're out there, since there're so many of them."

"So, they split up after coming to earth?"

"Yes, as far as I know. I don't know where they come from or why they came here; all I know is that she was waiting for something to happen and she felt like the time was close. She said I was the first one she'd turned in a thousand years, and I was special for some reason that she never explained."

"And the Chronolotians being here is what gave birth to the vampire legend," I said.

"Yes."

"So, what happened to you next?"

"The cravings started." Shane shoved his hair back once more as he stopped his pacing. "They were stronger than anything I've ever experienced." His voice was desperately quiet. "I started changing, too." He lifted his left hand and looked at the palm. "I took an X-ray of this," he said with a shrug. "It's quite sophisticated, really. It was painful when the cells changed, of course, but then . . ."

"What did you do? About the cravings?"

"What I had to do to survive."

"Shane—"

"I tried to justify it. I went after drug dealers and criminals, pretty much the scum of the universe. But it was still . . ." He looked at me and gave his hair another shove. His eyes were desperate, pleading, so very, very sad. "The cravings ruled me," he said finally.

I remembered how desperately ill I'd felt just a few days past, and that was just from caffeine withdrawal. It must have been a million times worse for him.

"Obviously you stopped," I said.

He nodded in relief. "Suddenly there were others like me. I might have been her first turn in a while, but I was only the first of many. I made a clean break from Lucinda. And I started hunting the ones she turned. The world started changing then. The pandemic. I moved in here. My aunt, as you recall, was kind of loopy. The rest, as they say, is history."

"Or a really horrible future," I added.

Shane nodded.

I dismissed him with a wave of my hand. This was a lot of information to absorb, and I was trying to make sense of it.

"So, where does the time-twister come in?" I asked.

"I don't know," Shane said. "You're the first person who's spoken of it. Maybe its appearance was the event she waited for all those years." He paced again, and I could tell he was thinking. "Maybe that's why she followed you. She knew the time-twister was in your house."

"That's why there were all those murders in the neighborhood," I realized. "She was hanging around, waiting."

"Makes sense."

"And, whoever placed the time-twister in my house placed it inside peroxide to keep her from getting to it because they knew it would burn her."

"Lucinda was hanging around in hopes that you'd open it up." Suddenly he grinned. "Why do you call it a time-twister?"

"Because it twists. Or maybe 'spins' is a better word. I don't know. I touched it, and it was like turning a key on a music box. Then it started spinning." I waved my hand in dismissal. I was still trying to figure out Lucinda's angle. After all, she still wanted to capture me.

"I wonder how long she'd been waiting." I rubbed my forehead. Too much information, not enough food. And I would gladly kill for a cup of coffee. Just like Shane would kill—

My musings were interrupted by a crash upstairs. We flinched at the sound and Jayne let loose with a questioning meow. The sounds of several pairs of feet on the wooden floor above made us realize that Berta and Owen were back. And apparently they'd brought company.

"Shane?" Berta called from the top of the stairs.

"I'm awake," he called back.

"We've got a problem," she said. "Denise has gone into labor."

"It's not her time," Shane said. We heard the sound of

Berta coming down the stairs, and then she poked her head through the curtain.

"Her water broke," she explained. "We think it's grief that caused it. That, along with the full moon tonight . . ."

"Denise is—was—Radar's wife," Shane explained to me.

"She's upstairs," Berta continued. "And it's a bright sunny day."

"Shit!"

"Women have been having babies for millions of years," I said. "She can do it without you."

"Not Denise. She's lost two already. If she loses this one . . ." Shane pushed his hair back from his forehead. "I've got to get up there." He was obviously upset.

"Can't she come down here?" I asked.

"We'd have to move the entire surgery down here. There might not be time."

I looked around his room and my eyes settled on the bed. "These are blackout curtains, aren't they?"

"Yes."

"Let's take them upstairs. Cover the windows and the door. We'll save one to cover you up and get you in there."

"We can't take that risk," Berta said. "What if someone comes in?"

I laughed. "Set Owen outside with his crossbow. No one will come in."

"Let's do it," Shane said, and he pulled down the curtain at the base of the steps.

THIRTEEN

Denise was terrified, and I couldn't say that I blamed her. As we hustled to place the blackout curtains over the tall windows in Shane's clinic, Berta told me about the two separate losses of babies in the sixth month of her pregnancies. She'd made it to the seventh with this one, and the couple had celebrated the achievement.

Now Radar was dead, and Denise's water broke just as they'd lowered his body into the ground.

Denise lay curled on her side on the exam table. Her body shuddered with sobs and most likely labor pains. Her mother stroked her hair and spoke encouraging words to her. Words of faith, strength, and hope. It amazed me to think of how many things I took for granted in my own time.

Shane was unbelievable. All I could think as I watched him with Denise was: What a waste. He could have done great things. Then again, maybe he was doing them.

Even though the start of labor was quick, the advance was slow. It was strange, being in the darkened room with a chandelier packed with candles. It was as if my body longed for the sunlight right beyond the curtains. Like forbidden fruit—knowing that I shouldn't let it in made me want it all the more.

Owen stood guard outside and dared anyone to even think about coming in. I heard Trent's protests in the hall, Berta calming him. Jayne roamed everywhere, and finally took up a position in a corner of the room.

Shane was worried.

"I'm afraid the baby might be in distress," he said to me in a soft voice. Claudia and Denise's mother had Denise up and walking in hopes that it would increase her labor. Shane stayed behind the curtains and took advantage of the time to check the dressing on my arm. We were both shocked to see that it was totally healed, and nothing was left but a narrow pink ridge in my arm where the gash had been.

"Maybe time travel accelerated the healing?" I offered as Shane ran a finger down the length of the scar.

"Maybe," he said quietly, and I shivered at his touch.

I don't know why I hung around. It's not like I could be of any help. But it was too fascinating to leave, and since I didn't really know any of the people waiting outside I'd figured I'd better stay where I was. From what I'd seen while hanging the curtains, the entire local population had migrated from the funeral to Shane's and now filled both the front and back yards.

"Why do you think the baby might be in distress?" I asked when I saw him frown at my arm. "In what way?"

"It's hard to say. There are a number of things that could be going on in there, and I have no way of knowing what it is. My biggest concern now is the cord. Where is it? Is it wrapped around the baby's neck? Or is it trapped against the baby and the bones of the pelvis? Either way spells trouble."

"Is there anything you can do?"

"Yeah," he said. "I could poke around in there and see if I can feel anything."

He held his hands out in front of him as if seeing them for the first time. They were wide, with long lean fingers and blunt-tipped nails. Not the hands of a surgeon, but strong hands that could get a person through a crisis. Or kill someone with one quick motion.

They were shaking.

"Are you okay?" I asked. In over one hundred years, surely he had done this before.

"The moon is full tonight," he said quietly.

"And?"

He quickly turned to look at me. "It's harder when the moon is full." I saw the hint of red in the centers of his pupils, which contrasted sharply with the bright blue all around.

"What's harder?" My mind was on delivering babies. And not being completely useless in the process.

"Staying focused on the task at hand." He squeezed his eyes shut. "And *you* make it harder to stay focused."

"Me? Why?"

"I don't know. I just know things have been . . . I've been different since you showed up."

So, once again everything was my fault.

"Suck it up, Doc," I said.

His eyes flared wide as I spoke. Maybe that had been a bad choice of words, but I continued. "You've got a couple of hours before sunset and a baby to bring into the world. It's not all about you."

For a brief moment I thought he might kill me. Or maybe try to. The look on his face was deadly, and I had a flash of what a rabbit might feel like while being hypnotized by a snake. Still, I kept my eyes on his and stood my ground, and after a moment he shook his head in disbelief.

"What's the matter?" I asked. "Are you so used to having

your ass kissed that you can't handle it when someone gives you a reality check?"

Shane looked at his instruments, all sterilized, all carefully arranged on the table. "Get Denise in here," he said. "Let's see what's going on with that baby."

I think it was Denise's fear that the child would die that kept it from coming. Or maybe it was her fear of bringing it into the world they lived in. What kind of future would the child have? It wasn't as if it could grow up to be a doctor or a lawyer or a movie star or President. All it would know of life was a fight for survival.

But, wasn't that how things were in the beginning? Wasn't that how new civilizations were made?

It had to be a scary prospect, but eventually there came the time in Denise's labor when nature took over. The baby had to come.

I'd never seen an actual delivery before, and even though I knew what to expect from my many weekend chick-flick DVD marathons, it was still an experience to watch. When the baby's head appeared, everyone in the room broke into wide grins. Shane seemed immensely relieved that it had begun. Denise seemed to gather some hidden source of strength, and she pushed out a tiny baby boy.

I knew they were afraid that he would be too small, that his lungs wouldn't be fully developed. Everyone held their breath as Claudia and Shane took the baby aside. He seemed blue to me, but I saw the tension leave Shane's shoulders as a tiny wail burst forth from the red little face.

"Where there's life, there's hope," Claudia said, laying the swaddled baby on Denise's stomach.

Shane went back to work, finishing up the birth, then quietly stepped away as the mother, grandmother and

Claudia made faces over little Daniel, which I realized had also been Radar's given name. I didn't even know how late the time was until Owen pushed aside one of the blackout curtains and gave a thumbs-up sign. The crowd outside broke into cheers. Night would soon be upon us.

Jayne and I followed Shane into the kitchen. He stood in front of the sink and splashed water on his face as I came in. Through the window, I saw the sky tinged with the pink of sunset. How long would it be before the moon appeared?

"I think I know why your prayers haven't been answered," I said.

He kept his back to me, but he was still so I knew he was listening.

"Because you're the answer to these people's prayers. Without you, they would be lost."

You'd think that by this time I would be used to the way he moved. Still, I jumped when he grabbed the front of my shirt and twisted it in his hand. I grabbed his arms as he pulled me upward and towards him.

"They're already lost." His eyes raged with fire. "I'm just prolonging the agony."

"As long as there is life there is hope," I repeated.

He released me just as quickly as he'd grabbed me, and I stumbled back towards the bar.

"This isn't life," he snarled as he stalked away. "It's a new course for the buffet."

FOURTEEN

I helped Berta clean up after we moved Denise, baby Daniel and Denise's mother into one of the empty upstairs bedrooms. We carried Shane's curtains downstairs to his room to rehang, and Berta took advantage of his absence to change the sheets on his bed. I noticed a bonfire out back when I carried the dirty linens to the porch, and saw that the yard held a long table covered with food.

"For the wake," Berta explained, as she followed me out with her own armful of dirty things from the birth. "They had it without us."

There was plenty left to eat, and I helped myself to a plate. Several cats eyed my food expectantly, and I noticed they seemed to be having a feast of leftovers. I sat down beside Trent on the edge of the porch. Jayne stretched out beside me and with an eye on my dinner.

"What's going on?" I asked Trent as I took a bite and then waved my fork toward Owen and Jamie, who were handing out weapons through the back door. Neither man seemed worried, but they also looked grim.

"Tick patrol," Trent said. "Everyone has to work tonight."

"Because of the full moon?"

"Yeah."

"So, how old do you have to be to go on tick patrol?" I asked.

"They start the training when you're fourteen. You can't go until you're seventeen."

"Sounds like a long wait," I said. He appeared miserable about it.

"After you teach me that ninja stuff, maybe they'll let me start training."

"Hmmm," I said. "It takes a long time to become a ninja. If you work very hard, then maybe by the time you turn fourteen you can be one."

"Really?"

The other night I'd promised him lessons because I thought I wouldn't be back. Now here I was, promising him he'd be a ninja.

There had to be something more to life than just these people waiting around to die. I refused to give in to Shane's jaded views—even if he was much older and therefore supposedly much wiser than me.

The moon hung large and round right over the treetops. The night was much warmer than the one before. I gave Jayne my leftovers and sat back against a post, listening to the sounds of crickets and peepers and the soft voices of people as some moved off on patrol and others started to clean up.

"Does Shane always go off when the moon is full?" I asked Trent.

"Yeah. He doesn't want to be around. He's afraid he'll hurt one of us."

"He's a considerate guy," I said. I noticed Jamie coming our way, and quickly looked around for Claudia, in case she wanted to scratch my eyes out or something.

"Here," he said, and handed me my sword and the long coat that I'd worn the night before. I noticed it was remarkably free of goop, as Shane had called it. "I hosed it off last night," he said when he saw my glance.

"Er, thanks," I said. "What am I supposed to do with it?"

"Protect yourself," he replied. "Shane said the ticks will probably try to grab you, and under no circumstances are we to let that happen."

My jaw dropped into my lap. "Why? Not why it can't happen, but why will they try to grab me?"

"Shane and Owen think it has something to do with the time thing."

"The time-twister?"

"Yeah. If they want you alive, then they must need you for something. If they need you, then us keeping them from getting you is bad for them and good for us."

"I get it," I said. "But I don't want anyone to get hurt because of me. Especially not after—"

"Radar wasn't your fault," Jamie interrupted. "It's a risk we all take every day. We all know it's bound to us happen sooner or later. It always does."

"But we wouldn't have gone there if—"

"When it's your time to go, it's your time to go," Jamie interrupted again. "It happens. That's all. If you stop to think about it, then that's all you'd think about. I'd rather think about living than dying."

I had to admit he was right. "So, what do you want me to do?" I pulled the katana blade halfway out to check it. Light from the bonfire bounced off the cool steel. It was clean, even polished. Jamie was thorough. I noticed his quiver was once again full of arrows. He must make them himself. "Do I patrol, too?"

"No," Jamie said. "Owen wants you to stay here where we can defend you if we need to. I just thought you should be ready, in case."

"Thanks," I said. Jamie nodded and turned to walk

away. He had a bounce in his step, which made me wonder. He was good at archery if last night was any in-dication, and he had a girl who loved him, but was it possible in this future?

"Jamie," I called after him. "Are you happy?"

He looked at me for moment, his head tilted as if he were thinking real hard about the question. He really was cute in a college-student, soccer-player kind of way. At last he grinned. "Yeah. I'm happy."

"Good," I said with a smile. I noticed Claudia latch on to him again as soon as he walked away. She also gave me a quick glance over his shoulder, so I waved and smiled.

"Like I said." I maintained my smile but talked quietly through it. "Not interested."

Yeah. Because I was still holding out for a manic-depressive soul-sucker who was way, way older than me. But he was a doctor, so that would make up for all the other stuff—or so I'd always heard.

"Not interested in what?" Trent asked from behind me.

"Going on patrol," I said quickly. "Because we have to start your ninja lessons."

"Really?"

"Yep. Really. Just give me time to run upstairs and get my shoes." Just in case, I thought, as I gathered up the katana and coat. I changed T-shirts, too. If I was going to be captured by Lucinda, I didn't want to be wearing something pink and sparkly. The one I chose was olive and had a big fish on it. It said *Kick Some Bass*

"Where are your mom and dad?" I asked Trent as we took a break from ninja training. I knew he'd get bored quickly with all the stretching that should be taught first, so I interspersed our little workout with some punch-and-kick techniques.

"Dead," he said. Jayne sat on the floor between us and rumbled contentedly while Trent rubbed his ears.

"I'm sorry," I said. "Mine died, too."

"Did you know them?" he asked.

"I knew my dad. My mom died when I was born. My dad died a few years ago."

"Ticks got mine," Trent said. "Shane found me on the road and brought me here."

"On the road?"

"Yeah." Trent rubbed under Jayne's chin and the cat stretched his neck for easier access. "Outside of town. I guess they were coming here because nobody knew who they were. Shane said he found me crying under a bush. I was just a baby, and ticks don't do babies."

Wasn't it nice to know that the ticks had some boundaries? Or maybe they just thought that if a baby grew up he would someday make more of a meal. Kind of like an egg versus a chicken argument.

I put my hand on my forehead. "I am so morbid," I said. But Shane's buffet comment had really brought me down from the wonder of baby Daniel's birth.

Plus, now I really wanted some chicken.

I could see it: Shane prowling the outskirts of town on a night a lot like this one, finding the wreckage of whatever possessions the small family had, finding the father dead, then the mother who'd fought till the end to protect her baby.

"Did Shane name you Trent?" I asked.

"Nope." He hadn't looked at me during his entire story, so I knew he was trying to be brave and strong. "It was written on my blanket."

"And now Berta and Owen raise you?"

"They take care of Shane, so they take care of me," Trent said. "But it's not the same as having a real mom and dad."

"Believe me, I know." While my dad was great, even after the horrible choice of his second wife, I'd always wondered what it would be like to have a mom.

An old saying rolled through my mind: *In a hundred years we'll all be dead, so what difference will it make?*

But not all of us were dead. And yes, things made a difference.

Trent was unable to hide a huge yawn. It was late. Probably well past midnight.

"Lesson's over," I said.

"But . . ."

"Tired people make mistakes," I said. "We want you to be perfect. And I'm too tired to teach right now."

"She's right," Berta said from the doorway. "You need to get a good night's sleep, then you can learn more tomorrow."

"We'll do this again tomorrow?" the boy asked hopefully.

"Yes," I said. "After you're done with your chores and lessons."

Berta smiled at me appreciatively and guided Trent from the room.

I was tired, myself, but didn't want to go to bed. For some strange reason I felt restless, so I threw my long coat on, picked up my katana and walked out to the front porch, Jayne at my heels.

"Merow?" he asked as I leaned against the railing.

"Must be the moon," I said. Jayne jumped up on the rail and I rubbed his ears as I looked at the huge orb that hung high in the sky. Stars were pinpricks around it, closer and brighter than I'd ever noticed.

"At least there's one benefit to having no electricity," I mused, looking in wonder at the panorama.

The bonfire still raged in the middle of the street. There were men and women gathered around it. Some sat in chairs, some sat beside blankets that covered others who slept, and some kept watch, their backs to the flames and their weapons ready. There was safety in numbers, yet Shane was out by himself.

Why should I worry? He'd been doing this for more years that I'd been alive, and he'd survived. But for some reason, things were different now. I was here. I changed things.

I changed things. . . .

I wasn't supposed to be here. I was supposed to be in the past. Had I changed the future by coming here? I'd certainly changed the past. Shane had been turned when I didn't show up. His life was changed for the worse. But what other effects had my time traveling had? Would I have gotten married, had children? Possibly one who found a cure for the pandemic?

Okay, so maybe I was being dramatic and overestimating my importance in the scheme of things. But what if I'd inadvertently saved someone's life?

Or, Shane might have saved someone's life. That made more sense. When he was changed, it would have been hard for him to practice medicine. What if his absence in the medical world meant the loss of someone who could have prevented all this? It was almost too much to comprehend. There was a very good reason why the time-twister had been hidden. Whoever did it must have realized the long-reaching repercussions of the thing.

So, why hadn't they destroyed it?

"I've got to destroy it." If Lucinda was using it to travel

back and turn ticks, or worse, just to feed, then she was wreaking new havoc on the future, making things worse and worse. I didn't understand how the machine worked, but I knew its capacity for evil was immense.

Jayne looked at me with his great green eyes as I spoke. The light of the fire was reflected, giving them a yellow glow.

Suddenly, he arched his back and hissed. I heard the yowling of several cats, and the people around the bonfire sprang into action.

I drew my katana and waited. Women and children ran to the house, and I stepped out into the yard as they filed past. Berta stood at the door, waving them inside as the men and women who were armed lit torches and encircled the house.

"You should come inside," she said. "We can't let them take you."

"And I can't let innocent people die to protect me," I said. I looked at the people surrounding the house. I didn't even know their names, yet they were ready to fight to keep Lucinda from taking me. Because Shane had said to protect me. Because Lucinda wanted me for some strange reason. Because they had to fight or die.

No, there was no way I was going to hide in the basement while that was going on, no matter what Shane said.

Jayne's growl rumbled low in his throat. His ears lay flat against his head and his tail twitched. Around the circle several other cats did the same. Above me I could hear cats in the trees growling and hissing.

"The trees!" I said. "Watch the trees!"

The cats yowled, and Jayne leapt from the railing with his claws extended. A tick dropped to the ground before me with a big grin on his face. As I swung the katana, he ducked beneath the arc of my blade.

Around me I heard yells, screams, the creak of tree branches and the sounds of battle. As the tick ducked a second time, Jayne landed on the back of his head with his front claws buried in the man's cheeks. Jayne's pointed teeth grabbed an ear, and the tick tried to shake and swat the cat off. I couldn't decapitate the tick without hurting Jayne, so I swung at the back of his knees. I knew he could heal quickly, but this would take him down.

Jayne hopped away as the tick fell. I buried the tip of my sword in the man's heart, hoping that it would have some effect. The tick screamed as I pinned him to the ground. He grabbed the blade with both hands and tried to pull it out. I was tired of messing around, so I jerked the blade out and with two hands swung at his neck. Head and hands went flying across the lawn, and the tick's body turned to dust beneath my feet.

Jayne flew toward me and I ducked. He used my back as a springboard and jumped into a tick who'd appeared behind me. I whirled around and slashed the tick across the chest. He staggered back, and Jayne obligingly got out of the way so I could take off the thing's head. The body turned to dust. Two ticks down, and I was goop-free.

Everywhere I looked there was a battle. I was in front of the house, and saw Owen, Jamie, Claudia and another man fighting to keep the ticks out.

"Get in here!" Owen barked.

"Busy!" I yelled back as a tick came toward me. I noticed the ones close to me were all turning to dust in death, while the ones on the perimeter were exploding. Which meant that Lucinda sent her best after me while the young ones were supposed to keep the rest busy. Why? What was so damn important about me?

I didn't have time to think about it; this was a full-out assault. I swung my katana as the tick attacked, and in the next instant I was surrounded by dust, which blinded me.

I felt arms wrap around my chest. I couldn't swing my sword. I heard Jayne yowling as I struggled against the strong arms. I felt hot breath against my neck. I stuck a foot out and braced myself against a tree trunk. I walked three steps up and flipped over, so my momentum took the tick with me. I used my coat to blind him as I twisted out of his grip and wrapped my arms around his neck. There came a popping sound as he struggled, and suddenly his chest was full of arrows. It took but a second for me to finish him off.

Jamie appeared, a big grin on his face, but I didn't have time to reply. More ticks were coming our way.

I didn't plan my moves; I just leapt forward. Act and react. Defend and attack. My training kicked in, and I was on autopilot. Even when I realized that the older ticks had backed off and let the younger ones take over, I kept on fighting.

Yet I couldn't help but think: how much longer will we be able to hold them off?

FIFTEEN

How many more were there? I couldn't count how many ticks I'd killed. My arms were tired, the katana had grown heavy, the hilt slick in my grip. I heard the sounds of battle all around me and wondered how we were doing. How many had we lost?

Was this all about me? It sickened me to think that people were dying because of me. But the alternative was also unthinkable. I didn't know why Lucinda wanted me, but I had a feeling it wouldn't be good for the human race.

The ground around me was covered with gore, so it was inevitable that I'd slip. As I swung the katana upward in a two-handed grip, I stumbled back and fell over a tree root. I hit the ground hard—hard enough to knock the air from my lungs and the sword from my grasp.

Instantly, three ticks came toward me. I took one out with a sweep kick, but the other two were able to grab my arms. I lashed out again with all my might, but they used their uber-strength and pulled me up and outward so that my arms were stretched and my feet dangled above the ground.

Nothing in Master Thomas's class had prepared me to

escape my present position. All I could do was scream my frustration.

The tick I'd taken down with the sweep kick stood up with a big grin on his face. "I just want a taste," he said. His eyes glowed bright red, and he licked his lips in anticipation.

No way was he going to touch me, and no way in hell was he going to suck a single day of my life out of me. I might not have been able to touch the ground, but I could still swing my legs. I let loose as he came toward me and nailed him in the balls. I'd learned from my experience the first night with Shane that a male tick was just like any other male: the family jewels were not to be messed with.

The two holding me laughed. It was a bizarre sight, them laughing with their glowing red eyes. I realized that one of them had scars on his hands, and I quickly made the connection. These were the vamps from the night I came through. The ones who were lounging in the parlor.

I was in big trouble. I looked around for anything, anyone who could help me. Everyone else was involved in their own battles.

Then I saw Shane. He came out of the shadows and ran straight toward me. The tick that I'd kicked was slowly climbing to his feet. As he stood to face me, Shane grabbed him from behind and twisted him around. His hand slammed the tick's chest, and the tick shuddered as his head flung back. He hung suspended by the thing protruding from Shane's palm until his body kind of caved in on itself and vanished in an explosion of dust.

"Stay back, *canibalis,* or we'll rip her apart," said one of the ticks who held me.

It was pretty obvious to me that *canibalis* was meant

to be an insult. It was also obvious what it meant. Shane had the look of a junkie who'd just made a prime score.

He laughed. "No, you won't," he said. "Your queen bitch needs her whole and alive so she can travel through time."

He sounded fairly confident of his strategy. Still, the possibility of being ripped in two felt real as the ticks jerked my arms. It hurt. I was pretty sure they'd dislocated my shoulder. I tried not to cry out, but it was hard. I kept my eyes on Shane.

That was when I realized that most of the fighting had stopped. All eyes were on Shane, me and my escorts.

Shane pushed his hair back from his forehead. "Wow," he said, and kicked at the dust of the creature he'd destroyed. "What a rush!" I could tell by the look on his face and the glow in his eyes that he was aching for a fight.

To bad he'd come too late.

My shoulders hurt. I swallowed and looked up at the sky in an attempt to keep from crying. The moon hadn't moved much; it was right where I'd seen it earlier. How long had we fought? It seemed like forever, but then again not long enough.

"Put me down," I said to the ticks holding me captive. The pain was unbearable. I didn't know how much longer I'd last, and passing out was not an option. Jayne stood nearby, and reached up to paw my boot as if he could free me.

I saw Jamie, his bow ready, an arrow notched. So, why didn't he shoot? Didn't he really think the ticks were going to rip me in half? From the look on Owen's face I'd say they were.

"Put her down," Shane repeated. "Or die. It's your choice."

"We're taking her," the more talkative tick said.

"Like I said, your choice," Shane replied. He smiled at me, then did that blink-of-an-eye thing again. He dove, rolled, and came up with my katana in his hand. He sliced off the arm of the tick on my left before either foe had time to react. Jamie nailed the other one in the heart, and Shane took off both heads in one arching swing of the katana. Dust exploded around me as I fell into a heap on the ground. My arms were paralyzed, as if they'd been pulled from their sockets. My shoulders and chest cramped, and I felt like screaming in agony.

Shane stood with his back to me. "I suggest you all leave town," he yelled at the remaining ticks. "Unless you want to go back and tell Lucy how you failed her tonight."

Through the haze of my pain I saw several ticks slip off. Did that mean it was over? Did we win?

Maybe the battle, but not the war. Shane knew something. Something about me.

Your queen bitch needs her whole and alive so she can travel through time. . . .

What did that mean? What did I have to do with everything?

"Hey." Shane knelt beside me on the ground. Jayne's nose was in my face, bobbing around as if looking for a wound. I gently pushed him away.

"Are you hurt?" Shane asked.

"You're the doctor," I said shakily. "You tell me."

He pushed my coat open and grinned when he saw my T-shirt. "Dressed for the occasion?" he asked.

"I thought it much more appropriate than the pink sparkly one."

After a moment he said, "I don't see any blood." He moved his hand over my left collarbone, and I made a face. "Looks like you've dislocated a shoulder," he added. He sounded disapproving.

"Me? You act like I did it to myself."

"Hold still."

I knew I wasn't going to like what followed. Especially when he stretched my arm and put a hand on my shoulder. I turned my head and felt a quick tug and his firm but gentle touch guiding my arm back into place. Lights spun around me as intense pain shot through my body. Then it was gone.

"Don't. Throw. Up," I said to my once again rebellious stomach.

"You're done," Shane said.

"Thanks." I looked up at him. "I think."

His hands on my waist were gentle as he lifted me to my feet. Hard to believe the guy had just sucked a tick's life from its body.

My head started swimming as soon as I got vertical, and I hung on to Shane's arms until the world stopped spinning. "What a mess," I said when I was finally able to focus. The front lawn was covered with ash and gore. It looked like the floor of a slaughterhouse. "Who's going to clean this up?"

"All of us," Shane said. He looked beyond me to Owen, who approached. "How many?"

"Eight dead and seven wounded," Owen reported.

Eight people dead because of me. "You should have let them take me," I muttered as Jayne twined around my ankles. I wasn't sure I meant it, though. I didn't really want to die.

"No," Shane said. He looked at Owen, who seemed to agree with me. "I found some things out tonight. No matter what happens, we can't let Lucinda get her."

"Why?" I asked. "What do I have to do with anything?"

"Later," Shane said. "I've got to take care of the

wounded." He followed Owen into the house and left me standing in the yard.

"You were awesome!" Jamie handed me my katana. "I've never seen anyone fight like you do."

I didn't know what to say. *Thank you* seemed kind of sick. Instead, I wiped the gore off the katana with a cloth he handed me, and looked around for the sheath I'd thrown aside as soon as the cats gave the alarm.

"Claudia," I finally said. "Is Claudia all right?"

"Yeah," Jamie said. "She went to help get the wounded in."

"I'm sorry," I said. "I don't know why this is happening."

"Abbey. It's not your fault. They always attack with the full moon. That's their feeding time."

"Aren't you sick of it? Don't you want it to stop?"

"Of course. But what am I supposed to do about it? This is my life. This is how it is. I don't know any different. All I know is what Shane's told us of the past and what I read in books. And from what I've read, it seems like it wasn't that different."

"Not that different? We don't—didn't—live in fear of being slaughtered by ticks every full moon!" I exclaimed.

"No, but you still had to find a way to survive." Jamie shook his bow and grinned at me. "I just use a different tool."

At least he had a great attitude. But, still . . .

A couple of guys I'd never seen before showed up with shovels and a wheelbarrow. They looked at me as if I was diseased, and I wondered if one of their loved ones had been killed. Jamie must have noticed it, too.

"Go on and get cleaned up," he said. "Take care of that arm."

"Yeah," I said. "Thanks."

SIXTEEN

I cleaned my katana, then hosed off my coat before going inside. Everyone pretty much ignored me or else looked at me as if I were a leper as I hung it over the back porch railing to dry. I can't say that I blamed them. Still, it was uncomfortable. I felt as if I needed to do something to contribute but didn't know what. Finally, I went into the weapons room. I figured that was a place where I could be useful.

The concept of time no longer had meaning for me. Before, I would have studied the clock and worried about getting enough sleep to face the next day. I knew tonight that sleep would elude me, so I might as well make use of my insomnia.

It was late. Or early. It didn't matter; all I knew was that there were blades that could all use a good cleaning and sharpening.

Through the window I could see the clean-up efforts underway. Tick remains—the gory kind—were dumped into the fire from wheelbarrows, while human bodies were laid on the porch and covered with odd pieces of tarp and plastic for burial in the morning. I saw piles of shoes and clothing lying on one of the long tables. Recycling was a morbid necessity.

Would civilization eventually run out of things left over from my century? The stack of T-shirts in my room was a testament to how much stuff had been available in my time and how much we'd wasted. How much longer could this society survive on goods scavenged from deserted shopping malls and warehouses, while the ticks simply popped back into time to do their shopping? And their killing . . .

They had to be stopped. But how? If only I knew why they wanted me. What I had to do with the time-twister. Shane knew something, but there were others who needed him more at the moment.

How long before dawn? I heard the steady creak of floorboards, which let me know that the house was full of people coming and going. How were the wounded faring? How many would survive? How many more battles would be fought because of me?

Jayne padded into the room and gave me a where-have-you-been-I've-been-looking-all-over-for-you sniff before tucking his front paws beneath his chest and settling down to watch me work.

The collection of weapons was unbelievable. I didn't know much about the guns, but the swords and knives were beautiful and lethal. Some of them were real collector's items and had to be worth tons of money. Of course, money was something else that didn't matter now.

I placed the last sword back on the rack, realizing there wasn't anything more for me to do. Berta kept the place spotless. But . . . maybe I could help her with the laundry.

I went back toward the laundry room with the intent of getting a basket to gather up the dirty clothes and towels from the night's surgeries, when the sound of angry voices stopped me. I ducked into the half-bath, in case the speakers were moving my way.

"How many more of our people are going to die because of her?"

I recognized Owen's voice. And I knew without a doubt to whom he referred.

"Just let them have her and be done with it," he continued. "Or better yet, negotiate a treaty with them for her."

"I'm not giving her up to them." Shane's voice. He sounded really tired. Did ticks get tired? He'd missed a day of sleep because of talking to me, and then there had been Denise and the baby. So, maybe he was.

"Look, Doc, I know she's got you thinking with your cock instead of your brain, but that doesn't mean you can't go ahead and have her first. Just do her and *then* give her to the ticks."

My first impulse was to run into the room and kick Owen's ass. Instead, I drove my nails into my palms and kept on listening. Jayne looked up at me and voiced a quiet meow. I put a finger over my lips and gave him the wide eye to keep him quiet.

"They need her to work the time-twister," Shane said after a long moment. I hoped he'd been contemplating punishing Owen too. "Somehow it's affected by her."

"What do you mean, affected?" Owen asked.

"I had a nice chat with one of Lucy's old friends, another ancient," Shane said. "Apparently, Abbey is a Time Guardian."

What the hell was a Time Guardian?

"What the hell is a Time Guardian?" Owen gave voice to my question, and I listened carefully.

"Something or someone that's been around a long time," Shane said. "She's a descendant of one of them, and she doesn't even know it. It's their job to protect the time-twister—or portal or whatever it's called. When one of them is around, no one else can use it. Because Abbey is here, Lucinda can't time travel. She's been using it freely for the past one hundred years because Abbey skipped through that time."

I rubbed my forehead with my hand. "What?" I mouthed to Jayne. This was so strange. So bizarre. So totally unbelievable. Of course, how was this news any stranger than what I'd been through in the past week?

"Why don't they just kill her then? Why do they need her alive?"

"When Abbey came through, she deactivated it somehow. They need her to reactivate it again."

"And this tick just told you all this."

"He did," Shane said. "Before I killed him."

That explained where he'd been earlier.

"Give her to Lucinda," Owen said. "Nothing will be different than before if you do, and maybe we can make things better for ourselves by giving her up. Maybe we can make Lucinda go elsewhere."

"I can't do it, Owen."

"Our people are dying. More than ever."

"So are theirs," Shane said. "Have you watched her? Have you seen her fight? She's helping even out the odds. Maybe even get them down enough so that we've got more than them."

"They'd still be stronger," Owen said. "Of course, if we had more fighters like her . . ." His voice trailed off, and I ducked back in the half-bath in case they decided to move my way. "I've never seen anything like it," Owen said finally. "Where did she learn that stuff?"

"It's because she's a Time Guardian," Shane said. "It's a part of her. Inherent fighting skills are a part of the legacy."

I slapped a hand over my mouth. It sounded like he was talking about Buffy: "One in every generation" and all that stuff. *Puh-leeze* . . .

But once again, the little voice in my head asked why was this any weirder than anything else that was happening.

No. There wasn't anything special about me. I wasn't a Time Guardian or anything beyond a scared, caffeine-deprived architecture student who desperately wanted to wake up from her horrible nightmare. My dad had been normal enough, and my mom died when I was born. My life was boring and, well, sort of normal. Lots of people had parents who died young. Lots of people had to work hard for everything they had. No big freaking deal.

But, if I *was* some descendant of Time Guardians or something, then which side had it come from? I had no known family. No one. No grandparents, no uncles, no aunts, no cousins—no one that I could trace my heritage to. I was an island. A vapor. There wasn't even anyone to know I was missing in my own time except maybe Joe.

And Charlie, of course. Poor Charlie.

"So, what are we going to do about it?" Owen asked.

"I don't know," Shane said. "But we aren't giving her up, so get that thought out of your head."

"It's not just my head you've got to worry about," Owen said. "If everyone else keeps seeing their friends and family dying for her, and for no apparent reason . . ."

I heard the sudden crash of a body forced against the wall, and Shane's voice came to me, strained, but clear. "There *is* a reason," he said. "And if they can't see it, they're free to pack up and go."

Pack up and go?

I should go. My being here was a problem for everyone, and my presence didn't really help them, no matter what Shane thought about my fighting skills. But where would I go? It's not like I knew anyone or had a place in mind. I didn't know anything that was out there.

The small window high on the bathroom wall showed the gentle pinkening sky of dawn. If I left now, could I get to a safe place before night came? What about food? Water? Weapons? My mind told me I should plan something out. That I couldn't just take off. But my gut said to go before someone else died.

Jayne decided he'd had enough of hiding, and began weaving around my ankles. His purr rumbled loud enough for me to hear. Maybe loud enough for Shane and Owen to hear. I needed to move before they realized I was listening in. I needed time to think.

I opened the door to walk back to the weapons room, and with luck sneak out the side door, when I heard Jamie. "Shane! Owen! You better come here," he called out. "We've got a delivery from the ticks for Abbey."

"Go on," Shane said to Owen. "I'll find her."

I heard Owen's footsteps and grumpy complaints fade away. Then Shane stood before me in the hall.

"You were listening." It was a statement, not a question.

"I was," I replied.

"And?"

"And what? I'm supposed to believe that I'm some sort of Time Keeper or Gate Guardian or something else just as weird—which actually isn't any weirder than anything else that's happened to me lately." I stopped and rubbed my forehead. I was very tired. "Why?" I asked Shane. "Why me?"

He shrugged. "Funny, I've been asking myself the very same question for the past hundred years."

We walked toward the front of the house, me in the

lead. I was curious to know what Lucinda had sent me. If only it were her head on a platter. . . .

A huge old trunk sat on the front porch. Shane stayed just inside the door, as dawn was quickly approaching, but I went out. Jamie and a few other men and women stood in the yard watching Owen jab it, a quarrel notched in his crossbow.

"Do you think there's one in there?" I asked.

"It's kind of heavy," Jamie said. "But I don't think there's a tick inside, if that's what you mean."

I took a good look at the trunk. My name was scrawled across the top in what looked like chalk. The leather was beat up pretty bad, but I recognized it. It had been in the basement of my house when I moved in. It had also been empty.

"So, I guess I should open it?" I asked.

"It's got your name on it," Owen barked.

I flipped open the latches and slowly raised the lid. I sneezed as a musty odor rose from the trunk.

"Hey, it's all my clothes and stuff," I said. I recognized a faded pink sweater on top, along with my running shoes thrown on the side. "I guess Lucinda and I have different tastes," I added as I dug into the trunk. I found my comb, my brush, my toothbrush; even my cosmetics bag was thrown haphazardly inside. "It's everything," I said as I kept digging.

Jayne put his paws up on the edge and looked down into the trunk. Suddenly, he hissed. He dropped onto his belly, lay his ears back flat on his head and growled.

"He must smell the ticks on the stuff," Owen said.

Berta stepped onto the porch and nudged the cat with the toe of her shoe. "Get on with you," she said. "We're too tired to care right now."

I felt something hard at the bottom, something maybe

covered with a garbage bag. "What the heck?" I said as I moved the clothes out and sneezed again. "There's something else in here," I said. "I can't figure out what it is."

Jamie came up to help, and lifted the garbage bag out just as the morning sun danced across the porch. The bag was stiff and shaped kind of weird, with strange angles jutting out. Jamie laid it down and sliced it open with his knife.

At first I thought the contents was an old fur coat. It was a strange color, kind of a dusky gray. But as Jamie pulled the plastic off and I saw the chain wrapped around the body . . .

"Oh God," I backed away and covered my mouth. "It's Charlie."

"Who's Charlie?" Owen asked.

I looked once again as I stood next to the porch rail. "My dog. She murdered my dog. Oh God." I leaned over the rail and emptied the contents of my stomach. I felt a gentle hand on my back as I collapsed over the rail, sobbing.

"Charlie . . . I'm so sorry. Oh, God . . . why couldn't she just turn him loose? Why did she have to kill him?"

"Shane," I heard Owen hiss. "It's daylight."

Tears blinded me. But that was better than seeing the horror lying on the porch. How long had it taken him to die? Did he wonder why? Did he cry out for me? Why? Oh why?

Strong arms scooped me up as I slid to the floor. I heard a strange sound, like a *pop*, and smelled something burning. I didn't care to know what it was; all I knew was my grief combined with anger. I didn't even know where I was or who carried me until I heard his voice.

"Shhh," Shane murmured against my hair. "It's okay. It happened a long time ago."

"Not to me," I cried out. "Why would she do that? Why would she send him to me?"

"Because she's evil."

"I'm going to kill her. I'm going to kill her. *I'm going to kill her.*" I said it over and over again as I cried. It was something to focus on. Something to motivate me. Somehow I would make things right. Make things better. But her death wouldn't bring Charlie back.

I don't know how long I cried. Maybe I was crying for more than Charlie. Maybe I was crying for myself and the predicament I was in.

SEVENTEEN

The flare of a match woke me. My head pounded, the empty thudding that only comes after intense grief. Still, I moved quickly and sat up as my surroundings filtered through the anger and sadness that still suffused me.

I was in Shane's bed.

I put my head in my hands. "What did I do?" This nightmare kept getting worse and worse. Jayne bumped my arm with his nose, but I ignored him. He walked over to the edge of the bed and spread his legs apart for his grotesque, usual morning ablutions. Cats could care less what anyone thinks. I, on the other hand, was absolutely mortified about what everyone was probably thinking at the moment.

"You fell asleep," Shane said. "I couldn't risk taking you upstairs." He stood in front of a bureau wearing nothing but his jeans. He turned away, and even in the dim light I noticed the bright red wounds on his back and arm.

"What happened?" I asked.

He looked over his shoulder at me and then at his arm. "I got singed," he said.

"How?"

He opened his bureau and pulled out a shirt. "When I carried you in."

I scrambled off the bed and moved closer to look at his back. "How bad is it?" I asked.

He wouldn't let me see. Instead, he whipped a Henley shirt over his head and turned to face me. "It's nothing." He grimaced as the fabric settled onto his skin. "It will heal. One of the benefits."

"Shane . . ."

He brushed past me. "Jamie buried Charlie for you. He said he'd take you there when you woke up." Sitting on the edge of the bed he pulled on some socks, then jerked his boots on as he talked. "Stay close to Jamie and get back to the house before full dark. Make sure you take your weapons."

"You think they'll come back," I said as he walked toward the staircase.

He stopped and turned to look at me. His bright blue eyes were hidden in the shadows, and candlelight lit the smooth planes of his jaw. He pushed his hair back.

"I can't imagine they'll quit," he said. Then he took off up the stairs.

The clothes from the trunk were all laundered and lying on my bed, courtesy of dear sweet Berta. I couldn't stand to look at them. Instead, I pulled on the jeans I found in a drawer and a T-shirt that said *I'm up, I'm dressed, what more do you want?* Then I pulled my hair back in its usual ponytail and went downstairs to find Jamie.

What started out as a bright and sunny day had turned overcast while I slept. Shane took advantage of the lack of sunlight to check on his patients. I heard him talking in the clinic as we walked past.

"Did we lose anyone else?" I asked Jamie as we walked down the street.

"One," he said. "I think the rest will recover."

I began to think about the stereotypical stories of vampires that I knew. "Do any of them ever turn?" I asked.

"I've never seen it. We always decapitate the bodies before we bury them," he said. "I guess you could say it's one of our laws."

"It seems so . . . gruesome," I remarked.

"It is." Jamie shook his head as if remembering. "But no one wants to come back and hurt their friends—or worse, their family."

"Has that ever happened?"

"Not in my time. But in the beginning . . . Shane said it was pretty bad."

"So, tell me about the rest of the world," I said.

"We have gatherings every three moons. When it's waning. We meet in a wide open area. Airports, Shane calls them. There's little cover for the ticks around them."

That made sense. An airport could hold a lot of people. And the land around one would be plenty clear, with wide highways going in and out.

"We meet with other humans to trade, talk, possibly find someone romantically . . ." Jamie continued.

"Is that where you met Claudia?"

"Yeah. With the communities so small, you've got to bring in new blood."

"Don't want cousins marrying cousins," I said.

Jamie nodded and laughed. "Yeah."

"So, how long have you two been together?"

"Since the last gathering. I finally persuaded her to come back here. She's something of a healer, so I'm still not sure if it was me or the chance to learn from Shane that made her decide to come," he said with a wry grin.

I looked around, making sure to check behind me in case Claudia was sneaking up on me with a deadly weapon. No one was there but Jayne and another cat that trailed along the pavement behind us.

"So, is the rest of the tick population like this one?"

"Pretty much the same everywhere. Except, we've got Lucinda, who seems to be the queen. We never knew what made this place her headquarters until now."

"You mean, the neighborhood is kind of seedy for royalty?"

"Yeah. Most ticks live in highrises in the big cities."

"Most ticks don't have time-twisters."

"It finally makes some sense," Jamie agreed.

"I wonder if there are any more out there—twisters, I mean." I looked at Jamie. He made a good sounding board. He looked at things simply, and was easy to talk to. His opinion wasn't clouded with emotion, and I didn't have to worry about him pulling a Jekyll-and-Hyde thing on me. "If there's one, then it makes sense that there could be more."

"I wonder how long it's been around," Jamie added. "And how Lucinda knew about it."

"It was as if she was hanging around waiting for me to open it," I said. "And oh my gosh. All those people she killed . . ."

"It's not your fault, Abbey," Jamie said. "You've got to quit taking on the world. It's a big place. There's enough guilt for everyone, believe me."

The way he said it, I knew there was something he himself felt guilty about. Still, it wasn't my place to question him. And at the present time, I just felt grateful for his unflagging friendship.

"Thanks for taking care of Charlie for me," I said as we walked through the stone archway into the cemetery.

He grabbed my hand and gave it a quick squeeze.

"Don't worry about it. It's a shame there's not more dogs around now."

"Yeah, I've noticed that. Why is it?"

"A lot of them got wiped out after the pandemic. They were abandoned and running in packs and got pretty vicious from what I heard. I've seen dogs at gatherings, but not many. And the people who have them want a lot for the offspring. No one from our community ever bought one. Anyway, we have the cats."

"The cats are okay," I said as Jayne and his buddy galloped before us. "But there's nothing like the love of a dog. I guess it's just another way Lucinda and her friends have changed things."

"And not for the better," Jamie added as we entered the cemetery.

I'd never been in this cemetery before, just by it sometimes when Charlie and I felt like a long run. My dad had been cremated and he'd said my mom was, too. The second wife had done something with his ashes. I never knew what.

It was a pretty place, even with the heavy clouds and the wind that rustled the leaves of the old oaks that were scattered throughout. Jamie led me toward a line of freshly dug graves, all marked with simple white crosses. Claudia and some other women were there, working to smooth the dirt out over the graves and surround them with stones.

We stopped in front of a marker that said *Charlie* on the crossbar and *a good dog and friend* going down the length.

Jamie didn't say a word as I knelt in the grass beside it. Instead, he walked away to join Claudia.

Jayne sniffed the dirt. I gave him a look that said

This is not a litterbox, and he walked off with his tail in the air.

"I'm sorry, Charlie," I said as I moved my hand over the surface of the grave. "I'm sorry I left you alone."

I felt tears well up again, and quickly wiped them away. They wouldn't help. Neither would the guilt over what he must have gone through a hundred years ago. A hundred years ago for him, yet I could still feel my dog's body pressed against mine beneath the covers and his head bumping my hand, the touch of his paw on my knee when he wanted to go out.

"I promise I'm going to make her pay. . . ."

My anger was tangible. I gripped the hilt of the katana at my side. I wanted to kill. I *needed* to kill. I needed Lucinda to suffer the way I'd suffered. I wanted her to hurt the way I hurt. But how could I accomplish it? I needed time to think. And for the first time since everything had happened, I was alone.

Jamie knelt beside Claudia, who seemed to take special care to fix the graves just so. She wasn't from here, yet she cared about the people. It was obvious that she and Jamie were in love. I watched him tenderly pull a piece of grass from her long dark hair. Did they have any chance for a future? Any chance for normalcy, maybe even children?

I reminded myself: to Jamie this *was* normal, and most likely to Claudia, too. It was normal to everyone who lived in this time and place.

Yet it could be better. The only way to make it so would be to get rid of the ticks. All of them.

Even Shane?

If ever there was a man in conflict, Shane Maddox was it. His conflict was worse than my own weird life. How much longer could he go on living this way, siding with humans? Wouldn't his true nature eventually come out? How many more years could he keep the demon at bay?

I wandered around the edge of the cemetery with Jayne at my heels. The history was obvious. Recent graves were neatly mounded, older ones sunken in. Wooden crosses gave way to carved stone and finally marble headstones. I looked at the dates. It was strange to see one ten years after my jump. Kind of like a scene out of *A Christmas Carol*. But which ghost was I—past, present or future?

Then I saw a name I recognized: Maddox. I knelt down to get a closer look. *Dr. Jonathan L., beloved husband*, and *Melody S., beloved wife*. They'd died the same year. At least they hadn't gone through the pandemic.

It didn't surprise me in the least that the adjacent headstone said *Shane Maddox. Beloved Son and Brother*. I traced the faded date of his death with my fingertip. Fifteen years after he was turned. Long enough to have a few wrinkles around the eyes, a touch of gray in his dark hair, maybe even a receding hairline or a bit of a belly.

Not likely. Not the Shane I knew. But people must have wondered. Especially if they never saw him in the daylight. He'd done it to spare his parents pain. Yet they'd had to bury two sons.

Two sons.

I looked around. The other son had to be close.

Jayne was the one who found him. He sat down in front of a nearby stone and meowed.

"If you tell me you can read my mind, I'm going to go abso-freaking crazy," I said, brushing some of the dirt and mold away from the letters and numbers.

"Sean Maddox." The numbers were faded and full of

grime, but I was able to decipher them. I did the math in my head: ten years old when he died. And he'd been younger than Shane by two years.

A tragedy. How had he died? Suddenly, or slowly, from some dread disease?

Shane would have been twelve when it happened. It must have been devastating. As devastating as watching your father get run down right in front of your eyes.

He took an oath to be a doctor. And he meant it. For all eternity if need be.

"I don't make promises lightly," he'd said.

Well, neither did I.

"Lucinda will pay." I touched the hilt of my katana. "Or I will die trying to make her."

EIGHTEEN

"Abbey!" Jamie's shout sounded worried. I stood up and saw him standing close to the entrance of the cemetery, his hands cupped for volume.

It would be dark soon. I waved to let him see me, to show him I was coming, and picked my way through the headstones to where he waited with Claudia. Jayne and his friend charged across the lawn to join us as we walked through the gates.

"Looks like rain again," Claudia said.

"Good," Jamie replied. "Especially since it's my night off." He waggled his eyebrows suggestively at her, and she smiled and clasped his hand.

I fell into step on the opposite side of Claudia. I wondered if Shane would go out and feed again. If all he stalked was ticks, now was a good time to reduce their numbers. Since Lucinda had no way to go back . . .

I was supposed to be a Time Guardian. What was that all about? Shane seemed convinced of it, from what he'd told Owen. From what I'd heard, Lucinda needed me to activate the portal. As long as I was around she couldn't use it. But there was also the fact that my presence around my friends put them in danger.

My friends . . . It was a strange train of thought.

How long had I been in this future world? A week? Maybe more? I'd shared more of myself with these people than I had with any in my own time. They'd definitely seen me at my caffeine-deprived worst. According to the way they talked about my fighting skills, they'd also seen me at my best. Were they my friends?

I slowed a bit and let Jamie and Claudia move ahead. Jayne looked up at me in confusion, but I just pointed at the couple and kept walking. They were so wrapped up in each other that they didn't notice.

I thought I could definitely count Jamie as a friend. We'd held an easy camaraderie ever since the first night out. And Claudia seemed over her "he's mine, so stay away" phase. Berta seemed to like everyone, and she had certainly been sweet and caring to me. I could still feel the gentle touch of her hand on my back when I'd discovered Charlie.

Owen? Well, he was just Owen. He was sheriff here. His first allegiance was to the safety of his people. And the rest didn't really know me; they just saw the damage my presence had seemed to cause. I couldn't really blame them for wanting me gone. At the very least, I couldn't take it personally.

Trent wanted me to stay. Trent liked me because I paid attention to him. It was hard being a kid in a mostly adult world, harder still, I imagined, under these circumstances. Maybe we could do some more ninja training when I got back to the house. I had promised him, after all.

Which left Shane. Where did he fit into the equation?

I had to admit I had feelings for him. But were they for the Shane I'd met in the past, or for the Shane I knew from the future?

In the past I'd watched him covertly on the El, deep in fantasies about wild uncontrolled sex with him. I hadn't even had enough courage just to walk up and say hi. Neither of us had. No, we'd both sat lost in our own thoughts without the courage to even speak to each other until we crashed into each other at Joe's.

Funny, how I'd met him just before all this weird stuff happened. How tiny changes made such big impacts in lives. What would have happened between us if I'd made our date? Would we have a different future, or would Lucinda have taken both of us? Why had Lucinda turned Shane? She'd told him he was special for some reason, that he was the first in a long time. But what was it about him that made him special? Beyond the obvious. Sure he was hot and a doctor, but surely that wasn't it. That would be ludicrous. If she wanted hot she could have turned Brad Pitt.

Did Lucinda turning Shane have anything to do with me? Her actions in the ER that night had been strange, but now that I knew her story it made more sense. Maybe she'd been looking out for me, waiting until I unlocked the twister. Of course, she sure had made a point out of meeting Shane. All of this just couldn't be one big coincidence, could it?

A Time Guardian. What exactly was a Time Guardian? The disaster with Charlie had blown every other thought out of my head, but now that I had time to think about it I realized that I really needed to get the answers from Shane and find out everything he knew.

And to thank him for being so kind to me last night.

The wind whipped the tail of my coat around my calves, and dead leaves swirled in a vortex down the street. Jayne and his buddy—encouraged or frightened,

I couldn't tell—took off at a full gallop, their tails straight up like antennae. Jamie and Claudia laughed at their antics.

"When is the next gathering?" I asked, as I moved once more up beside them.

"As soon as the moon wanes," Jamie said. "There will be a group of us going."

"Will you join us?" Claudia asked.

"I'm thinking of it," I replied.

I was thinking of how best to protect my friends and get rid of Lucinda. I was thinking I might have to choose . . .

Shane was in his clinic. I found out the chamber behind the exam room held two rows of narrow beds. Five of them held patients.

"Hey," he said when I walked in. "How was it?"

"Nice." Why did I suddenly feel like crying again? "It was really nice. What Jamie did—and how Claudia made it look." I quickly wiped beneath my eyes. "Can we talk?"

"Sure," Shane said. Once again he was ER Shane—kind, sympathetic, all bedside manner and concern. We walked out to the broad front porch, and I sat on the banister while he took a seat in an old swing. Jayne jumped onto the cushion of an old wicker chair and proceeded with his evening ablutions. Inside I could see Berta bustling about, lighting candles and shooing Trent from the door. Poor kid. I gave him a nod—yes, ninja lessons would continue—which made him smile.

"Yeah!" he said, and clenched his fist in victory. Then he ran off.

Shane grinned and shook his head. The first pattering

of rain hit the leaves as I settled back against a post. The air felt good, fresh and clean, cool on my skin.

"How are the patients?" I asked as I unstrapped my katana and leaned it against the railing.

"I sent one home, and the rest should recover," he said. He pushed the swing back and forth by flexing his knees, and the chains that held the swing squeaked. I nodded in time to the swing.

"How's your shoulder?" Shane asked.

I placed my hand on it and flexed my arm. "Fine," I said. I felt no pain at all. Not even a twinge. "I forgot all about it."

"Hmm," Shane said. I could tell he was in total doctor mode. Should my shoulder hurt?

He waved as some people walked up under the trees to shelter from the rain. "I didn't want the injured to be unprotected in case of another attack, so most everyone is coming back here tonight," he explained.

"Are the attacks worse because of me?"

Shane leaned forward and rubbed his hands over his face. I could tell by the set of his shoulders that he was worried. "Worse than what?" he finally said. "They always come to feed. Last night they had an additional purpose. Was it any worse? No. Was it more violent? Yes. Have we lost people before? Yes. Does that answer all your questions?"

I let him continue with his tirade because I knew he was tired and frustrated. He probably needed to feed, too, but I hoped that could wait. My stomach's gentle rumblings reminded me that I myself had gone an entire day without food. Somehow, eating was way down on my priority list.

"Tell me about the Time Guardian thing," I said.

Shane leaned back in the swing and crossed his

arms. He looked at me, intently, as if studying me and seeing me for the first time. I returned his gaze, captivated by his bright blue eyes.

He must have been a beautiful child. I could see him with snow-white hair and chubby cheeks and dark-lashed eyes that would melt the cruelest heart. It was good that he was a doctor. Good that someone so obviously blessed had wanted to give something back.

Make that formerly blessed. Now he was cursed.

"The tick I killed was an old one," he began. "An ancient, one of the originals. He was the second since I turned. I've come across very few, apart from Lucinda."

"He was the second ancient that you've killed?" I asked.

"Yes." He smiled briefly. "At least that will help for a while."

"What?"

"Kill. Feed. I won't have to. When you take an old one, it lasts a while."

"So, the tick you killed out here last night?"

"You mean the one who wanted to snack on you?" he asked.

"Yeah. You didn't need to . . ."

"Strictly for the buzz," he said.

"Thanks." I rolled my eyes, and he laughed. "So what's the deal?" I asked when his mirth faded to a sly smile.

"Remember how I said it wasn't all about you?" he said. "Well, it *is* all about you. At least, the time-twister is."

"Why?"

"A balance of power. The Chronolotians can live forever. Someone has to make sure they don't abuse that power."

"And that's me?"

"It was supposed to be."

"What do you mean, supposed to be?"

Shane got up from the swing and sat on the banister next to me. I got the feeling I wasn't going to like what he was about to say, and I raised an eyebrow in question.

"You told me that night in the ER that you have no family."

"No one," I agreed. It was amazing that he remembered, considering how long it had been.

"There's a reason for that."

"Why?"

"Lucinda . . ."

"Lucinda? How? Why?"

"That Time Portal was sent here millennia ago for safekeeping by the Time Guardians. That's why the Chronolotians came. They wanted it. While the Time Guardians are not immortal, they do have powers. Incredible speed, strength, rapid healing . . ."

I touched my arm where I'd ripped it open. It had healed incredibly fast: in less than a week. And my shoulder . . . it was as if that had never happened. Now that I thought of it, I'd always been a fast healer, but this was insane. As I'd been told, my powers must be increasing.

"You should see the way you move when you're fighting," Shane continued. His eyes pierced me, as if he were trying to see inside. "It's unbelievable."

"The same with you." I turned away. I couldn't take his unabashed admiration of my combat skills. Especially since I wasn't particularly aware of them.

"It's because of the balance of power," he replied. "The guardianship is handed down from generation to generation. Your ancestors managed to keep the portal a secret. Whenever they thought they were close to being discovered, they would move it. And that's how it came to be here."

"But the house . . . it was just pure luck that I bought it. I didn't know anything about it. And I certainly didn't know there was a time-twister in it!"

"Maybe not so much luck, as someone pushing you in that direction."

"Lucinda?"

Shane rubbed the bridge of his nose. "The tick I killed didn't know that part. He just knew that Lucinda had found the Time Portal and was using it. And now she couldn't, because a Guardian had shown up. He came here to try and partner up with her."

"So, where does the part about Lucinda being responsible for my being an orphan come in?" I asked.

"I don't know for sure." Shane looked over at me. "But this tick implied that was the case."

I nodded. Once again, this was a lot to absorb. Could Lucinda be in any way responsible? My dad's death had been an accident; I'd seen it happen. And my mom died in childbirth. But what about my grandparents? My dad had said my mom grew up in a foster home. And his parents had both died young. There was no one to ask . . .

Except Lucinda.

Shane sat patiently on the banister. I wondered if he was afraid that I would have a meltdown or something.

"Did you catch this tick on his way in or out?" I asked. "To talk to Lucinda."

"In," Shane said.

"It would be bad if they did partner up," I surmised.

"Yeah. Bad for us."

"If the old ones are so powerful," I asked. "Then how . . ."

Shane interrupted, "I guess you could say I disarmed him." He grinned. "I cut off his left arm."

I burst out laughing. "You are so bad." I punched his arm, and he grabbed mine.

"I *am* bad," he said. He grabbed at my stomach, trying to tickle me, and I fell off the banister onto the stairs. We collapsed against each other in laughter. I fell into a complete girly moment as he tickled me. I twisted away, but he grabbed me around the waist and turned me.

We both stopped. Looked at each other. Shane slowly and tenderly pushed aside the hair that had fallen from my ponytail into my face.

"Abbey . . ."

He was going to kiss me. I could see it in his eyes, in the way he looked at me, in the way he moved his lips . . .

"Shane! We need you in here." It was Claudia. Standing in the doorway, she was holding it open and looking nervous. "Roger's fever's gone up."

Shane looked down at me and then his eyes changed. Not red, not glowy, just closed off, as if he were embarrassed. As if he'd almost made a tragic mistake. He followed Claudia into the house.

I stood on the porch, practically dumbfounded. What had just happened?

I looked around to see if anyone was watching, but there was no one. They must have all gone round back while Shane and I were talking.

I picked up my katana and looked at Jayne, who seemed just as confused as I was.

"Can we do ninja stuff now?" a voice asked.

It was Trent, peering through the door.

"Yeah," I said. "Now would be the perfect time for ninja stuff."

NINETEEN

My body was on a totally different schedule than ever before: sleep all day, fight all night, wonder about crap in between. It was the wondering that was killing me.

The pattering rain on the roof should have been blissful; instead it kept me awake. I finally kicked off the blankets and perched on the open windowsill, Jayne on my lap. I had no idea what time it was. I'd lost all sense of it except for at dawn and dusk, preparing to fight or sleep and trying to figure things out in between.

The rain was not to blame for my lack of sleep, however. It was Shane. The inside of my head was so twisted up with him that I couldn't think of anything else. I wanted him to kiss me. I wanted it so bad I could taste it. Which made his recent about-face all the more painful.

At the same time, part of me was glad. Part of me was having a major fit because he wasn't technically human anymore. Was he?

He sure did look human. Human perfection, to be exact. And he acted human . . . except for when he was sucking the life out of ticks and his eyes got all red and glowy.

"Jayne." I leaned over and buried my face in the cat's

thick fur. "What should I do?" Jayne's answering rumble was soothing, but it did nothing to solve my dilemma.

Not that it mattered much, what I thought. Shane had made it apparent that he'd been grateful for the interruption. He'd disappeared into his clinic for the evening and not come out; at least, not when I could see him.

I'd taught Trent ninja moves until he was staggering from tiredness. Then I'd found Owen, Jamie and Claudia gathered around the kitchen table.

The steady rain had seemed to discourage the ticks from attacking tonight, just as Jamie had predicted. Owen seemed to think they were busy plotting another way to get to me. Jamie was more optimistic: he said they were getting seriously outnumbered, and had decided to stay in and lick their wounds.

None of us believed the problem was just going to go away, however. Lucinda wanted me—no, she *needed* me—so she could use the time-twister.

The easiest solution was to kill Lucinda. Of course, walking up to her house—no, *my* house—to do so seemed impossible. And she had yet to show her face outside of it; she was sticking close to the time-twister.

No, there weren't enough humans to mount an attack. Not yet. As long as we kept killing ticks, someday the odds might be in our favor. But right now it would just be a suicide mission.

I wasn't ready to die. And I surely wasn't ready to ask anyone else to die for me.

The best solution for everyone would be for me to leave. Owen didn't come right out and say it, but I know that's what he was thinking.

"I guess I'll be moving on, Jayne," I said. The cat looked up at me, stretched out a paw, snagged his claws into my T-shirt and meowed.

"Well, if you insist," I said. "But you can come only if you walk. I'm not carrying your fuzzy butt anywhere."

"Whatever you think is best," Shane said when I told him my plan. I was going to the gathering and not coming back.

So much for any please-beg-me-to-stay fantasy. Which I wasn't really sure I'd wanted.

Shane checked on the last patient in his ward. Things had been remarkably quiet since the night of the big showdown, and now that the moon was growing smaller every night it was almost time for the gathering. A wagon was at this moment being loaded in front of the house with goods for trade. I was relieved to know that we were going on horseback instead of walking. With my limited scope of the new world I was living in, I had not realized that there was any organization in place. I knew that the people living here had other homes besides Shane's. It had just never occurred to me that there were farms inside the safety zone, with horses and sheep and cows. What were once backyards now melded together into garden plots and pastures. That was how this community fed itself. The ticks left the farms alone.

"I just feel like, if I'm gone, then Lucinda won't have an excuse to attack," I said, even though Shane had agreed with me.

"You're right," he said. He didn't look at me, just continued checking the wound on the feverish man who lay on the narrow cot.

"I told Berta I'd look after Trent until I figure out where to go," I added.

"Good luck with that," Shane said. "I'm sure he's

pretty excited about going to a gathering. This'll be his first."

"Yeah," I said to the back of his head. I hung around a few more moments, and when he finally turned and looked at me again, it was as if he'd forgotten I was even there.

So much for romantic fantasies. Of course, all of my fantasies involved Shane not being able to suck the life out of my body with the palm of his hand. I still couldn't figure out how to get around that little problem. Not that it was an issue.

The T-shirt I wore was bright blue and said *Over It.* As in, I was. Still, I couldn't help but look back as our crew rode away from Shane's house before dawn. No Shane anywhere that I could see. Just Berta, waving a tearful farewell with a side of admonishments for Trent to behave.

"I will," he assured her from behind me.

Jayne found a bed deep inside the wagon we rode in, and disappeared into its depths. At least he cared that I was leaving. At least he wanted to be with me.

Jerk.

Heavy fog swirled around our caravan as we rode in a direction I'd yet to try since coming here. We were moving away from the city, toward the suburbs. I hoped it wouldn't take too long to get to our destination.

It had been a long while since I'd been on horseback. Jamie must have known, because the horse I rode seemed old and resolved, content to plod along in the middle of the line, its nose right up against the tail of Claudia's horse. Which was fine with me. I'd had enough excitement in my life lately. The last thing I wanted was to land on my tail. Luckily, Trent stayed pretty still behind me. I think it was Owen's threat to skin him if he heard any reports of the boy acting up that kept him silent and wide-eyed behind me.

There were thirty or so in the procession. Most were families, some with small children, and some with older teens. Janet was part of the group. She was with Burton, her husband, and three sons, all somewhere in their teens. There were also some single guys around Jamie's age. I figured they were probably hoping to get lucky like Jamie had. I wondered if the teens were the soldiers-in-training that Trent was so anxious to join.

The group was remarkably quiet, maybe because of the fog that pressed around us. The only sounds were the creak of wagon wheels and the occasional jangle of reins.

It's scary, not being able to see what's around you. But it was going to be dawn soon, so the chance of a tick attack was slim. We'd had no sign of them since the big assault. Still, I kept my hand on the hilt of the katana that I'd looped over the horn of my saddle.

My horse stopped suddenly, its nose on the haunch of Claudia's horse. The beast tossed its head as I pulled it back and away—I didn't want to get kicked by some moody mare protesting over the invasion of personal space.

"What is it?" I asked Jamie.

"Someone's coming toward us," he said. I noticed he had a gun stuffed into the waistband of his jeans.

I kept my eyes front, and my hand on my katana. We were so close to home; surely there wasn't about to be an attack. I felt Trent move and realized he was peering around my back.

"If something happens," I said, "go hide in the wagon. Got it?"

"Yes, ma'am." I felt his nod against my back.

I noticed a definite relaxation in Jamie's shoulders,

and felt myself relax along with him. "It's Shane," he called back to me.

Shane. So that's why he hadn't been around to say goodbye. He was out. He'd said he wouldn't need to feed for a while, but was that why he was out here? Had he been on a rampage?

He materialized out of the fog next to Jamie's horse. "The way's clear," he said. "I've checked all the way to the city limits. . . ."

He looked at me as Jamie and Claudia nudged their horses ahead. His hair was damp, and curled wildly around his ears. The wetness darkened the ends in sharp contrast against the golden blond, and the world around us was gray, which made his eyes seem even more vibrantly blue.

He gripped my ankle and squeezed tight enough that I could feel his strength and heat through my boot.

"Abbey."

My heart jumped into my throat. The swirling mass of emotion that was my constant companion once again battled inside me.

"I wish things were different," he said.

"Yeah," I said. Different. As in, I wish you weren't a soul-sucking monster and we were back in our own time a hundred years ago drinking coffee at Joe's. Or how about: I wish I'd talked to you the first time I saw you on the El. "Me, too." Who knows what could have happened between us if not for all the lost time?

"Take care of yourself," he said.

"You, too," I replied. What else could I say? Shane gave my ankle another squeeze, and then he let go. I kicked my heels into the side of my horse and it took off at a trot as if anxious to be on its way. Or maybe it just sensed safety in numbers.

A scene from *Pirates of the Caribbean* played in my mind, the one at the end where Will Turner tells Elizabeth that her fiancé will be relieved to know she's okay, when Will really should have kissed her. Then Johnny Depp tells him that, if he was waiting for the opportune moment, that had been it.

Of course, I didn't know what it was I wanted Shane to do. How could I, when I didn't know what I wanted? If only things were different.

I turned around for one last look. All I could see was the fog.

TWENTY

"Holy campground, Batman," I said as we rode down the cracked pavement of the road around the airport. As far as I could see the runways were covered with tents.

"Who's Batman?" Trent asked. So much for me being witty with cultural references. Trent's question triggered a picture in my mind: Shane, once more materializing out of the fog, running full out, his coat flying around him. The only thing missing was the black mask with the pointy ears.

"Here, I guess you could say Shane is Batman," I said. I held Trent's arm as he slid down from the back of the horse. "Stay close!" I yelled as he took off after some of the older boys, which meant he would totally ignore me. So much for my responsible-guardian moment.

I dismounted. I was stiff from a long day and another long morning in the saddle and wanted nothing more than some peaceful yoga stretching and a nice comfortable bed. I had a feeling both would be in short supply.

Our group went to work, immediately setting up camp with tents and beach-type awnings. I felt as if I were at a giant festival of some sort. Everywhere I looked there were tents and flags and vendors selling food and clothing and scavenged goods. And all of it was available for barter. Our group had their own stores to set up, and I was interested to see what kind of trading would go on.

Jayne popped out of the wagon just as Claudia handed me a pile of blankets. The cat jumped up on the seat and started a bath.

"Yeah," I said. "You take it easy while the rest of us do all the work."

We spent the early part of the afternoon setting up tents and arranging our own little neighborhood campsite while the kids ran and played. Trent checked in occasionally, if only because the parents of the boys he was with had laid down the law and they were scared not to. Trent had no such compunction where I was concerned, but still he presented himself before me, immediately taking off again as if everything would disappear if he didn't see it at once. I was a little intimidated by the responsibility of being the one to look after him, as neither Owen, Berta nor Shane was around to do so.

"So, what happens now?" I asked Jamie when we were done setting up our temporary homes.

"Janet and Burton go to the Gathering Council," Jamie informed me. "The rest of us will look around until the festival tonight."

"There's music and dancing," Claudia added as she wrapped her arms around Jamie's waist.

"Cool." Music and dancing sounded like a nice change from killing and dying.

The air still held a chill, even though the sun felt warm, and I pulled on my coat. I noticed Jamie did the same after carefully placing his gun in the waistband of his jeans. I picked up my katana and arched an eyebrow in his direction. He nodded, so I strapped it on and secured it to my thigh. Apparently there could be more than music and dancing tonight.

I looked around for Trent but didn't see him as we three adults walked toward the rows of vendor tents. Jayne trailed along behind us, meowing loudly as if to make sure we knew he was there.

The vendors were arranged by comparable goods. We passed rows of kitchen gadgets that reminded me of a Williams-Sonoma store. Knives, silverware, spatulas, spoons—all were neatly arranged in plastic bins placed on tables. No Braun or Geralia were anywhere to be seen. Whoever figured out a way to bring back coffee would make a killing.

Next, there was an assortment of cookware and bowls and all kinds of grilling accessories, followed by an assortment of linens, some of them high quality, though most of them homemade.

Another tent held all kinds of dishes: everything from fine china to your everyday variety of Corelle. I'd always been a sucker for dishes, and stopped to admire some of the stoneware pieces.

"This is nothing," Claudia said. "Wait until you see some of the handmade pieces."

"Pottery?" I asked hopefully.

"Yeah," she said with a smile.

I couldn't believe that we were bonding over something as simple as shopping. All it took was her realizing that I wasn't after Jamie. And how silly of her. How could I be after Jamie when I had somebody else constantly on my mind? I couldn't even help but wonder what Shane was doing at that very moment, and more importantly, I couldn't help but wonder if he missed me. I hadn't given a thought to where I would go after the gathering; I just hoped that something would give me a sign, a direction, something to grab on to. A purpose.

We moved from household goods into clothing. Tents upon tents held stacks of everything imaginable. I picked up a gold T-shirt that said *Remember Cedric Diggory* on it.

"Harry Potter," I laughed.

"Who?" Jamie asked.

"Harry Potter." I started to explain about Harry Potter, then changed my mind. It was way too complicated.

"Did you know the guy who owned that?" Claudia asked.

"Kind of," I said. "Do any of these tents hold books?" I asked.

"Yeah," Claudia said. "They're usually on the far side."

We moved on. I noticed the crowd was growing. I saw people of every race and age as we moved down the row. Some of them shopped and dickered with the vendors, while others stood in groups and talked. Snippets of a conversation caught my ears as we walked by.

"Did you hear?"

"They've got a tick."

"An older one."

"I hear they're going to fry her tomorrow."

"That should be interesting," Jamie commented.

"Indeed," I said. If only it were Lucinda being left out in the sun.

That thought started my mind on a runaway train of an imagined future. With Lucinda gone, the ticks would fall. I could go back because the threat would be over. But . . . then what? Settle down? Live happily ever after with a demon doctor who wouldn't age? How long before he got tired of me? How long before I got old and he got bored? And would he always be able to control himself?

If only I could go back to my own time. If only there was some way to stop this from happening.

Trent and his posse crossed our path. I grabbed his arm to stop him. His face was flushed, and he was damp with sweat.

"What are you up to?" I asked suspiciously.

"Nothing," he said. "Just looking around."

His face seemed pale, and I stuck a hand on his forehead. "Are you sick?" I asked.

"No!" he protested. I read his mind. Sick meant missing out on everything. Give me a little responsibility and I already was in full-out mom mode.

"He's just excited," Jamie said. "You guys check in with us before the entertainment," he said.

"Okay," Trent agreed, and wriggled out of my grasp. He took off in the direction of his friends, and I lost sight of him in the crowd.

"He'll be fine," Jamie assured me. I figured he knew more about it than me, so I let Trent go. It *was* all kind of exciting, and would be more so to a ten-year-old boy who'd never been anywhere. I know I was certainly caught up. Everywhere I looked there seemed something new to see, yet familiar.

"I'm starving," Jamie said.

"Me, too," Claudia agreed.

"I could eat," I added.

Jamie led us down an aisle, and my nose was soon assaulted with a variety of smells that took me back to the county fair. My mouth watered as we stopped in front of an old charcoal grill that held an assortment of spicy sausages.

"How do we pay?" I asked Jamie.

He took a small bag from inside his coat. I noticed as he dug around that his coat lining held an assortment of weapons in webbed pockets. Which reminded me that the gathering wasn't all fun and games. I felt the hilt of the katana through the pocket of my coat. The small blade hidden inside the dragon would be handy if things got ugly.

Jamie's bag held small pieces of jewelry, along with some coins. The cook picked up a gold chain and nodded for us to help ourselves to sausages.

"Is *everything* up for trade?" I asked Jamie as Claudia quickly fixed us plates.

"Yeah," Jamie said. "You've just got to have something the other person wants."

"Jamie's arrows are a high commodity," Claudia volunteered.

"I'm lucky enough to have good tools," Jamie said. "And the heritage. The art's been passed down from generation to generation in my family."

"Hopefully we'll have a son to pass it down to also," Claudia said with a shy smile.

And life goes on, I found myself thinking. The human race always finds a way to survive, no matter what the odds. Yet I couldn't help but feel that maybe there was something I could do about the current predicament. I was supposed to be a Time Guardian, whatever that was. I just needed answers. But where was I supposed to find them?

Jayne's claw in my jeans reminded me that he was hungry also. I knelt down and fed him part of my dinner just as the sound of a gong echoed through the rows.

"The general meeting is over," Jamie said. "Now comes the fun part."

The crowd moved as one, and I saw the tents thin out

as we approached the building that at one time was the airport. A large stage was set up in between two concourses. As we moved closer, I saw a huge board with all kinds of notices attached. Mostly there were drawings. Some were crude, some were fantastically detailed; all featured descriptions. Missing people. Tick fodder, as Owen had so quaintly put it. Part of the buffet.

"Come on," Jamie said. "It's a part of life," he reminded me when he saw the look on my face. "Some people refuse to let go."

"Could you?" I asked. "If it were Claudia?"

There was a moment of uncomfortable silence as the pair looked at me, stricken, both denying what was a distinct possibility. Jamie pulled Claudia to him and she wrapped her arms around his waist.

"It's not *going* to be Claudia," he said. "Or me."

"Why not?" I asked. "What makes you two so special?"

"We've got you," Jamie said simply, and he turned with Claudia and walked away. His arm around her waist was firm, and he placed a tender kiss on top of her head.

I stood and watched them walk away, Jayne twining around my ankles. "They've got me," I said to the cat. "And I've got nothing."

TWENTY-ONE

The sun was just setting behind the airport building and the stage. An excited buzz settled over the crowd as we all jockeyed for position to better see what was about to happen. Jayne decided he was too short and much too vulnerable on the ground, and used my clothing to climb up into my arms. I held him and followed Jamie, who pushed through toward the side where we could climb up on the side of a wagon to watch.

I realized the stage was several old flatbed trailers placed side by side and end to end to make a large platform. The tires had rotted away, but since there was no need to move the trailers, what difference did it make? I had to admire the people of this time for their efficiency. They used whatever they had at hand.

Torches lit the stage and the surrounding area. Two huge drum sets were set up as if a rock concert was about to take place. Of course, there was a definite lack of electrical cords or speakers, but still something immense seemed about to happen. They even had the jetways that used to connect to planes stretched out so that whoever was to appear could walk directly onto the stage from the concourse.

To my amazement and complete embarrassment, a

man appeared on the stage with a boy, his hand firmly gripping the boy's neck. The boy was obviously in a great deal of trouble.

"Trent," I said in disgust.

"Whatever he's done, it's not good," Jamie said. "That's the Constable holding him. We'd better go see what's up."

"I'll go," I said. "He's my responsibility."

Jamie raised an arm in acknowledgment of Trent, and I shouldered my way through the crowd with Jayne still in my arms. People laughed and applauded as Trent squirmed beneath the firm hold of the Constable.

I noticed Janet and Burton were already at the stage and both looking over the crowd—for me, I figured. One day as a parent, and already I'd failed miserably. Now I had a good idea as to why kids got spankings; not that I'd ever deserved one.

By the time I got to Janet and Burton I was more concerned about how Trent looked than the trouble he was in. He looked horrible—pale and sweaty, and his eyes were weak and watery, with huge dark circles beneath them.

"What happened?" I asked as we were herded down the jetway. I dropped Jayne, but the cat stayed right on my heels, meowing as we walked briskly up the tunnel.

"We caught him in the restricted zone," the Constable said. "If we had known he was one of yours," he continued, speaking directly to Janet, "we would have just handed him over to you."

"He's with our group," Janet explained, "but he's not one of mine. He's orphaned."

"He's mine," I spoke up. "At least today he is." I put my arm out to stop the Constable and pulled Trent away from him. The boy's lower lip quivered but he kept quiet as I drew him to my side. "So, what exactly are the charges, or the damages, or whatever it is that you get for going in the restricted area?"

The Constable leveled his gaze on me, sizing me up. I shoved Trent behind me and pushed back the side of my coat so that the hilt of my katana was handy . . . and visible. Jayne crouched beside me and flicked his tail; a low growl rumbled in his throat.

The Constable's eyes flicked from Jayne to the sword and then back to my face. "Is this your first gathering?" he asked.

"Yeah," I said as I crossed my arms. "Having a blast so far."

"She's part of your group?" he asked Janet.

I was happy to see Janet and Burton shoulder up beside me. "She is," Janet said.

"Are we done here?" I asked.

The Constable gave me one last look. It was a long one. "We're done. Just make sure he stays out of trouble."

"Oh, he will," I said, sounding very much like a parent. Now where had that come from?

Janet gave me a pleading look as she and Burton followed the Constable back out the jetway. I could hear the noise from the crowd as they cheered some announcement. A man stepped forward—a deputy, no doubt—and led us into the building and pointed toward the exit.

I took Trent by the arm and we followed. The airport looked remarkably preserved. The built-in seats still defined the waiting areas. The walls were covered with graffiti but the area was pretty much free of trash. I noticed a group waiting down the hall—most likely the entertainment, since a couple of them held guitars and one held a pair of drumsticks that he twirled around his fingers.

"Rock on," I said, and turned Trent in the direction indicated by the deputy.

Trent seemed shaky, and stumbled after me. I stopped and once again did the forehead check.

"You're burning up," I said. "You're going back to camp."

The fact that he didn't protest made me realize how sick he was. As soon as we got outside I picked him up, and he wrapped his arms around my neck and put his head on my shoulder.

"So, tell me about going to the restricted zone," I said as we made our way around the crowd. I saw that Jayne was following.

"Carson dared me," Trent said. "Dared me to see the tick."

I rolled my eyes. Carson was Janet's youngest, and a few years older than Trent. He should have known better.

"You've seen ticks before," I said, deciding to save the would-you-jump-off-a-bridge-if-Carson-did lecture for later.

"Not up close."

"How close were you?"

"Real close. She's in a cage."

"What does she look like?"

"Real pretty." We were away from the crowd now, and heading in the opposite direction from everyone else. I got a few sympathetic looks from some moms as I held on to Trent. He was slippery and soaking wet. My neck where his head lay felt hot and sticky.

"Older than you but still pretty," he said as he stifled a yawn.

"Prettier?" I teased. The sun had set and we made our way through the campsites lit by torches.

"In a way," he said.

"Oh, thanks," I said. I wasn't offended, though. I definitely wasn't the glamorous type. I leaned more toward Jennifer Garner than Jennifer Aniston. Not that anyone in this time had a clue to who either of those two were.

"They said she was old. Like Shane is," he continued.

"Who are 'they'?"

"The guards. We heard them talking about her. That's when Carson dared me to go see her. They said she was one of the first ones turned, and that she lived with one of the old ones. Like Lucinda."

"I wonder how they caught her?"

"They said they found her in a house in the middle of nowhere. She was waiting on the old one to come back for her."

"You know something, Trent?" I said, at last seeing the banner that marked our camp. "You'd make a pretty good spy.

"A ninja spy?" he asked.

"Yep. A ninja spy."

As I walked up to our tents, one of the women from our group approached. "Is he sick?" she asked.

"Yeah," I said. "Running a mad fever."

"Mine too," she said. "Too bad Shane didn't come."

"Yeah," I agreed. "Too bad."

"Put him in with mine," she said. "I'll watch over him."

"Thanks," I said. I carried Trent into the tent and put him on a pile of blankets next to a boy close to his own age. "Was he running around with you today?" I asked.

"Yeah," Trent said as he made himself comfortable. "But his mom made him come in when she saw he was sick."

"Guess I should have done the same," I said. "Were you around anyone from outside our group that was sick?"

"There were some boys that we hooked up with. One of them left 'cause he said he didn't feel well."

I put my hand on his head again. Definitely a fever. Could it be some kind of virus spreading throughout the gathering? I tried to blot out thoughts of the pandemic that had wiped out most of mankind; there wasn't much I could do.

The other mom came in with some water for Trent. "I'm Nora," she said. "Todd's my son." She ran a head over her child's forehead. The boy stirred restlessly in his sleep. "Go on back, I know it's your first gathering. You shouldn't miss it."

"Okay," I said. I started to rise then knelt back down. "Trent," I said. He blinked and turned to look at me. "Where was she—the tick?"

A slow smile chased across his face. "Are you going to talk to her?"

"I might," I said. I *was*. If she was truly old like Shane, and had been traveling with an ancient, then just maybe she knew something. Something about me. Something that could help.

"The building we were in," he said. "She's underneath. In a cage. We got in under the jetways."

I nodded, my mind quickly forming a picture. She was probably down in the baggage area. There would be cages down there where bags had been locked up for storage. The boys could have sneaked in from the runway side; I could probably go in from the baggage-claim side.

"Get some rest," I said. Then I slipped out into the darkness with one thing on my mind: It was time to have a heart-to-heart with a tick.

TWENTY-TWO

It dawned on me that I was listening to a Nickelback song as I worked my way around the crowd slow-dancing in front of the stage. The lyrics of "If Everyone Cared" carried over the dancers, and I had to shake my head at the irony.

"I'm alive," I said to Jayne. "Does anyone care?"

Lucinda did. But only because she needed me. And with luck I was about to find out why.

The cat and I made our way around the crowd and dipped into the shadows beyond the concourse. I took a moment to let my eyes adjust to the darkness. A tall hurricane fence met the building, but parts of it were peeled back and it was a simple matter to slip through.

The route to the Arrivals dropoff was down below. The long-term parking was beyond, so I worked my way around and took a walking tunnel beneath the road. At first I moved slowly, cautiously, since it was black as pitch, but Jayne trotted on without a care so I followed, confident that he'd give me warning if someone appeared. I stopped at the tunnel end to scan the area.

The only visible light came from deep within the building. Because of the road overhead it was like being in a cave. I figured since I couldn't see anyone, they couldn't see me, so I stepped out and followed the curve of Jayne's tail toward the glass doors.

The main doors of the terminal were broken out. It was a simple matter to step through. I reached for my katana and then thought better of it; if I drew my weapon I'd just be asking for violence, and chances were that whoever I ran into would have guns. I didn't want to kill anyone; I just wanted to ask questions.

Like, why me?

Through the darkness I walked. To be safe, I drew the small Tanto blade from the katana hilt and slid it up into the lining of my coat sleeve. At last I saw a soft glow spill from behind the swinging doors that led into the back area of the luggage claim. I felt Jayne near my ankles. He was waiting for me to make a decision on where to go next.

I headed toward the luggage carousel on the far end, away from the glow. I crawled through the hatch and rolled off the side, away from the direction the light came from. Beyond, I saw a group of five men and women standing around. Their attention all seemed focused in the same direction, away from me, so I moved behind them with Jayne padding along.

I realized they were standing behind and below the stage setup. They were listening to the band and talking, basically having a good time. But where was the tick? Surely not here, hanging out and chatting. I kept to the darkness and the ever-changing shapes along the back wall.

It suddenly occurred to me that Jayne might be a liability instead of an asset. He wouldn't like coming across a tick, and would probably pitch a fit, but he might lead me right to her.

"I guess we'll just have to play it by ear," I said under my breath as we passed the group gathered at the door.

In the darkness beyond, I saw a fence that stretched from end to end across two walls. Dim lanterns were hung on it. I glanced toward the chatting guards and was relieved to see that they were still gathered at the main door, all looking upward and outward. I crept on until I got to the fence.

Trent had been down here in the light of day. If they were saving the tick for tonight, then they would have had to provide precautions to protect her against the light. Yet, Trent said he saw her. He'd even said she was pretty. She had to be here somewhere.

She was. I saw her in profile, moving to the edge of the fence, looking at her guards. The light from two lanterns hung on either side of a door poured over her face. Long golden blond hair cascaded down her back, and her figure in skintight black leather pants and a silky cami was unbelievable.

There was also something vaguely familiar about her. Something that nudged at the edge of my mind.

Jayne hissed, and the tick turned toward the sound. I nudged Jayne with my foot and he hunkered down on the floor with a low growl rumbling in his throat as she glided toward me.

I looked toward the group once again. To my amazement, the guards all stepped outside into the darkness as if summoned.

I stepped closer to the fence . . . and immediately wished I hadn't.

"Hello, Abbey," my father's second wife purred.

"Sheila?" I gasped in disbelief, then quickly looked at to door and back. So far we were good. Sorta.

I couldn't think of a thing to say. My mind could not

comprehend that Sheila was standing before me, one-hundred-plus years from the last time I'd seen her.

"So, you finally figured it out," she said.

How did she know about me? She didn't seem surprised that I was alive in this day and time.

"Yes, I did," I said, as my mind scrambled to find some logical explanation. Just when I'd accepted things for what they were, I'd had another bomb lobbed at me.

Sheila was a tick.

"And when did *you* figure it out?" I asked quietly.

"Before your father died," she said. She seemed to be enjoying herself. Of course, we never had gotten along. Go figure.

Jayne's growls grew stronger as Sheila played with the diamond pattern of the fence. "Who's your friend?" she asked, looking down at Jayne. She made a face at him as his tail whipped back and forth.

"Before Dad died?" I ignored her comment about Jayne and once more made sure that we were alone. "How?"

She looked over toward the door and smiled. "Get me out of here, and I'll tell you all about it."

Yeah. Right.

I crossed my arms and stared at her. "I don't think so, Sheila. You haven't given me a reason why I should believe anything you have to say."

"You came looking for me, remember?" The look she offered was confident, but also full of disdain. In other words, it was the usual look she'd given me back when I was a teenager and we were supposed to be one big happy family. The your-father's-going-to-do-whatever-I-say-because-I'm-hot-and-am-good-in-bed look.

I hated her. Still.

"Obviously you want to hear what I have to say," she continued.

"Maybe I just wanted to get a good look at the tick they're going to fry," I said.

"They won't fry me," she said. "At least, the men won't want to." She arched her back and stretched lazily, ending with a flip of her hair. "Why should they let all this go to waste?"

"I always knew you were a slut."

"Well, here's something I bet you *didn't* know," she said with a sinister smile. "Your precious daddy's death was no accident."

The anger that swelled inside me kept my jaw from dropping to the floor. "What do you mean?" I ground out between clenched teeth.

"Come on, Abbey, get me out," she said. "Then I'll tell you all about it."

I slid my katana out of its sheath and through the fence in one fluid motion. The point of it pressed right into Sheila's navel, which was exposed beneath the hem of her cami. She backed up and away, her blue eyes flicking between my face and the blade. Jayne let loose with a yowl and smacked a paw against the fence.

"Put the weapon down," a voice said.

Stupid. I'd got so caught up in Sheila that I quit paying attention to what was around me. Stupid, stupid, stupid.

I felt the cold steel of a gun barrel next to my ear, and carefully pulled the katana out of the fence.

"Drop it," the voice said. It was a man, and Sheila quickly went to work.

"Thanks," she purred. "I'm sure she wants to kill me."

"At least some things never change," I said as I lowered my blade to the floor.

I saw Jayne disappear into the darkness—so much for sticking by my side. Inside I was kicking myself for being such an idiot as I stepped away from the fence with my hands in the air. I should have told Jamie what I was doing. He could have backed me up. Or . . . he could have wound up in as much trouble as I seemed to be in now.

"What were you doing?" the man with the gun asked, herding me toward the light.

"Just wanted to chat," I said. "Is there anything wrong with that?"

"Yeah," Sheila said. "We're old friends. *Ol-l-ld* friends," she emphasized.

I rolled my eyes. "Hardly," I said. "Not then, and definitely not now."

"What does she mean, old friends?" the man asked.

"It means I knew her a hundred years ago," Sheila informed him. "Now, why is it that she's still around?"

"Don't move a muscle," the man said, and he put his gun once more to my temple. "Hey!" he yelled for his friends. "Get in here quick!"

The gang ran in, all asking questions.

"I caught one," my captor said excitedly. "I caught another tick!"

"I am *not* a tick," I said as carefully as I could. I could feel his hand shaking with excitement.

Sheila laughed. "Try telling him what you really are," she said. "Maybe that will work."

How did she know? I didn't dare move, yet all I could think about was tearing through the fence and forcing Sheila to tell me everything before I sliced her head off.

"I guess there's only one way to find out," one of the women said. "Hold her."

Two men grabbed me by the arms, while the first kept his gun pointed right at my forehead. The woman pulled a knife from her boot, grabbed my hand and sliced the palm. Blood oozed out for a quick moment; then the wound healed magically before our eyes.

"I can explain that," I said. But could I? Whatever change I'd suffered since coming through the twister was really accelerating my powers.

"Yeah," she said. "You're a tick."

"Get a cat," I said. "They go crazy around ticks. See what one does around me." I was grasping at straws. Luckily, none of them was wearing a sword. I was pretty sure my powers excluded growing a head back after it'd been sliced off.

"Sorry," she said. "No cats."

"Jayne?" I called. "Here kitty, kitty, kitty." *Fair-weather friend. Stupid cat ran at the first sign of trouble.*

I knew I wasn't being fair to Jayne. After all, he'd help me take down several ticks, but still, I sure could have used him.

"Lock her up," the woman said. "I'll go get Stu."

"Wait," said the man with the gun in my ear. "We can't put them together. They might try to kill each other."

"You're right," the woman said. "We'll figure something out." She gave me one last look. "Prepare to fry," she said, and spat in my face.

I couldn't help it; I laughed. "Okay," I said as she walked away.

TWENTY-THREE

Stu, the Constable, was not happy to see me again. After making several accusations about using a kid to spy for me, he walked away in a huff. The other group's solution to the they-might-kill-each-other-before-we-want-them-to-die problem was to wrap several lengths of chain around me and the back of an old rolling desk chair. Then they plopped me down in front of Sheila's cage.

"So you two can catch up," one said. I felt some satisfaction that they were ignoring Sheila as she tried her best to look sexy and alluring for the men.

"Yeah," I said. "Thanks." I noticed the one who'd found me had walked off with my katana. I filed that away for later reference.

Sheila and I stared at each other for a long moment as the footsteps of the guards faded behind me, and the band played something with a heavy drumbeat. I imagined the crowd really enjoying themselves now, working up some excitement until the prize captive was carried out. Now they'd get two for the price of one.

I just hoped things hadn't changed. If tick suntans were the plan, I had nothing to worry about.

Unless someone got antsy.

Sheila walked over to the fence and stood before me. She traced a well-manicured finger down the links in the fence. "You should have got me out when you had a chance," she said.

"Hey, the way I see it, come morning you'll be nothing but a pile of dust and all I've got to worry about is getting the end of my nose burnt," I said. "I can wait. I'm actually looking forward to getting a little color."

"I see you haven't lost any of your attitude," Sheila said. "It took every bit of patience I had not to slap you across the room at times."

"Well, gee," I said. "My life is complete. I can now die happy, knowing I pissed you off." I stuck my foot on the fence and rocked my chair back. "*Eventually*," I added.

She tried desperately to hide it, but she was scared. I could tell by the way her eyes flicked over the fence as she looked once more for any way to escape.

"Maybe if you sleep with them they'll let you go," I said. "It's always worked in the past hasn't it—sex for favors?"

"It worked easily enough with your dad," she snarled back.

Ouch! I did not want to discuss my dad's bad choice. "Why did you marry him, anyway?" I asked. "Sure he had money. But not that much."

"I got an offer I couldn't refuse," Sheila said. "Eternal life."

I took my foot off the fence and sat forward. "You weren't a tick when you married my dad. I saw you in the daylight plenty of times."

"Eternal life was my reward for killing him. I married him for the cash."

"*You* killed my father?"

"I arranged it."

I must have been past the point where anything

would surprise me. Or maybe it was the fact that I was pretty much immobilized. Or it could have been that I'd known all along. At any rate, I didn't even blink when she said it. I just said, "Why?"

"They needed you to open the gate," she replied.

All calm that I'd felt vanished. I wanted to scream. I wanted to cry. I wanted to tear the fence down with my bare hands and chop Sheila into a million pieces. But all I could do was sit and force back tears.

"What did killing my dad have to do with me opening the gate? How did they expect me to open it? I didn't even know what it was, or where it was. It was all just a big twist of fate that I wound up with the house where the gate is in the first place. . . ."

"Not necessarily," Sheila said.

The look I gave her showed my doubt.

"You were being played, my dear," Sheila said. "Just like your parents and your grandparents."

"You're crazy," I said.

"You asked," she replied.

What she said didn't make sense. But she did know something about me. She wasn't surprised that I was in this time. And she knew about the gate.

I decided to try a different tack.

"Who changed you?" I asked.

Sheila smiled, as if remembering something pleasant. "His name was Gavin," she said. "You should have seen him. The most gorgeous man who ever walked the earth."

"What happened to him?"

"I killed him."

Weirder and weirder, I thought.

"Why?"

"For the rush. I wanted to know what if felt like to take time from a Chronolotian. It surprised him, I must say."

"I can imagine," I snapped. It didn't surprise me, but I knew her. "So, what, you've been snacking on humans ever since?"

"Sort of," she said. "Until I hooked up with Marco. That's who I was waiting on when they found me. Something must have happened to him. He was supposed to meet with one named Lucinda. I believe you know *her*," she said.

Now she wanted information from me. I could tell by the way she looked at me. It was the same look she'd had when my dad pulled out his wallet.

Marco. Shane said he'd killed an ancient who was on his way to meet Lucinda. I made a leap of logic.

"I hate to be the bearer of bad news, Sheila, but Marco is dead." I didn't really hate it, but she was being agreeable. Sort of.

"You killed him?"

"No, a friend of mine did."

She accepted the news silently. She must have really liked him.

"My turn," I said. "How did you do it? Arranging my father's death."

"Anything can be bought. I knew he was meeting you for lunch, I knew you'd be at that sidewalk café. It was an easy enough thing to find someone willing to run him down so that it looked like an accident. Actually, I was hoping they'd get you, too, but since your father hadn't bothered with a will it didn't really matter."

"But I thought your friend Gavin wanted him dead to get to me."

"Gavin thought that with your father out of the way we could control you. But I didn't want to have to deal with you. After he changed me I killed him, took the money and took off."

"Lucky me," I said.

"I did do you a favor," she replied. "Gavin would have come after you."

"Thanks," I said dryly. "So, what about my mother and my grandparents?"

"I'm not sure of the details. Like I said, Gavin had traced the lineage but didn't know where the gate was. Your mother was raised in an orphanage. I'm guessing her parents were killed for the same reason yours were."

"But my mom died in childbirth," I said.

"She was attacked and went into labor early," Sheila said. "Your dad spared you the details. He didn't want you to have to deal with the fact that she was murdered."

"Who attacked her?"

"Gavin—or so he said. He thought he'd kill your mother and take you. Somehow she got away. Some of those superpowers you're supposed to possess, I guess. Before your mother died she told your father that you would never be safe. So your father changed his name and yours and moved around a bit before settling with you here."

"How do you know all this?" I asked, incredulous.

"Marco told me," she said. "He managed to put everything together. The funny thing is, your father moved you back to the city your grandmother ran away from trying to protect your mother. Of course he'd have no way of knowing that. . . ."

"What happened to my grandparents?"

"You'll have to ask Lucinda about that. It seems she found the gate but didn't know the lineage. Gavin found the gatekeepers but didn't know where the gate was. Very amusing. In any event, your family has all been played."

I shook my head. Everything sounded so bizarre. Yet

here I was, one hundred years in the future, chained to a chair and talking to my father's murderous ex-wife who happened to be immortal as long as she could suck the life out of someone's chest.

"Enough about me," Sheila said abruptly. "What have you been up to?"

"Since you left me penniless?" I said. "Working and putting myself through school."

"How did you wind up here?" she asked. "In this time."

"Strictly by accident," I said. "How did Lucinda think that I would someday end up buying the very house that held the gate?"

"Don't know," Sheila said. "You'll have to ask her about that."

"If only it were that simple," I said.

Sheila shrugged. "Not my problem."

She turned away, and I knew the conversation was over. Apparently, so was our time alone. Our jailers had returned.

TWENTY-FOUR

As I'd expected, the crowd was ready for some blood. I don't know what the speech given previous to our appearance was about, but I'm pretty sure the two of us were blamed for everything wrong with the world, including the lack of coffee. The crowd greeted us with jeers and screams of outrage as Sheila and I were dragged onto the stage.

We were chained to two posts. The posts were embedded in tires filled with concrete. I could barely shift mine, and saw Sheila trying to move hers. Because of the chains it was difficult to get leverage. Instead, I concentrated on obtaining the small blade still hidden in my sleeve.

I wondered how Sheila's powers compared to mine. Which one of us was stronger? From what I could tell, she wasn't going anywhere. But then again, she could have been faking it.

"Is this the world you envisioned when you were planning my father's death?" I asked her.

"It was for a while," she said as Stu stepped away, seemingly satisfied that we weren't going anywhere. He held up his hands in victory and the crowd roared its approval.

"He must be up for reelection," I said. Sheila smiled

faintly, and shook her head as she squirmed against her bonds.

She was facing a horrendous death, I realized. I knew from the burn I'd seen on Shane's back that when the sun rose she would go up in flames. Not a pleasant prospect. And not something I really wanted to watch. Yet here I was with a ringside seat.

I couldn't work up any sympathy for her. She'd murdered my father and most likely countless more in the past hundred years. I wondered what Stu would do when I didn't go up in flames.

Stu shushed the crowd by waving his hands, palms down, and they looked up at him with anticipation on their faces.

"Let this be a message to all who think we will lie down and die," he began. I rolled my eyes. The Constable definitely had a flair for the drama.

I looked out over the crowd. He had their attention. Were there any ticks out there? There very easily could be.

I spotted Jamie, Claudia, Janet and Burton squirming through the crowd, trying to get to the front. Jayne was in Claudia's arms, and the cat jumped onto the stage when she got close. He made a point of walking through Stu's legs before he stopped and hissed violently at Sheila.

"Jayne, if I didn't say it before, I'm saying it now," I said as the cat wound his way around my ankles a few times before sitting down in front of me. "I love you."

Stu tried to go on with his speech, but he soon realized that there was more attention focused on me and Jayne than there was on him.

"She's not a tick," Jamie yelled. "Let her go."

"Yeah, let her go," Claudia echoed. Meanwhile, Burton

boosted Janet up on the stage while the five who had guarded us earlier walked over to Stu. I motioned with my head toward the one wearing my katana, and Jamie looked at him and then back at me before nodding with an evil grin.

"I can vouch for her," Janet said. "She's not a tick."

"You vouched for her before and I believed you. Then we caught her trying to free that one," Stu said. He indicated Sheila.

Janet gave me a questioning look.

"I just wanted to talk to her," I said.

"The tick says she's one," the woman who'd cut me said.

"Oh, and you believe her?" I asked.

"We cut you and you healed," the woman said. "Only ticks have that ability."

"She's not a tick," Janet repeated. "Believe me. I know her. She has abilities, but she's not a tick. She's killed many of them. She's our best fighter."

"How come we've never seen her before at the gatherings?" Stu asked.

"She just joined up with us," Janet said.

The entire she-traveled-through-time-and-is-a-super-hero thing was too out there to believe; I prayed Janet wouldn't mention it. I didn't think it would help me at this stage of the game. I just needed to wait things out; when the sun came up I would be fine.

The people closest to the stage were trying to listen, but the ones behind, who couldn't hear or see very well, started grumbling. Stu knew he was losing the crowd, and I was afraid of what he might do. Especially since the sword-stealer was stroking the handle of my katana.

"Test her!" The audience had figured out what was going on, and a chant began.

"Acid!" someone yelled. "Throw some acid on her!"

"Yeah," I muttered. "Throw some acid on me. What real human burns when acid is thrown on them?"

Sheila struggled desperately against her bonds as a bottle was handed to Stu, who flourished it over his head like he'd just won an Oscar. Considering he was hamming it up, the award seems appropriate. I was relieved to see the bottle just held peroxide.

He twisted off the top and flung a wide arc of liquid at both of us—aiming for our faces, of course. Sheila screamed in agony. I'd closed my eyes for self preservation, but rubbed my wet cheek on my shoulder. I opened my eyes to find all faces turned toward me.

Sheila cried out in pain, again. Huge blisters marred her face and the skin bubbled away, leaving raw tissue exposed in several places on her porcelain-white skin. I sneezed and looked at Stu.

"I *told* you," Janet said as Jayne questioningly pawed at my knee.

"What you gonna do, Stu?" I asked. "Kill an innocent person?"

"If you're so innocent, what were you doing sneaking around back there?"

"Just wanted to talk," I said. I looked over at Sheila. She had her head tilted forward and her hair veiled her face.

"You could have asked," Stu snarled.

"Yeah," I said. "I bet that would have worked."

"Let her go," Janet said.

"She broke the law," the katana-stealer said. I guess he was embarrassed at having caught a non-tick and making such a big deal out of it. He pulled my sword out as if to make a point. Jamie's hand snared his ankle as he stepped forward, and he fell flat on his face. The blade slid toward me. Jayne jumped away and I stamped my foot firmly down on the sword to keep Katana-stealer from taking it back.

Jamie heaved himself up onto the stage, Claudia and Burton right behind. I noticed some other familiar faces forming a barrier between me and the crowd. I had friends. Brothers in arms. People willing to stand up for me, even though I'd cost them loved ones. I was overwhelmed.

Jamie put his gun to the back of Katana-stealer's head. He was busy trying to jerk the sword out from under my foot. I used the toe of my other boot to shove his head back until he could see Jamie's weapon.

"Turn her loose," Janet said as Burton drew his own gun. "Now."

Burton and Jamie got the five guards together by waving their guns, and Stu had to admit defeat. He handed his keys to Claudia, who quickly unlocked the chains around me. I shrugged out of them and moved to pick up my katana. The guy who'd stole it lunged for the blade, but I flung my dagger and saw the point bury itself between his outstretched fingers.

Jamie jerked the guy to his feet and pulled the blade free as the guy yelped in fear.

"Help me," Sheila begged as I made a wide arc with my blade to intimidate anyone who had ideas about rushing us. She raised her head. I saw the deep tissue of her face as her jaw muscles clenched in pain. Across her nose everything was gone, revealing nothing but the cartilage that formed it.

With two hands I swung the katana. I felt the tip nick the post as I severed her head. It flew off and rolled until it landed at Stu's feet, and Sheila's body dissolved into dust.

"How's that for a showstopper?" I said. The crowd screamed behind me.

TWENTY-FIVE

•

As it turned out, the beheading was not the show's final act. We formed two lines on the stage, Sheila's head lying between us. It slowly disintegrated, and Jayne sniffed at the remaining dust as the rest of us watched each other and wondered who would make the first move.

Instead, a man ran onto the stage with his hands in the air. "You've got to stop," he said to Stu. "There's an epidemic."

Stu and his posse looked shocked. Our group took advantage of the situation to leave the stage.

I heard the announcement as we made our way through the crowd toward our camp: "Please don't panic," Stu said. "Go to your campsites. Anyone who is running a fever should report to the hospital tent."

"Trent's running a fever," I told Jamie and Claudia.

"We're not taking him to that hospital," Jamie said. "It will be packed, plus they won't have the skills Shane does."

"Shane's too far away," I said.

Jamie grabbed my arm. "You don't understand," he said. "Look around." He pulled Claudia and me into a space between two tents. Already, hysteria had set in.

People were running to and fro, jerking tents and awnings down, throwing things into bags, shrieking and crying. It was madness.

"There's no way to cure these things," Jamie said. "Not in crowds like this. We've got to get out of here if we're going to do anyone any good."

I nodded. Even though the pandemic had happened a couple of generations back, the knowledge of it was still in the forefront of the people's minds. Some world. You could either die from ticks or disease, and basically that was all there was to look forward to.

Jayne clawed his way up my leg and into my arms. It was getting dangerous for him on the ground.

Things weren't much better at our camp, though there was at least some semblance of order. Tents were broken down, the horses were waiting to be saddled and the wagon was ready to be loaded. I ducked into the last standing tent, the one where I'd left Trent. Jayne stayed where I dropped him and sat down as if he did not want to go inside.

"He's gone," Nora said as I entered. She sat on a stool and regarded me with a tear-stained face. "Dead."

"Trent?" I gasped. I dropped down beside him and put my hand on his head. He was burning up, not dead.

"Todd's gone," she said.

I looked over at her son's pallet. The boy was still, quiet, his face pasty white. I grabbed his wrist to feel for a pulse and found nothing. I bent my head over his chest, hoping to hear a heartbeat, feel his breath . . . There was nothing there.

"I'm sorry," I said. "Nora. Where is your husband?"

"He went to find a coffin." I could barely make out her words; she spoke so quietly. "So we can take him home."

I moved back to Trent. What should I do? What did one do for a fever in this time? There was no aspirin, no pain-relievers, and no ice to help cool him down.

"Trent?" I used a cloth lying by his pallet to wipe his face.

"Shane," he murmured. "My head hurts."

"Yeah," I said. "Shane." I gathered him up in my arms. "Shane will know what to do."

Jamie and I rode ahead and through the night. We took turns holding Trent in our arms as we traveled, only stopping to briefly rest the horses and relieve ourselves before moving on. We got to the outskirts of town just as the sun came up, and it was mid-morning when we approached Shane's house.

"What happened?" Berta asked as she came onto the porch.

"An epidemic of some sort," I said wearily as I handed Trent over to Owen.

"Little Todd died," Jamie added as we dismounted. A man I'd seen once or twice took the horses and led them off.

Berta made a little sound and put her hands to her mouth. "Oh, bless poor Nora and Bobby," she said. "Are they bringing him home?"

"In their wagon," Jamie said. "We left Claudia behind to be with her."

We'd also left Jayne behind, as there was no way to carry him on horseback. I couldn't help but miss him as I staggered past the dozen or so cats lounging on the house's wide front porch.

"How long has he had this fever?" Berta anxiously laid her hand on Trent's forehead. He didn't move. He hadn't made a sound for several hours. I'd tried to keep him hydrated, but since he was practically unconscious it was impossible.

"Since yesterday afternoon," I said. "He had a headache too.

"Take him down to Shane," Berta told Owen.

We trailed after him; Berta, Jamie and I. I wasn't sure how Jamie and I were still standing. We'd been up for forty-eight hours straight after not getting much sleep on the way to the gathering. All I wanted was a shower and to crawl into bed. Instead, I trooped through the house and wondered how Shane would react when he saw I was back.

Or if he would even care.

"I haven't seen much of him since you all left," Berta said nervously as we tromped down the darkened staircase. "He's been keeping pretty much to himself."

So what else was new? Shane had the franchise on moodiness as far as I was concerned.

A light flared from a match, and candlelight flooded the basement as Owen pushed aside the curtain.

I heard Shane's growl. "What is it?"

"The boy," Owen said. "Trent. He's sick."

I came through the curtain just as Shane and Owen lowered Trent onto the couch. Berta grabbed the first candle and lit more, handing one to each of us to help Shane examine him.

"What happened? How long as he been sick? Was anyone else sick?" Shane barked questions quicker than my muddled brain could compute them, and he pulled off Trent's shirt and bent down to listen to the boy's heart and lungs.

I looked at Trent's thin chest. At the protuberant ribs underneath his skin. At the pale face and dark shadows beneath the sheen of sweat that covered him. "Todd died," was all I was able to get out.

Shane stopped what he was doing and looked at me. I felt my body sway as exhaustion, long held at bay by fear, finally set in.

"Take her upstairs and put her to bed before she gets sick, too," he said, and bent back to Trent.

Jamie took my arm. "We can't do anything else here," he whispered. "Let Shane take care of him."

I started to protest but realized Jamie was just as tired as I was. We both stumbled up the stairs. I stripped off my clothes, took a cold shower that only served to further numb my senses, and finally fell facedown on my mattress wearing nothing but a towel. I don't even remember closing my eyes.

It seemed like only a few seconds before I felt someone touching me. A hand smoothed my hair back from my forehead and trailed over my bare shoulder. I wanted to stay where I was and snuggle into the warmth of the touch, but my mind screamed danger as I swam up through the deep fog. I opened my eyes and found Shane standing over me, his face hidden in the darkness. Deep purple shadows fell across the wall. It was evening.

"I need your help," he said.

I dragged my hand through my hair and slowly sat up, catching the towel, which had slipped.

"How long did I sleep?"

"A while."

"Trent." Words were hard to form. I felt like I was still in a dream. "How's Trent?"

"I don't know." I heard him strike a match, and light filled the room as he lit the candle on my nightstand.

I blinked the sleep from my eyes and looked at Shane. His eyes were dark and desperate, and there were lines grooved around his mouth. He was worried.

"What can I do?" I looked around the room for my clothes, and realized that I'd probably dropped them in the bathroom. Along with my katana. *Nice, Abbey. Real smart.*

I hitched up the towel again and slipped from the bed.

"I need to do a spinal tap," Shane said.

"A spinal tap?" I managed to slide on some underwear while still covered with the towel. "Why?" I gasped. "Do you have the equipment for that?"

"I think he's got meningitis."

"Can you cure it?" I asked.

"I don't know." He ran his hands through his hair. "I won't know until I know what kind. If it's bacterial . . ."

I quickly yanked on a T-shirt and my spare pair of jeans. Shane gave a slight quirk of his lips as I dragged a comb through my tangled hair and pulled it up in a scrunchie.

"What?" I asked.

He trailed a finger over my chest, and I felt it all the way down to my toes. My body reacted to his touch, almost melting. I looked down, away from those blue, blue eyes to keep from throwing myself into his arms. I saw the words on my T-shirt.

Don't make me call in the flying monkeys.

"We could use some flying monkeys around here," Shane said.

"As long as they're on our side," I agreed.

He looked at me for a long moment. His hand cupped my cheek and his thumb moved over my lashes, wiping sleep away. For a moment I could swear time stood still.

I felt the pad of his thumb glide across each one of my lashes. I heard the steady thump of my heart, and felt my lungs slowly expand with the air inhaled.

Kiss me, I thought.

He tilted his head a bit, and the candlelight caught his eyes. I was afraid to look, afraid I'd see the red glow. All I saw was deep, deep blue, like twin sapphires. I exhaled.

Voices sounded in the yard. The front door slammed. Footsteps pounded up the stairs.

"Jamie!" Claudia called out. Shane stepped back, and once more the spell was broken.

"They're back," I said.

"Trent was asking for you," Shane replied. "Hurry up." He turned and walked away.

TWENTY-SIX

Jayne sat in the upstairs hall, his tail lashing back and forth like a snake. He was obviously displeased with me.

"Join the club," I said as I ran down the stairs.

Trent had been moved to the clinic. He lay curled on his side on the metal table, the knobs of his spine exposed to a lantern that sat on a nearby rolling cart. A huge needle lay next to it. Berta stood next to him and wiped his face. Shane was by the window, watching the commotion outside as he pulled on a pair of rubber gloves.

I swallowed the bile that rose in my throat, which was considerable given the fact that I couldn't remember the last time I'd eaten.

Berta bent over and spoke in Trent's ear. "Abbey's here," she said. She looked up and smiled at me encouragingly.

"Hey," I said as I walked up to the table. "You finally woke up."

"Shane said I should go back to sleep." I had to bend down to hear him; his voice seemed so distant. " 'Cause it's gonna hurt."

I looked up at Shane, who was watching the two of us. "Anesthesia?" I mouthed. He shook his head, no.

"Yes, it's going to hurt," I said to Trent. "But you're a ninja now. And ninjas are brave and strong."

"Do ninjas cry?" he asked.

"Sometimes," I said. "When something *really* hurts." I didn't want him to be worried about trying to be brave.

"Ninjas are way cooler than pirates," Shane said.

There he was with that line again. I wondered exactly what it meant, and I gave him a puzzled look.

"Do you know any pirates?" Trent asked.

I arched an eyebrow at Shane. "A few," I said. "But I know a lot more ninjas. And he's right. They are cooler."

Shane picked up the needle and handed me a piece of plastic. He pointed toward his mouth with his finger, and I quickly got the meaning.

"Put this in your mouth, and when it hurts bite down," I said. Trent obliged. "That's what the cool ninjas do."

"You're going to have to hold him," Shane said.

I took Trent's upper body, and Berta took his legs. I watched as Shane dabbed the base of Trent's spine with alcohol and then inserted the needle.

The noise the boy made was wretched. Trent clamped his teeth down on the piece of plastic, and tears poured from between his clenched eyelids. I tried to soothe him. I don't even know what I said beyond "Ninjas are cool," over and over again, but he seemed to respond, smiling up bravely at me when he could.

Shane backed off the plunger on the needle, and a cloudy liquid filled it. I was surprised; I'd expected blood. Shane frowned when he saw it.

"It's over now," I said as Shane pulled the needle away.

Trent didn't answer. He'd passed out—from the pain or the fever, I didn't know which.

Shane held the vial up to the candlelight, and looked at it closely before placing it on a tray.

"What?" I asked.

He didn't answer. Instead, he picked up Trent and carried him to the wardroom. I stood at the door and watched as he gently placed the boy on a cot, and Berta pulled a blanket over him.

The look on Shane's face was grim as he passed me again. He picked up the vial and left the room. I trailed after him with Jayne bringing up the rear as we once more went downstairs.

Shane attacked his worktable. He lit several candles and prepared a slide with the fluid drawn from Trent's back. I leaned against the edge of his sofa as he examined the slide and then went over to his desk and pulled down one of the thick books that sat on the shelf above.

Jayne looked up at me questioningly as Shane flipped through innumerable pages. Finally I saw Shane settle on a page and study it intently. He slammed the book shut and dropped it on his desk with a thud. He leaned over the desk with his back to me, his hair falling across his face. I watched as a long shudder moved down his spine.

"What is it?"

"Bacterial meningitis."

"Can you cure it?"

He laughed. It was mirthless, almost sinister. The sound gave me chills, and I rubbed the goosebumps on my arms.

In one movement he suddenly swung his arms and cleared his desk. Books, papers, binders, pencils and pens—everything went flying to the floor. Jayne jumped and ran under the bed. I heard a low growl in the cat's throat, and his eyes glowed with a strange gold light.

"How can I cure it?" Shane asked in a hoarse voice.

"I've got nothing to cure it with. Nothing. No meds. Those were gone a long time ago, used up in the pandemic, where once again all I could do was stand back and watch people die."

"We'll go to the hospital, to doctors' offices, pharmacies," I said. "We'll find some."

Shane shook his head like he was talking to a child. "What do you think people have been doing for the past hundred years? I myself have cleaned out every stockpile of medicine in this city." He stretched his hands in front of him, spread the fingers, arched the palms. He looked at them as if he'd never seen them before.

"I used to think my hands were for healing," he continued. He turned the left one over, and in a heartbeat his eyes took on that red glow that frightened me so. I watched with my stomach churning as that *thing*, that stabber, that life-sucker extended out of it. He held it up for me to see.

"This is all I'm good for," he said. "This. Taking life. Killing. Ending it." He took a step toward me. I wanted to retreat, but the sofa was already pressed against my back. "I *could* save him," he said. His voice was speculative. "I could change him."

"No." I shook my head. Fiercely.

"Why not?"

I didn't like the look on his face, or the fact that he'd taken another step closer.

"Save Trent. Save you. I could save everyone. Then we could all live happily ever after—at least while we aren't trying to kill each other off." Shane took another step. He turned his palm over again so that the thing in his hand stood straight up. I couldn't help but look at it. "How 'bout it, Abbey?" he said. "Want to live forever?"

I looked into his eyes. The red glow was still there, but it covered something else.

"No," I said.

"Think of all the fun we'll have," he continued. He took another step.

"Stop it, Shane," I said. I grabbed his hand and wrenched it away. It was an old move, one I'd learned in my karate class: twist the fingers back, and the body will follow. "You said you couldn't change us before. What are you doing?"

The weapon in Shane's palm retracted, and I watched the skin close over it so that his palm once again looked normal. It amazed me to see the opening coincided with his lifeline. If I traced it would it run on continually? Did eternal life show in patterns on the skin?

I looked once more at his face. His eyes lost their red hue as he looked at me for a long hard moment, but I felt rage and frustration simmer beneath their surface. Suddenly, he fell to the floor. It was if all his strength left him at once. He sagged down, his back against the couch and his head on his knees.

"No matter what I do, I can't stop it. I can never stop it," he said. His voice was shaky. Was he crying? "It never ends," he continued. "I've nothing but an eternity of death."

I knelt down beside him. I touched his hair and let my fingers trail through the silky blond strands. He looked up at me. His eyes were dark, practically navy, and they filled with tears.

"I told myself a long time ago not to care. Doctors aren't supposed to get personally involved with their patients. I try to keep everyone at a distance because I know in the end they're all going to die."

I realized then his pain. His loneliness. His solitude. And the reason why he always ran hot and cold with me. He was scared of caring for anyone. He'd watched so many people die through the years: his brother, his parents, his friends and the people who lived and worked in this small community trying to stay alive. And now Trent was dying. Trent, who was probably as close as he'd ever come to having a child of his own.

I wrapped my arms around his shoulders, pulled his head under my chin. I stretched my legs out so that one went behind him and the other over his lap, and I pulled him close.

His body was tense, his muscles rigid. I stroked his hair and held on tight until I felt him relax against me. His arms crept around my waist and he wrapped his hands in my shirt. I felt it bunch up and move, exposing the bare skin of my back. He let out a long sigh and moved his head up on my shoulder so that I could feel the brush of his breath on the skin of my neck.

We sat still for a long, long moment. I continued to run my fingers through his hair. Jayne came out from under the bed and lay down beside me, his paws tucked up beneath his chest. His rumbling purr seemed louder than normal as it broke the deep dark silence that surrounded us.

"No one touches me," Shane said quietly.

I didn't understand, but said nothing, just continued with my fingers in his hair.

"They're all afraid to touch me," he said. "Afraid if they touch me they'll become infected. They don't mind when I touch them, as long as it's medicinal, but they won't touch me."

I nodded. I felt his lips move against my neck as he spoke again.

"Physical comfort is a precious thing," he said. "You're the first person to give it to me in one hundred years."

I didn't know what to say. I'd only done what I wanted, gave him what I felt he needed. I'd offered comfort. It was the most natural thing in the world.

"Abbey . . ." His voice trailed off as his hands freed themselves from my shirt and his fingers caressed my back.

I felt that touch down to my core. Heat coiled inside me. It bubbled and twisted and spread from the center of my body to follow the trail of his hand, which moved gently up my spine.

"Abbey," he said again. I turned toward him as he lifted his head from my shoulder.

"Abbey," he whispered as I looked into his eyes.

They were blue. Very blue. For a moment I'd been afraid they'd be glowing with red fire. Instead, I saw something more dangerous.

Dangerous, yet so very very tempting.

Our lips met. The heat that came with his touch exploded with his kiss. I wanted to feel him, to touch him, but I was afraid that when we touched I would ignite and burn like a supernova.

There were worse ways to go.

Shane's hands moved down to my hips, and he twisted and lifted me so that I straddled his lap. I felt him, hard and pressing against my jeans, and my body lurched, seeking, throbbing, wanting, while our tongues teased and twisted between our mouths.

He moved his hands once more, up and down my back, into my hair, pulling it loose from the scrunchie and flinging that away. I heard Jayne give out a questioning meow and we pulled apart, both out of breath, to watch him attack the hair-tie like it was a full-grown mouse.

But only for a moment. Shane's hands continued their exploration of my back, then encircled my waist. He rubbed his thumbs on my stomach. The muscles there jumped and clenched, sending spasms down to my toes. Shane smiled and kissed me again, and I wrapped my hands in his hair and ground myself against him.

He groaned. His hands moved up and skimmed over my breasts, and I pushed down against him. I grabbed the tail of his shirt and pulled. I wanted to feel him. I wanted to touch him. We stopped kissing long enough for me to peel off his shirt, and he did the same for me. His hand touched my cheek, then trailed down my neck. I placed my hands on his shoulders and leaned back as his mouth followed the trail of his hand. He supported me with his left hand in the small of my back. I felt my hair dance against his arm as I continued to press against him.

This was crazy-fast for me, but I couldn't stand it. I wanted more. I wanted it all.

"Shane." I tried to speak but all that came out was a gasp.

His mouth trailed back up my body, and his other hand came round as he pressed me full against the hard plane of his chest. I wrapped my arms around his neck as his hands moved down and cupped my behind. I felt him stand, was amazed at the ease with which he did so. I didn't let go, just wrapped my legs around his waist until he lowered me to his bed.

The light was behind him. I could not see his face as he knelt over me, his hands on the fly of my jeans. I reached up and undid his pants, even though my hands shook. We slipped off our clothes until nothing stood between us. I wanted him. God help me.

Was it right or was it wrong? Was he human? Was he more? Was he less? He was Shane. He had shown me his soul, the danger and the need. The evil and the goodness.

I shook with fear. With want. With necessity. My body shivered with cold, yet my blood boiled inside me. Shane touched me and I cried out.

He pulled his hand back, as if afraid of hurting me. I grabbed his hands and then just as quickly pushed them away, reached for his hips. I couldn't speak. Instead, I leaned upward and kissed him as I guided his hips toward mine, wrapping my legs once more around his waist. He pressed into me and I felt everything I was surge forward, form and swell around him until he was buried deep inside.

"Shane," I whispered.

He laid his forehead against mine as we lay very still. I knew by the way he stiffened against me that he was afraid to move.

"Please," I said. "Please."

His lips touched mine and then he moved, pulled out with a tantalizing slowness that made me want to weep before he pressed into me once more. We found a rhythm and moved as one until I felt my body soaring above the bed and my soul spinning round and round until it exploded into a light so bright that it was blinding.

I'm not alone, I realized. And his voice calling out my name was the last thing I heard before time ceased to exist.

TWENTY-SEVEN

If only time *would* stop. As my breathing returned to normal and my brain returned to full function, I wondered if it was possible for me to make it stop. I wanted nothing more than to lie tangled up with Shane for eternity.

His arms were wrapped around my waist and he curled against me as I wrapped my fingers in his thick blond hair. The curtains around the bed sheltered us on three sides, with the fourth open to the candle on the nightstand. It was as if we were closed in our own little world. A world without sickness, a world without death. A world where we were two people who needed, nothing more. A world where time did not exist.

Could I stop time? Wasn't that my purpose—to guard time? Whatever that meant, which moment could be more precious than this one?

I felt Shane's hands against the skin of my back, the fingers spread and the palms flat, as if he wanted to secure his hold. His head lay right over my heart; its weight seemed to magnify the beating. I felt the thump against my chest in time with the pulse in his neck.

"How long has it been?" I asked him. "Since you made love."

He rolled us over so that we lay on our sides and faced each other. His hand caressed my cheek and pushed my hair away from my face. I did the same for him, pushing back the fringe that fell over his eyes so I could see the clear bright blue in the candlelight.

"I've never made love," he said. "Until now."

Not the answer I was expecting. I moved my head away to look at his face.

He grinned at me. "I've had sex," he said. "Lots of sex. Do you want me to name them all? It has been one hundred years after all. Lots of time for sex. Plus, there's all the hot sex I had while I was in college and med school. And, oh yeah, I can't forget about the hot closet sex with the nurses in between the twenty minutes of sleep I got everyday while interning."

"I could kill you, you know," I said evenly. "One swing of my blade and you'd be nothing but dust."

"I might have taken you up on that offer early today." Shane's mouth moved to my neck. "But now, not so much."

His mouth sent shivers down my spine, and I felt a slow boil begin once again.

"How 'bout you?" he asked as he nibbled his way down my stomach. "How long has it been?"

"This was my first time, too." I gasped as he ran his hand up the inside of my thigh. "Making love."

He stopped suddenly and moved so that he lay on top of me; we were stomach to stomach, thigh to thigh, our bodies molding into each other. His hands cupped my face.

"Abbey," he said. He looked at me for a long moment, his eyes steady upon mine as if he were looking into my soul. "I've had very little peace since I was changed. And not much happiness. Then you showed up and things really got twisted." He stopped for a moment, as if to think about what he truly wanted to say. I stared up at him, amazed that he was speaking to me so honestly.

"I didn't want you to go, but I understood why you did," he said. "And I am so glad you came back."

He kissed me. A kiss that branded me. A kiss that claimed me. A kiss that told me that he'd meant it when he said we made love, that it wasn't just sex. A kiss that was so tender yet so powerful that tears slid down my cheek.

He traced them with his thumb as he kissed me again. All I could do was hold on as he showed me exactly what he'd meant by "making love."

When the pounding in my heart subsided, and I lay trembling and exhausted in his arms, I realized that we were not alone.

"Shane?" Berta said from the other side of the bed curtains.

Shane growled in frustration as he moved from my side. On the floor, Jayne jumped up as Shane stood and quickly slid on his jeans.

"What is it?" he asked, his tone more civil that I expected. "Is it Trent? I didn't mean to leave him for so long."

"He's the same," Berta said. "But there are more. Claudia just fainted, and one of Janet's boys is feverish."

Berta didn't know. She didn't know the diagnosis. Would Shane tell any of them?

And . . . *Claudia?*

Berta couldn't see me, but she had to know I was there. Shane's face was grim as he pulled on a T-shirt. He stopped and bent to kiss me gently before he left.

"What are you looking at?" I said to Jayne as I heard their footsteps fade up the stairs. The creak of boards overhead let me know there were a lot of people in the house.

"I hope I didn't scream or anything," I added as Jayne butted my hand with his head. I scratched his ears. "If I'd known it was going to be this good I would have jumped Shane the first time I saw him on the El," I confided.

The cat yawned.

"Yeah, I know, my sex life is boring. Or it was until now."

I stretched luxuriously among the tangled sheets. Though I hadn't said, I had just doubled my sex life in one evening. There had only been one other time. But after experiencing the difference between having sex and making love, I was more than willing to repeat this experience.

How long had we been down here? Long enough for Shane to feel guilty about abandoning his patients. Life with a doctor. Is this how it would have been if we'd gotten together in a normal time? Would I always be second to his patients?

I shook my head at my wonderings thoughts. How could I complain? Shane had definitely given me his full attention. My body still tingled with the after-effects.

How much time had we stolen away, I wondered. It seemed like forever. Of course, when your life suddenly changes, what's happened before the change seems to belong to a totally different person, as if you were reincarnated. Like, my life before the time jump was nothing but a distant memory. Except for Charlie, there was nothing to consider. If only he had come with me. Could he have come with me?

I didn't want to get melancholy over my dog. There was nothing I could do for him now.

The rumbling of my stomach brought my mind back

to the present. Time to eat. Time to sleep, time to fight, time to make love—there were no longer hours on the clock; there were just blocks of time. Each one was to be filled as needed. Each one was to be enjoyed and lived to the fullest.

I couldn't help but wonder how long my block of time with Shane would be, how long before the demon waiting inside took him over again and he pushed me away.

"We need to quit wasting time," I said to Jayne as I climbed from the bed.

TWENTY-EIGHT

There were now four patients in the ward behind Shane's clinic—Trent, Claudia, one of Janet's sons, and one of the older teen boys who'd traveled with us. Only one candle lit the room since the patients suffered light sensitivity along with the headaches, fever and stiffness in their limbs.

Beside each bed sat a loved one, tenderly ministering. Berta was with Trent, Jamie with Claudia, Janet with her son, and the mother of the teen who I recognized as Denise's mom was with hers. They each wiped a fevered brow and spoke tenderly, in hopes that the patient would hear them through the haze of the fever.

Claudia, the last one to get sick, seemed to be making up for lost time. Her fever was higher than the rest, and she was out of her head and ranting when she wasn't tossing back and forth on the bed.

"What can we do?" I asked Shane as we walked out to the front porch.

He shook his head. I knew why he didn't want to voice the words. If he took away hope . . .

Instead, he sat down in the swing and leaned against me, his hands on my hips and his cheek pressed against my stomach. I could tell he was tired by the set of his shoulders and the dark circles under his eyes. He had fed off an old one. He'd said that would last a while, but I could not help but wonder how long "a while" was in his concept of time.

"I heard you got into trouble at the gathering," he said finally. He took my hand and pulled me down on the swing. It was amazing how easy it was to be with him. And kind of surprising to experience this public display of affection.

"Who?" I said. "Me? Trouble?"

"Nothing but, since the day you showed up," he replied. He traced a finger up my arm. "Then and now," he added.

I looked at my arm. There was no trace of the wound from the night we met. Not even a scar.

"What happened?" he asked.

I explained to him the events, why I'd wanted to talk to a tick and my surprise at finding she was my former stepmother. Then I told him what Sheila had told me.

"Your family was murdered off because of the time-guardian thing?"

"Apparently," I said. "From what I know, my mother was raised in an orphanage on the East Coast. I never knew her. She died when I was born, and she told my father that it wasn't safe for me there, that whoever went after her would come after me. So my father brought me here, not knowing that here was where it all started. Sheila was told that my grandmother was attacked and went into hiding when she was pregnant with my mother, and the same thing happened to her that happened to my mother. She died but the child survived. I guess my grandfather, like my father, was killed by ticks. It just so happened that my dad was an orphan also. I guess maybe that was what brought them together in the first place."

"The Chronolotians have been after the time-twister all this time?"

"For generations, I suppose. If it's been here as long as the Chronos then it had to have been in the Eastern Hemisphere at the beginning. I guess maybe my ancestors brought it to the States at some time to hide it. I don't know. Sheila said that the Chrono that turned her said they traced the lineage and found my grandmother. Then it took him a while to find my mother again. Apparently Lucinda found the gate but couldn't activate it without a Time Guardian."

"Why did the Chrono turn Sheila?"

"He thought he could control me through her after they killed my father. Instead, Sheila killed him and hooked up with Marco, the ancient you killed before the gathering. That's how they found her—she was waiting on him."

Shane nodded as he absorbed the information. I'd barely had time to digest it myself, what with worry about Trent being foremost in my mind.

"Shane," I said. His question had triggered a thought. Something had happened the night I went to the ER; Lucinda had paid special attention to him, even taking the time to read his name off his ID tag. I didn't think it was random lust anymore. "I think Lucinda changed you to get to me." I kept my eyes on his face as I said it.

"But we didn't even know each other," he said. He looked at me kind of funny, as if he were remembering. He picked up a strand of my hair and rubbed it between his fingers. "Not really," he added. "We never got a chance."

"Maybe Lucinda thought there was something between us."

Shane rubbed his forehead with his hand, another sure sign of his exhaustion and worry. "It doesn't matter why. It's in the past and can't be changed. What does matter is that I've got four people lying in there that are more than likely going to die unless I can come up with a miracle."

"Is there anything I can do to help?"

"Yeah. Get Jamie out of there. And Berta and Janet. We've got to make sure no one else is exposed," he said. "If they catch it and pass it on we could lose everyone."

"I can take over for them," I said. "I had a vaccine," I said.

"When?"

"January." I shrugged. "You know, *my* January. At the campus clinic. They were free, so I got one along with a flu shot."

"The campus clinic?"

"Yeah." I looked at him in confusion. "At the University. Where I used to be a student."

Shane grabbed my arms and grinned. "There's a clinic at the University."

"Um," I said. "Yes. There's a clinic at the University."

"I never checked the University Clinic," he said.

Suddenly I understood where he was coming from. "Maybe it's time for a trip down memory lane," I said.

"You could show me around," Shane agreed.

"No," I said. "You need to stay here in case their symptoms worsen." He started to protest but I touched his lips with my fingers. "You're the only one that can save them," I said. "And it's going to take a while to get there. We can't chance you getting stuck somewhere when daylight comes."

"Maybe you should wait until daylight," Shane said.

"Trent and Claudia and the others might not have that long." I said. "I'll be fine."

Jayne jumped from his perch on the porch rail as Shane and I moved to go into the house. He looked at me questioningly, his tail vertical in the air.

"You're not going, either," I said. "It's too far, and I don't want to carry your fuzzy butt."

Jayne sat down and proceeded to lick his fuzzy butt, as if I'd pointed out a dirty spot. Shane grinned at the cat and then pulled me into his arms.

"I'm not sure if I'm happy with you taking off again," he said. "I just about went crazy the last time you left."

"But this time you know that I'm coming back," I said.

He cocked his head to the side and looked down at me. "Why *did* you come back?" he asked.

"I could feed your ego and say I came back because of you, but that's really not it. And it wasn't because of Trent, either—I know Jamie and the others would have gotten him home. I came back because, when I was up there on that platform and Stu and the others were screaming for my blood, this community stood up for me. Even though I'd been nothing but trouble, they said I belonged with them and they vouched for me. It's the first time I've ever had that. For so long it was just me and my dad. We moved around a lot, and after he was gone I didn't have time to make friends or form any bonds. I couldn't run out on that. If they were willing to fight for me, then I figured the least I could do is come back here and fight for them."

He touched my cheek.

"And yeah," I continued. "There was you, too. I had to know . . ."

"Know what?"

"If there was something here." I placed my palm on his chest over his heart. "Something between us. I . . . thought there might be."

His fingers lifted my chin, and he kissed me.

"There is," he said. "And it's the one thing I'm not going to fight anymore."

TWENTY-NINE

Jamie went with me. He was anxious to feel like he was doing something to help Claudia and the others, and it was a way to get him out of the sickroom. I was worried that he was already over exposed.

Jamie took his bow, a pistol and a sword. I took my katana. We both wore empty packs and had instructions to bring back anything that looked medical.

I knew Shane wanted to go, but Trent was out of his head and throwing up. I said a prayer that the boy would last long enough for us to get back with some meds. The right meds.

It had to be close to midnight when we left. There was no moon. We'd left with the waning, and now it shed no light since it was between the earth and the sun. Which probably explained why Shane seemed more at peace. Would he become restless again as the moon became new?

Only time would tell.

It was a long way to the campus, especially on foot; we had to cross from one side of the city to the other. The night was quieter than any I'd ever experienced. I had locked Jayne in my room so he wouldn't follow us, but we still had a few cats trailing. After the first hour or so they left, as if they knew the journey would take them away from familiar territory.

Sounds that you become accustomed to, so accustomed that you don't even hear them: cars, sirens, TVs, radios, people talking, even the hum of electricity. You notice their absence much more than you notice them. The only thing we heard as we entered the heart of the city was the skittering of rats and the fluttering of bat wings.

If it was so quiet, then why did I feel like someone was following us? Jamie felt it, too. He kept looking over his shoulder, and I noticed he had his pistol tucked into the front of his waistband where it was handy.

Objects were ghostly in the darkness, the streets deep valleys between the skyscrapers where the wind whirled and carried paper and leaves that piled up against the windows and abandoned cars. Old newspaper kiosks and mailboxes were tossed helter-skelter, as if a child had pitched a tantrum and kicked his toys out of the way. Spooky.

"How much farther?" Jamie asked.

"A couple of blocks," I said. I pointed south. "Through there." We had to pass through the art district, an area full of quaint shops and sidewalk restaurants. It was also the place where my dad was run down. Murdered.

I was used to traveling to class on the El. Tonight I'd changed the route so we wouldn't pass Tick Central. I knew it would take longer to do so, but hoped we could make back the time in the daylight-hours return.

I spared a look up. Stars peppered the sky, and a few clouds hung lazily about. There was no wind, which meant the rattling we heard behind us was made by something living.

Jamie and I took off at a run. I led him through an alley that was a popular shortcut to the restaurant district. I didn't even blink an eye when we ran across the intersection where my dad died. We ducked into a deep entryway and held our breath as the blood pounded in our ears. I could tell Jamie was straining to listen, the same as I was. I placed my hand on the hilt of my katana.

We stood there for an eternity; then Jamie touched my arm and we silently moved on, sticking close to the building and the deep dark shadows.

We crossed another street, this one a row of coffee shops and bookstores with apartments over them, and then the pavement turned to grass. We paused under an oak that seemed significantly larger than the last time I'd seen it. A hundred years would do that, I supposed. Its branches spread over an area that I recalled was a place to sunbathe on a nice spring day. As I peered upward through the branches, I wished that my newly acquired powers included some sort of Spidey sense. Were we being followed? Maybe I *should* have brought Jayne.

We stayed there for a while, willing ourselves to become a part of the tree until we were sure no one tailed us. Then I pointed toward the university building that held the library and student services, which included the health clinic.

Jamie and I moved on. Our destination was behind a science building and close to some dorms. There was another quad, and I realized by the bizarre look of the landscape that one of the old giant oaks had fallen and crashed into the library roof. It was also pinned up against the door. I guess it had been too much to hope that we could just walk in the front entrance.

We climbed over the branches that still held dry leaves, even though the tree had to have fallen years before.

There was no way we could get through the doors; the trunk of the tree blocked them too neatly.

The library windows were high, plus there were bars across them—one of the necessities of a college close to the inner city. The windows were broken out but the iron was still in place. I guess nobody wanted books bad enough to break through.

Of course, this gave me hope that we would find meds inside. Could we be lucky enough to be the first ones in since the world had gone to hell?

If we could get in.

Jamie and I circled, peering up into the darkness, trying to find a way in. The back of the building held a fire escape, but the ladder was too far over our heads for us to be able to climb up. We completely rounded the building, and I began to be afraid we were going to have to wait until daylight, which was still hours away.

We returned to the front face of the building, squeezed in and climbed over tree branches, then ducked under some others, all the while trying not to trip over the squashed and broken remnants of the shrubberies that used to grace the facade. We came to steps that led up, and at the end of a sidewalk that led right up to a wall noticed a dark square about chest high. I pushed on it and it gave an eerie squeak.

"Mail chute!" I said.

"Where does it lead?" Jamie asked.

"Probably the basement." I grinned in the darkness. "And the campus post office."

"Will we fit?"

"Only one way to find out."

I took off my coat and pack and slid my katana from its sheath. Meanwhile, Jamie dug in his pockets and pulled out a tube.

"From Burton," he whispered. He snapped it and shook it, and I realized it was a neon glowstick. He pitched it into the chute, and we heard it slide down the sheet metal. A green luminescence settled around eight feet down.

"Here goes," I said. With the katana straight out before me, I slid headfirst down the chute. Cobwebs hit my face and I tried not to freak out at the thought of spiders crawling in my hair.

As I got close to the light, I saw that there was about a four-foot drop to the floor. I dropped my katana and grabbed the end of the chute. The sword clattered to the ground.

"Are you okay?" I heard Jamie call in a behind me as I tried to ease my way out without falling on my head.

"Yeah," I said. My voice sounded strangely loud, magnified by the chute. I finally wiggled my way out and was able to stand. I sneezed and picked up my katana as I looked around.

My coat and pack came down the chute. "Will I fit?" Jamie called down.

"Take off your coat," I said. "Send your stuff first."

I found a canvas bin that was supposed to catch the mail and wheeled it under the chute as I heard the rattling of Jamie's bow, quiver, pack and sword sliding down. His coat hit next; then I heard him grunt as he wiggled his way in.

"My shoulders," he said. "It's tight."

"Stretch out your arm," I said as I peered up the chute. He managed to wriggle free, and I grabbed his wrist and pulled him through.

"Got any ideas on how I'm going to get back out?" he said when finally standing on the floor.

"Nope," I said. "But we'll figure something out."

Jamie gathered his things and we moved on.

It seemed as if no one had been inside since the campus closed down. Thick dust coated the floor, and the tiny footprints of mice could be seen crisscrossing it. The biggest challenge, besides trying to see with nothing but the green glow to guide us, was trying not to sneeze our heads off.

I began to feel confident that we would find something to help Shane, med-wise. Especially when we got to the main floor and saw that the dust was thick on this level also.

The thing that must have saved the clinic was the fact that it wasn't labeled as one. The door simply said STU-DENT SERVICES, and surprisingly it was locked.

Jamie whacked out the window with his elbow, and we both cringed as the glass hit the floor. It sounded to our ears like a giant explosion. We froze in place, as if the sound of our breathing would make as much noise as the shattering glass.

"We better move," I said finally. Jamie nodded in agreement, and he opened the lock from the inside.

I led the way. As soon as we got inside the clinic, Jamie opened cabinets and drawers and emptied the contents into his pack. I went to a closet in the back corner. When I'd had my shots, the P.A. had gone in there to get them. The door was locked, and I rattled it in frustration.

"Have you come across a set of keys?" I asked Jamie.

"No," he said. He pulled out his knife and jammed it into the lock. A couple of twists and he pulled the mechanism free and the door swung open.

"How'd you do that?" I asked.

"We all have our gifts," he replied. He snapped another glowstick, and I used it to examine the shelves in the closet.

"Jackpot," I said. "We've found a pharmacy." The shelves were full of tiny bottles with labels too difficult to read. Plastic bins held syringes, more bottles and vials. Jamie and I loaded our packs; then Jamie started ramming things into the many pockets inside his coat and pants.

"Can you even move?" I laughed.

"Yeah," he said, and his coat clinked as he picked up his bow. "But I'm not going out the same way I climbed in."

"Maybe we can shinny down a drainpipe," I suggested as we made our way back to the main hall.

We tried the front door, just in case, and found it chained. No luck there. We moved toward the back door and it was the same. We went to the second floor.

As we passed by a window, something outside caught my eye. I grabbed Jamie's arm and we took cover on either side, cautiously peered out.

It took us a while to see them, but finally three figures emerged from the shadows of a building. I didn't need Jayne around to confirm what I already knew.

Ticks.

Headed our way.

Jamie and I ran on silent feet toward the back of the building, and looked out a window. I dared not blink as my eyes scanned the darkness. I heard Jamie's sharp intake of breath, and he pointed toward the corner of the quad. There were more.

I motioned up, and we took off up the stairs. We kept going until we hit the top floor.

Heavy banging from below let us know they'd caught our scent. There was no need to be quiet now; the important thing was to get away.

I led Jamie to a door that led to a fire escape. Miraculously it was unlocked, and we hustled onto the platform.

"You've got to get back," I said. I handed him my backpack. "I'll distract them."

"No," he said. "I'm not leaving without you."

"Jamie." I grabbed his hand. "Without the meds, Claudia, Trent and the rest will die. You've got to get the meds to Shane. I can handle this group."

Even in the darkness I could see how troubled he was. He had to choose between Claudia and me, and I know there was no choice to be made.

"What do you keep telling me?" I asked. A feeling of urgency was growing within me. Even though the ticks had not caught up, it was just a matter of time until they did. "We do what we gotta do. This is the way life is. It's not your fault you have to go."

Jamie bowed his head.

"Go," I said. "You said you wouldn't lose Claudia because you've got me. You're right. Let me do my thing."

He finally nodded. Grabbed me and gave me a quick hug.

"I'll draw them," I said. "You take off. Get to the El and follow the tracks all the way back."

"What should I tell Shane?" Jamie asked.

Shane?

"Tell Shane . . ." I felt a wry smile quirk my lips. "Tell Shane that I'm the coolest ninja he ever knew."

"Abbey—," Jamie started to say, but I brushed past him and moved down the fire escape, taking the steps as silently as I could. There were no ticks in sight, which was a good thing. It meant they still didn't know where we were. With any luck, the only one they'd be after was me.

The drop to the ground was about fifteen feet. I lowered myself down until I hung by my arms, then let myself fall. I flexed my knees so I'd roll. When I came up, I drew the katana and crept toward the corner of the building.

I looked up at Jamie. He stood flat against the building, blending into the darkness. If I hadn't known he was there I would never have seen him.

"Let's hope he stays invisible," I said to myself, then stepped onto the sidewalk directly between several buildings.

If Jamie was going to get away, I had to make sure all eyes were on me. I walked bold as brass down the sidewalk until I got to the quad in front. Three ticks were poking around the mail chute. Another three were standing back and looking up at the building. I held the katana out in front of me, the end pointed down and my hands steady on the grip.

"You guys lose something?" I called out in a clear voice.

As one, they all turned to look at me. They seemed dumbfounded. Even though it was dark I could see their jaws drop. Out of the corner of my eye I saw a movement. Jamie was on the move.

I took off running in the opposite direction.

THIRTY

It worked. They seemed to be following me. Now I just had to lose them.

I knew my pursuers had tick powers—extra speed and extra strength. But since I was the guardian, I should have those, too. Shane said he'd seen me do unbelievable things. I had to believe that whatever destiny had dropped on me would see me on equal footing with my enemies.

My boots pounded the pavement, and as I left the campus behind I knew that I was running faster than I'd ever run before. But was it fast enough? I only hoped that Jamie had enough sense to stay out of sight and keep to the El.

It should be daylight soon. If I could just keep these six away long enough, when the sun came up I would be able to stroll back without any problems at all. I hoped.

I recognized the area of town I was in; we'd toured it for one of my classes. Old industrial buildings had been transformed to lofts and galleries. I hoped I could find a place to hide in one—or at least lose some pursuers there.

I could hear them behind me, coming around on

both sides. Which meant that Jamie should be free and clear.

Please, God, let Jamie be free and clear.

I turned and saw more than the original six after me. Were they telepathic? How had others known to join the chase? Or was it random, just a lookey-what-we-found luck?

I heard them whooping it up in the predawn light. They were trying to corner me in one of the darkened alleys. With the tall buildings surrounding us, they could be in shadow for hours. Definitely long enough to eat me, or whatever they did.

I ran into a large brick apartment building. The inside was a disaster trash, broken furniture, and a flurry of mice that squeaked and scattered as hard as their little legs would carry them. I needed to get up high where the light would protect me. I bolted up a flight of stairs just as I heard a door thrown open below.

I was trapped. Up more stairs was my only chance. I heard yells and laughter at my predicament follow me as I climbed. What I needed now was sunlight. A lot of it. Roof access was my best bet. I could only pray as I chugged up the staircase.

Desperation is a great stimulant. There seemed to be no roof-access door, so I tore through the top-floor apartment and scrambled out onto a fire escape.

Other ticks were on it, too, on their way up. I stole a look at the sky. It was lighter, but the sun still hadn't made an appearance.

"Please, let it be a bright sunny day," I said as I found footholds and climbed to the flat roof of the building.

I was trapped. And I had too many pursuers to fight. I could hear them coming at me from all directions, and they were excited. Maybe Lucinda had promised who-ever brought me in some Scooby snacks. Whatever it was, they were properly motivated.

I was, too. I ran around the top of the building, look-ing for an escape. No way down, but just maybe . . . I sheathed my katana and took a deep breath. I took off running as hard as I could, and jumped.

The roof I aimed for was a story shorter than the one I'd been in. As I leapt, the first glimmer of the sun ap-peared on the horizon.

I let my knees give as I landed and rolled.

Technically, my plan should have worked. In my mind I rolled gracefully to my feet, pulled the katana from its sheath and let the sunlight glint off its blade. Ticks scattered in all directions, fear in their eyes.

What really happened is the dry-rotted roof gave way. I crashed through, landing on a hard floor several sto-ries below. I lay still, too stunned to move. My heart pounded in my chest as I struggled to regain breath.

I finally rolled over on my side and I tried to get my bearings. It was pitch-black inside, and I realized that all the building's windows were covered. Tables and chairs littered the floor. A table had broken my fall. I was lucky I hadn't broken my back. Chalk it up to being a Time Guardian, I guess. There were benefits.

My brain finally computed that I was in a dance club. I remembered going here one night with a group from school to celebrate the end of a semester. Floors and floors of your favorite tunes! It seemed like several life-times ago.

"Move," I said, in hopes it would motivate me. I man-aged to get to my feet just as the doors on the floor be-low banged open. I looked up through the hole in the roof and saw that dawn had come. Unfortunately, it was still dark inside this place.

The ticks outside were in trouble. One mistake and they would fry. But the ticks inside were already celebrating.

"She's trapped!" one of them yelled.

"Someone get Lucinda," another added.

Maybe I'd get lucky and she was on the roof. Fried tick for breakfast. I could practically taste it.

Or maybe it was fear that had made my mouth go dry. I was in big trouble.

The building was dark and the windows were covered. Lucinda and her gang would be elated. Still, I wasn't about to give up. The dance club had a catwalk around the top. The stairs were missing but I had to give it a try. As I heard the sounds of running footsteps below, I grabbed a support post and shinned my way up.

"Going somewhere?" a cool voice asked.

Lucinda. She sounded much the same as she had that night in the ER.

As I rolled onto the catwalk, I heard the ringing of metal posts as other ticks started to climb. I popped the small blade from the hilt of my katana, and stuck it into the black-painted plywood that covered the windows. I was able to pry up enough to get my hands behind it. I pulled with all my strength, and was rewarded with the sound of wood splitting. Old plywood, old nails and a window casing with a bad case of dry rot helped. The first rays of morning sunlight poured through, and I stood in the middle, turning to face the two ticks that were now approaching from either side of me.

My katana was long enough to slice into the shadows as the two ticks pondered their assault. I stood with the blade raised over my left shoulder, and wondered which would be the first to work up enough courage to attack.

The angle of the sunlight favored the one on my right. He dove for me, his intent to knock me into the darkness. I met his dive with a vicious downward stroke that found his shoulder. I wrenched the blade back as his friend came for me, gave him an upward punch with my elbow and he staggered backward into the window. It cracked, and he teetered in shock as the sun's rays fried his skin. He shrieked, and I kicked him through with a loud crash.

The wounded tick staggered to his feet, and I ducked as he swung wildly with his good arm, then I followed up with his decapitation. I kicked his headless corpse over the rail and dust exploded over the group waiting below.

I looked over the side and saw Lucinda and her gang. "You're running out of minions," I said.

"And you will eventually run out of daylight," Lucinda replied.

"Hey," I quipped. "I've got all day."

But I didn't even have that. I looked out the window. There were clouds to the west. And it was a straight drop down to the fried vampire corpse below. At least fifty feet, and nothing but worn brick to climb.

"There's no way out," Lucinda informed me.

Duh.

"Here's an idea," I said. "Why don't you take your Shadow Booty Clan and go on home."

"Can't, my sweet," Lucinda replied. "You know that the sunlight is bad for my complexion."

"Everybody wants to be a comedian," I said. "Even the Queen of the Ticks."

"You won't find me so funny if you keep wasting my time."

"I would say bite me, but I know you'd love it." So much for me getting the last word.

The angle of the sun quickly changed, as it is wont to do in early morning. It was higher in the sky now and light poured onto the dance floor. I heard the tick gang move around, each finding a position to wait until darkness doomed me.

I wouldn't wait. I moved to the next window and yanked on the plywood. When it came off, I threw it below with a clattering crash. More sunlight. I looked up to judge the angle. How much time would I have if I kept working my way around the room?

Not long enough. If only there was some way I could get back up through the hole I'd crashed through. I looked hopefully toward the ceiling. It was too high; even Shane with his uber-hops would have a problem getting through.

Pretty much screwed. That summed things up.

Lucinda knew it, I looked down to see her sitting in a chair, as if she had all the time in the world. Which she did.

There were eight ticks around her that I could see. Possibly more beneath me. Where had they all come from? I'd dusted two already, and I knew more had been caught in the daylight. How many had I killed since I arrived? Was there any way to know?

Another thing bothered me. This group had been quiet for some time. How and who were they feeding on? Were there other humans around? Humans close by? Maybe there were some who had gone into hiding and did not realize that there was still some semblance of civilization? At one time this had been a thriving city with a population in the hundreds of thousands. Could one hundred years, a pandemic and the presence of life-sucking aliens knock everything down to just the group of a hundred or so that tried to survive here? Or were there others—others who didn't know about Shane and the gathering and what hope remained to humanity?

If I wanted answers to these and all my other questions, I couldn't think of a better time to get them. I scanned below me once more and saw that the ticks were pretty much in a standby mode. I leaned back between the two windows and looked down at Lucinda, who sat on her chair like a queen on a throne, minions ready to do her bidding.

"Hey, Lucy," I said. "Let's talk."

THIRTY-ONE

The Queen Tick crossed her legs and placed her folded hands in her lap. Then she looked up at me and arched an elegant eyebrow. With that look, she made me feel like a flea-infested churl who'd been summoned to lick the boots of royalty.

I decided to show off. I was the Guardian, wasn't I? I did some fancy moves with my katana that had the ticks on the catwalk fading into the shadows. Lucinda motioned with her finger and they climbed down. She covered her mouth politely as she yawned, then looked at me expectantly.

"You have the floor," she said.

I was surprised that she didn't look at a watch. Of course, she wasn't wearing one.

I wondered if Chronolotians thought of them as calorie-counters.

Now that I had the opportunity to talk, I really didn't know where to start. There was so much I didn't know, so much I needed to know, and so many things that I knew I didn't want her to know.

Shane had spoken of things that Marco told him before he died. Lucinda didn't know about Marco; Shane had intercepted him before he arrived. Would Lucinda's story match the one Marco and Sheila told?

"Why me?" I finally asked. "What's so important about me?"

"You're the Time Guardian," she said. She didn't seem hesitant to answer my questions.

"Yeah, about that." I swung the katana at some dust motes dancing in the sunlight around my feet. "What exactly *is* a Time Guardian?"

Lucinda flicked something off the sleeve of her leather coat. "The Time Guardian is the one chosen to guard the portal. She who controls time, controls the universe," she said. She sounded bored.

"She?" I asked. "You make it sound all 'Buffy,' like I'm the chosen one."

She smiled. "Ah yes. Joss. He was very entertaining."

"You know Joss Whedon?" I asked.

"Who do you think inspired his Buffy movie?" she replied.

I saw the rest of the ticks snickering. Either she was yanking my chain or she really knew him.

"I hope that you don't think I've spent all my time just sitting around waiting for you to show up," she said.

"If I recall, you spent quite a bit leaving bodies lying about."

"One does what one needs to do," she agreed.

"Yeah," I said. "One does need to murder innocent people, doesn't one?" My voice dripped with sarcasm that she ignored, so I went back to my questions. "What makes me so special? Why am *I* the Time Guardian?"

She nodded approvingly. "So, you accept the fact that you are the Guardian?"

"Well," I said, "it's not any weirder than anything else that's happened lately." I did another fancy twirl with the katana, just in case any of the ticks thought they could sneak up on me. "It's pretty obvious I'm something. But why me?"

"The Guardianship is passed down through the female line from one generation to the next. It has been so since the gate was given over to your care."

"My care. You mean my ancestors' care? Who gave it? Did the former gatekeeper just walk up to my ninety-times-great-grandmother and say 'Here, I don't want this anymore, you do it'?"

"I do not know how it began. I just know that Earth seemed a pleasant place to pass the ages." Her speech seemed more cultured now. As if before she'd been just playing along.

"What happened to your planet?" I was suddenly extremely curious about her race. "Where did you come from? How did you get here?"

She raised her hand as I fired off questions. "It does not matter what came before. The years and the things those hold are too numerable to mention. You wish to know how you came to this place. These things I will tell you."

I opened my mouth to speak, then immediately closed it. She had my attention. But I also realized that while we talked I would lose my daylight. I moved to the next window and ripped off plywood. She watched me carefully and seemed oddly proud when I cleared the next two windows and settled down between them.

"So, tell me," I said.

"The gate came to this city after your first World War. Your great-grandmother felt it was no longer safe where it was."

"Because you'd found it."

"Yes," Lucinda said. "They hid it well. So well that it took me a while to find it even after I traced them here. And they took extreme precautions so I could not get to it."

"The tank . . . the peroxide . . ."

"Acid." Lucinda practically spat the word. "Then they disappeared."

A thought occurred to me. "Why couldn't you just get someone to bust down the wall and break the tank?"

"Because a Time Guardian must pass through to open the gate. As long as the Time Guardian is present in the same time as the gate, I cannot pass through."

"But once I passed through, you had one hundred years of free use until time caught up with me. You needed me to go through and disappear."

Lucinda nodded. "You understand how it works, I see."

Not really, but I was beginning to. There was so much I wanted to know, needed to know. I shrugged.

Seeing the position of the light, I moved to the next set of windows. They were on the southern side of the building. How much longer would I have? I had to make the most of my time.

"Can I control where I go?" I asked. "Can I pick a time?"

"You can pick the precise moment in time," she said. "All you have to do is think of it."

"I wasn't thinking about this time when I came through," I said. "I wasn't thinking of anything but the time I was wasting." I looked at her questioningly. I felt very confused. "How did I wind up here?"

"Perhaps you were called," she said. "Perhaps someone needed you."

"Shane?" I gasped.

She gave me a knowing look.

"But, I barely knew him. I'd just met him. He even blamed me for what happened to him."

"You've always known him," Lucinda informed me. "He is the one chosen for you."

I rubbed my forehead. The familiar ache had started—the one that showed up frequently now. The result of too much information and not enough sleep.

"I sensed it that night in the emergency room," she said. Standing, she walked as close as she dared to where sunlight poured upon the floor. She was smiling. It almost seemed as if she enjoyed the memory. "I could smell you on him," she continued. "I knew then that he was your lifemate. It has always been so—one is made for the Guardian to be her helpmate. One who will easily believe because he loves her. One who will stand by her side and sacrifice everything to protect the gate."

"That's why you changed him," I said. "Because of me."

"It is," she agreed. "If I could control him, then I could control you and thus the gate. I did not realize you were so close to opening it. Or that you knew so little. If I'd known, I would have just waited and killed you instead."

"Then you could control the gate for eternity, because I have no daughter to be the guardian."

"Yes," Lucinda said. "It was a simple matter once you disappeared to go back and change the title of the house so that I could assume ownership."

I shook my head. "Which is why the bank suddenly said there was a problem."

"Yes," she said.

"How did you even know that I would buy that house? Or did you meddle with that too?"

"I made sure the house was available," Lucinda explained. "I knew the gate would speak to you, call out to you, especially since your forbears had lived there. The house holds the blood of your lineage. It was destined to be yours. I just made sure it was there waiting for you."

"You can change the past?"

She nodded once more. "Anyone can, if they have the proper opportunity. But it is a dangerous thing to change the past. You don't know what effect it will have on the future. And a traveler must never be in the same time as her past self. It could lead to disaster if the two came into contact."

"You seem to have no qualms about traveling into the past and screwing things up," I said.

"I know what I'm doing." She shrugged. "You do not."

"I guess you like this future," I said.

"It was coming along nicely until you showed up."

"You've got an unlimited supply of victims," I noted.

"She who controls the gate, controls the world."

"Did you have anything to do with the pandemic?"

She laughed. "No. That was a result of human stupidity. I must admit, it did make things easier. There was such chaos."

"You've seen it all, haven't you?" I said. I moved to uncover the next window. The tick waiting in the darkness nearby moved back as more sunlight poured through.

The sun was high in the sky now. It was approaching midday. I couldn't help but wonder about Jamie. Had he made it back? I had a feeling that if they'd captured him they'd taunt me. The ticks all seemed cranky. They probably didn't like being away from the safety of their lair during daylight hours. I couldn't blame them. I could think of several things I'd rather be doing myself at the moment.

Shane . . .

"I was right," I said, as things pieced together in my mind. "It *was* my fault he got changed. Only my fault."

"Such is the life of a Guardian," Lucinda said. "It is not without its risks."

"But he didn't ask for it," I said. "He didn't get to choose. For that matter, neither did I."

"Destiny chose," Lucinda said. She smiled up at me. An evil smile. "How does it feel to know Shane is with you because he has no choice?"

"What do you mean?" I asked.

"He was destined for you. He can't help but be attracted to you. Maybe more so now that he is changed. You are a danger to him now. And if there's one thing we enjoy, it's the challenge. We have so few of them."

I noticed her minions nodding in agreement. They all seemed rather smug at the moment. I wondered if that was a side effect of their condition.

"Tell me, Abbey," Lucinda continued. "How is Shane doing? It's been a long time since we were . . . *together*." I heard her gang snicker at the comment. "He always was a bit moody," she said. "Is he still running hot one minute, cold the next?"

How did she know? I tightened my grip on my katana. Was it true? Was Shane with me because he had no choice? Was the attraction I felt for him some sort of cosmic plan? Did we have a choice?

I resisted the urge to rub my forehead. As if that would make the pain and confusion and frustration go away.

"Do not feel sorry for your doctor." Lucinda continued. "If I have one regret in my lifetime it was turning him. He does not appreciate the gift I gave him."

"Maybe you should have asked him first," I said. "Maybe you should have asked all of them." I swung my arm out to encompass the ticks in waiting. "How 'bout it, guys? Did you get to choose if you wanted everlasting life?"

"Yes!" they said as one, and Lucinda smiled.

"Idiots," I growled. I swung the katana in a flip over my wrist. "Guess she didn't tell you it wouldn't be easy."

"It's been nothing but a party till you showed up," one of them yelled.

"Yeah, you go ahead and believe that," I muttered. I scanned the ticks waiting in the darkness. "Your group looks a bit lean, Lucy," I said. "Are you having trouble finding food these days? Is there an embargo on heart-sucking?"

"Things will return to normal once you reactivate the gate," she said calmly, returning to her chair.

"What makes you think I'm going to reactivate the gate?"

She smiled and shook her head like I was a petulant child. "You have no escape," she said. "Darkness will eventually come. It always does." She stretched out her hand like she was checking her manicure. "You will find reactivating the gate much more pleasant that the alternative." She *tsk*ed, as if she had a hangnail, then looked directly at me. "I'm sure you appreciated how much your dog suffered. Can you imagine how much worse it will be for your friends?"

"Bitch!" I yelled. I gripped the rail of the catwalk. I wanted nothing more than to jump over the side and take her head for what she'd done to Charlie. For how she'd made him suffer. For all the things she'd done through the all the years she'd been on earth.

But there were too many of them. The ticks looked up at me expectantly. I could practically see them licking their lips.

"I found your dog to be an annoyance. Just as I find you to be one." Her voice was no longer pleasant. It was firm, commanding and downright scary. "You *will* do what I want." She was no longer chatty; she was telling me what to do, and expected me to do it. "You will *quit* wasting my time."

Maybe she realized she was being too bossy, because suddenly she changed her tack. "I appreciate your desperation," she said with a wave toward the sunlit windows. "But you will eventually run out of daylight."

I moved to the next window, but I knew she was right. I looked at the sky as I flung the plywood behind me. I was fine for now, but when the sun moved to the west and began its descent, the skyscrapers would block it. I heard movement below and realized Lucy and the ticks were changing their position; moving with the sun.

She was right. I was in deep trouble.

THIRTY-TWO

I couldn't believe I'd dozed off. Luckily, stealth was not my attacker's strong suit and the creak of metal jerked me awake with katana in hand.

I was so tired. More days than I could count of high stress had taken their toll. It must have shown. The tick coming toward me didn't even stop. It must have been luck that guided my hand.

I lashed out with the katana and hit the tick in the calf as he came over the rail of the catwalk. He stumbled toward me as he lost his balance, and I rammed my knee into his gut. His head jerked up, and I sliced through his neck, then dove toward the window as he exploded in a mess of gore.

"Rookie," someone laughed below.

I flung some of the slop off my arm and went to work on the western-facing wall of the building. I started to fling the wood covering down below, but stopped myself as I saw the ticks gathered and waiting. How long had I dozed? Long enough for one of Lucinda's gang below to come after me.

Stupid, stupid, stupid.

Making mistakes would be the surest thing to get me killed . . . eventually. There was no doubt in my mind that Lucinda would make me suffer before she ended it. She'd bragged about killing Charlie. About what would she do to one of my friends if she had them in front of me.

What if they had captured Jamie and were saving him to coerce me later? Or worse, what if they had Trent? Or Shane? What would I do when it came down to it? Would I open the gate? It was the only thing keeping me alive. Once I opened it, I was as good as dead. Get me out of the way, Lucinda had full control. Earth would face an eternity of her traveling back and forth, creating more ticks and using the rest of the population to stay alive until there was nothing left.

Was that why she and her friends left their home planet? Had they taken all the life there?

Now was not the time to ask more questions. Now was the time to figure out how the heck I was going to get out of there.

I figured I had an hour or so before things got really hairy; the sun was over the top of the highest building that I could see. I needed a way out and fast.

Down was out of the question. I knew I could fight, but I didn't think I could take that many by myself. And there was always the possibility that there were more outside, trapped in other buildings and just waiting for the streets to fill with shadows so they could emerge.

The windows seemed impossible. It was a straight drop all the way down. There had to be a fire escape somewhere, but as the only side of the building I hadn't seen was the north side, as old and decrepit as it was, I had a feeling that the fire escape was long gone.

Which left: up. The hole I'd crashed through. It was on the opposite side from where I was now, and looked just a little too high.

Maybe, just maybe, I could use the rail to climb up. The angle was impossible, the distance unbelievable, and the chances of me doing it improbable, yet I had to try. As far as I could tell, that was the only way out. What I would do once I got up there could be figured out later.

It was either this or die fighting. Having Lucinda capture me wasn't an option. It was time to do something.

With a scream that came from deep within my diaphragm, I kicked out the window before me. I ran to the one beside it and did the same. Then I picked up some nearby plywood and threw it sideways, like a giant Frisbee, at some ticks who were already charging one of the posts in an effort to climb up. It knocked them back long enough for me to get to the other side of the catwalk, and with luck to the hole in the ceiling.

As they figured out where I was heading, more ticks jumped on the posts and began to climb. Hands grabbed at me from below, and I swung my katana in a wide arc. I stepped up on the catwalk rail. The hole was too far. I needed something to hold on to, but the only thing was the rail beneath, which meant it was impossible for me to reach up.

My balance was precarious, and I hopped back down as a tick appeared on the catwalk. This one was armed with two chair legs. He swung them at me like clubs, and I had to duck back out of reach. Another tick came at me from the side, this one with an entire chair in his hands. He forced me back like a circus lion. I swung my katana, but their weapons kept them out of my reach. They were pushing me back against the wall.

Using the wall as a brace, with my leg I pushed against the chair. The tick holding it stumbled back, but the other one swung his weapon and hit my upper arm.

It went numb immediately, and it took all my concentration not to drop the katana.

I was done for. My choices were to surrender or drop five stories to the pavement outside. Some choice.

Suddenly, the room flashed with bright light and an explosion sent me teetering backward toward the window. To my surprise I saw an arm covered in black reaching for me. Since I didn't like the alternatives, I grabbed hold and wound up lying on my back on the roof.

Shane?

"Playing Dr. Doom?" I asked, as I lay on my back and looked up at his face, which was deep within the confines of a black-hooded cape. Jayne stuck his nose in my face and meowed.

"I just thought it was a nice afternoon for a walk," he said.

Behind him stood Owen. He was holding what looked like a whiskey bottle with a rag sticking out.

"Care for a cocktail?" he asked. Lighting the rag, he dropped the bottle into the hole I'd been pulled through. Another explosion rocked the building, and flame shot up through the hole at us. He grinned.

Shane yanked me to my feet. "Is that thing glued to your hand?" he asked, indicating my katana, which scraped against the bricks. I looked down. I couldn't believe I still held it.

"Guess so," I said. "What now?"

"We leave," Shane replied.

I heard shouts from below as he led me to the north side of the building. A long thick board stretched from this roof to an adjacent one. A narrow bridge. A very narrow bridge.

"How did you find me?" I asked.

"Your friend," Shane pointed at Jayne. "We started on

campus and he took it from there. We heard the glass breaking and figured it was you."

I plucked at his cape. "What is this?" I asked. "Where did you get it?"

"Berta." Shane explained. "She whipped it up from the blackout curtains after Jamie got back and told us what happened."

"Jamie made it back?"

Shane nodded, but I could tell something was wrong.

"The meds?" I asked.

"They're fine. But Claudia . . ." He stopped to gather his words, but Owen interrupted him.

"They're scattering," he said.

We looked down and saw ticks pouring out of the dance hall as flames licked the sides. I spared a moment to hope that Lucinda might be trapped, but saw her stalk out with her black leather coat flapping around her. She stayed in the shadows cast by the nearby buildings.

"Get them!" she yelled, and pointed up.

Jayne took off across the board bridge as if it were nothing. Shane took my hand firmly in his gloved one. "Don't look down," he said.

"Don't let go," I replied as I felt the board bow under our combined weight. He squeezed my hand and we practically skipped across, fearful that if we settled in one spot the wood would break.

Owen dropped another Molotov cocktail, then followed us as the ticks swarmed toward the building to which we'd crossed.

Shane drew a sword from beneath his cape. "In the mood for a fight?" he asked.

"All day long," I said, steadying my grip on the katana.

Jayne took the lead as we found a door and pounded down the stairs beyond. When we got to the bottom,

Owen opened that door and flung through another bomb. I scooped up Jayne, put him beneath my coat and we all jumped through the flames and into the street.

Shane met our attackers head on. He flung back his cape—we were now in the shadows—and sliced his way through a tick who exploded into dust.

Owen and I moved onto either side of him. Instead of attacking full-force, however, the ticks stood back. Lucinda and two other ticks stepped forward. Were they her generals? I put Jayne down, and he gave out a disgusted hiss before slinking into the shadows.

"Shane," Lucinda said. "How delightful to see you."

Shane shrugged out of his cloak and handed it to Owen, who stepped back behind the two of us. The ticks on either side of Lucinda showed weapons. One held a bo staff, and the other a set of tonfas.

"Make sure no one sneaks up on us," Shane said to Owen, but he kept his eyes on the trio ahead.

It's funny how people rise to the occasion. As I watched Shane stare down Lucinda and the two warriors who stood before us, it occurred to me that never in his wildest imagining as a med student would he have imagined himself one day in a street fight with immortals. He probably thought that all of his battles would be fought in the ER against silent diseases, against the intrinsic stupidity of people.

Of course, what was the thing he always said? Ninjas are way cooler than pirates? As a boy had he imagined being a ninja? Like Trent. Had he had pretend fights with his brother with broomsticks and plastic nunchakus? I know that I never imagined myself to be in this predicament. Even through all my self-defense classes, I thought the worst that would happen was a mugging.

Here we stood, side by side, both holding swords that

were hundreds of years old, ready to kick some major ass. It was them or us. Plain and simple. A truth as old as time itself: Only the strongest survive.

Lucinda smiled at Shane as if he were an old friend. The sun was vanished now. The buildings cast long shadows, but most of the light was from the fire burning inside the dance hall. It brightened the alleyway.

"Let's stop this nonsense and talk," Lucinda said to Shane. "How about a truce? You give me her"—she tossed her head in my direction—"and I'll make your little community off-limits. Kind of like a living memorial."

I felt the skin crawl on the back of my neck. I was fairly certain of Shane's answer, but wasn't sure of where Owen stood. Me for the safety of all of them? It was something to be considered. If Lucinda could be trusted.

"I don't think so," Shane said. "I've grown rather attached to Abbey."

"For now," Lucinda purred. "But she will get old eventually. Then what are you going to do?" She looked me up and down, and I knew that she found me lacking in some way. To be honest, how could I compare? She was perfect. Perfect body, perfect hair, and perfect skin— once you got past that evil-life-sucking-demon-that-wants-to-take-over-the-world shtick.

"You know he can't give you a child," she said.

To tell the truth, it wasn't something I was considering at the moment. But I was the Guardian, and without a child from me that Guardianship would end and Lucy would eventually win. I wondered if that was part of her plan all along.

Lucinda chewed on a perfect nail as if considering something. "Here's an idea," she said finally. "You choose a companion to spend your days with, and I'll change her for you. Was there someone you had a crush on back in the day? Jennifer Aniston? Maybe Angelina Jolie?" She shook her head. "No, I can't see you with her. Scarlett Johannson maybe?" Her eyebrow rose. "How about it, Shane? Anyone you want."

"I've got who I want right here beside me," he growled.

My heart swelled. Seriously. It seems corny, but that's the only way to describe it. Shane loved me. *Me.* Lucinda said it was his destiny, but still it was sweet to hear. To see. To have proven. Whatever events and DNA had come together to form him and make him my soul mate were still there, unchanged even though he'd gone through Lucinda's curse.

He still chose me. And he was willing to fight for me.

God, I loved him. And I was going to tell him. Just as soon as we got out of this mess.

THIRTY-THREE

"I want them both alive," Lucinda said. "We'll need him to make her cooperate."

Shane grinned. "That should make things interesting," he said. "Since we don't care if we kill all of you."

"And to think you used to be a humble little doctor," Lucinda said. "I hate to waste potential on someone such as you. You could have had it all, Shane. You still could have it all."

"No thanks," he said. They stared at each other for a moment. The past hundred years of fighting was probably passing between them. And the wasted potential of his life as a doctor instead of Lucinda's minion.

"Go on home, Owen," Shane said as the bo-staff tick twirled his weapon. "Don't get caught up in this."

"I'll stick around for a while," the sheriff replied. "You might need someone to carry your sorry ass home. Besides, I like to watch your girl there fight. Kinda makes up for her sass."

Shane and I stood shoulder to shoulder and watched as our two chosen challengers showed off their moves. I almost imagined myself in the middle of a low-budget action movie.

Shane touched my arm in silent communication. I

was to take the one with the tonfas. He would take Mr. Bo Staff. That made sense. I'd had more experience with tonfas—if you could call my lessons experience.

They attacked, and Shane and I met them. My guy was good. My first move was strictly defensive. He used his weapons with tick speed, and I quickly surmised that if not for my Guardian powers I would be toast.

This was not like the other battles I'd fought, where ticks flew forward in an attempt to overpower me and I basically surprised us both by whacking off their heads. This was a battle of two skilled warriors, the winner to be determined by who had the most skill . . . or luck.

I couldn't spare a moment to see how Shane was doing. I heard the grunts as the hard-as-concrete bo staff struck his sword, the ringing of the sword's steel. I felt the flap of his coat as he spun and twisted.

The most important thing was for us to not get trapped. When we'd started we had the building we'd escaped from behind us and the burning one to our left, an alleyway in between. We had to get in a position where we could move and possibly escape if the option presented itself.

If we could hold on that long.

Owen seemed to know what we needed. He threw another one of his cocktails, and flames ignited between the four of us who were fighting and the rest of the ticks. Shane and I took advantage of the flash to move into the alleyway. Owen had disappeared, and I realized as I dashed toward the street that I'd lost sight of Lucinda. I also had no idea where Jayne was. I could only hope that the cat would find us, because I sure couldn't take the time to look for him.

The surviving ticks would now have to go around the

block to catch us. Meanwhile, Shane and I still had our opponents to deal with.

We needed a diversion. Something more than the weapons we were using. It would be handy if the burning building would collapse on them both, but we didn't have time to wait for that to happen. Nor did we think it likely.

Shane and I were on the same wavelength. We both ran as hard as we could to a storefront across the street, leapt through flinging shelves and displays behind us. The two ticks were on our tail, and it wouldn't be long before their friends caught up. As we crashed through a door we found Owen coming back. We threw a shelf across the door to block it just as he spoke.

"Dead end," he said.

"We need a diversion," I panted.

"I'm open for ideas," Shane said. He threw his weight against the door to counter that of our attackers.

I looked around. The flames from across the street lit up the room through a small round window in the door. "It looks like an old hardware store," I said.

"You want to use your skills at deduction to get us out of here?" Shane snapped.

"I'm working on it," I said as I spied a wheelbarrow. I jerked it upright. The handles were still attached, but the tire was flat.

"What's that?" I asked Owen, pointing toward the corner.

He jumped as he went back to examine it, then dragged forth a mannequin dressed in hunting gear.

"Do you still have Shane's cloak?" I asked.

"Yeah," he said. He looked confused but handed it to me.

"Any of your bombs left?"

"Yeah."

"Empty them on the fabric," I said. I stood the mannequin in the wheelbarrow. I threw Shane's cloak over it, and Owen doused the fabric with alcohol.

"Did you ever see *The Princess Bride*?" I asked Shane.

"Um, yeah. Um . . . *oh* . . . "

" 'I am the Dread Pirate Roberts,' " we said at the same time.

"What are you talking about?" Owen asked.

"This is what we like to call a holocaust cloak," I said. "We're going to push this out, light it on fire and then run like hell while they try to figure out what's going on."

"You two are crazy," Owen said, but he handed me a box of matches. He took hold of the wheelbarrow handles. "I'm ready whenever you are."

I looked at Shane, who nodded. He had a big grin on his face.

"On three," I said. I counted down, and on three Shane slid the shelf out of the way while I lit the cloak. The thing flamed up and Owen opened the door. Shane grabbed one of the handles and Owen took the other. They both let loose with a deep roar, and shoved the wheelbarrow out. It screeched, crashing into the two guys who'd been fighting us. Their clothes caught fire and they leapt back, surprised. The wheelbarrow continued in a straight line across the street.

As we saw ticks dive out of the way, we realized our diversion had worked. I bolted through the door after Shane and Owen. We were soon running as hard as we could down the street, cutting back toward home as we ran.

We ran until we couldn't run anymore. We finally pulled up in a darkened doorway with stitches in our sides.

"I think we lost them," Owen said.

"I can't believe that worked," Shane replied.

"And you thought ninjas were cooler than pirates," I added.

Shane's hand brushed my cheek. "I *still* think they are," he said—right before he kissed me.

"Can you two save that until we get back?" Owen asked.

We heard a noise, and all three of us readied our weapons and stood, breathless, until a loud meow broke the silence.

"That cat has to have more than nine lives," Owen remarked as Jayne trotted up to us. The feline had a where-have-you-been look on his whiskered face.

All I knew was, I was glad to see him. I bent down and scooped him up, and made ridiculous baby sounds as I petted him.

"I hear you're the one who found me," I said to the cat, who purred loudly.

"But we're the ones who saved your ass," Owen pointed out.

"Thank you," I said. "And thank you for not trading me to Lucinda." I looked at both of their shadowed faces in the darkness. "You gave up a lifetime of peace for me."

Shane shrugged. "It's not like we could trust her," he said. But beneath his casual demeanor was more. Things that I hoped he would tell me later tonight.

"If I wanted her to have you, I would have saved myself the trouble and stayed home," Owen said. "Berta was frying chicken when we took off, and there had better be some left by the time we get there."

"Well, let's go," I said. "I'm starving."

THIRTY-FOUR

We did not speak again until we saw the bonfire burning brightly in the street in front of Shane's house. It was a strange feeling for me; the welcoming scene gave me a sense of home that I'd never felt. There was even a cheer from the people gathered round when they realized all three of us had returned safe and sound.

"I need to tell you something before we go in," Shane said as we walked up the porch steps. He took my hands and led me to the side. "Claudia died," he said. "Her fever spiked and she had a seizure."

I nodded, unable to speak. I couldn't help but remember Jamie and Claudia at the gathering, and Jamie's assurance that nothing would happen to either of them. Had it been a premonition on my part, or simply a horrible coincidence?

"It happened right after Jamie got back. He was with her." Shane rubbed his forehead. "I was sorting through the meds. . . . I didn't have time to treat her."

"I'm so sorry," I said. "You know it wasn't your fault."

"I know. Jamie was pretty torn up about it. He wanted to come back out with us. I had to hit him, knock him out so he wouldn't come after us. We were afraid he'd do something stupid."

"Like going out in the bright sunlight even though it could kill you?" I glared at Shane. He looked as tired and worn as I felt. A hot meal and sleep would help me, but unfortunately he couldn't have the luxury of the same. He needed another kind of hot meal. How long would it be before he gave in to his need again?

"I couldn't leave you out there." His fingers touched my cheek and then my hair. "Especially with dark coming."

I looked at the scene in the street. How would the people feel if they knew they could have traded me for a lifetime of peace? How would Jamie feel? It wasn't the ticks that had killed Claudia, just horrible circumstance. "He loved her," I said.

"He does," Shane replied, and I had a feeling from the way he looked at me that he wasn't talking about Jamie.

We went inside.

The clinic held a feeling of peace now, instead of the desperate urgency that had crushed everyone when Jamie and I left. Trent and the others slept soundly on clean sheets and wore T-shirts—Berta was responsible, no doubt, her very presence a comfort to those around her. Janet dozed on a cot next to her son's.

I went to Trent's bed and touched his forehead, and was relieved to feel it cool and dry beneath my hand.

Thank you, God.

Claudia's cot seemed out of place, glaringly empty though the blankets were washed and it was neatly made up. Had they buried her already?

Shane checked his patients, reassuring himself of each one's condition with the touch of his hand. Lucinda had called him a waste of potential. She didn't have a clue as to his value. As a man or as a doctor. If only there was a way to destroy the demon inside him without destroying the man.

"Go and eat," Shane said. "I want to check vitals again."

I agreed to go, mostly because I wanted to find out about Jamie. Jayne trailed after me as I went to the kitchen. I found Berta and Owen sitting at the table.

Berta gave me a hug and fixed me a plate. I didn't bother to sit, just ate quickly and listened as Berta told Owen about Jamie waking up from his sudden nap, courtesy of Shane.

"Where is he now?" I asked, feeding Jayne some scraps and wiping my hand on a towel.

"The poor dear went back to their place. He said he was going to make her a coffin," Berta said. "He took her body, too," she added in a whisper, as if it were a secret.

Owen gave me directions, and Jayne and I slipped out the back and made our way down the street to Jamie's cottage. It was quaint. Small and slope-roofed, it had gingerbread trim and a rosebush rambling over the porch rail that was covered with pink buds ready to explode with scent. The place looked like something out of a storybook, with its windows glowing with candlelight against the darkness. I'd never noticed it in my own time, since it sat back off one of the alleyways behind the bigger houses that lined the street. It must have been a gardening shed or a guesthouse when it was originally built, many many years ago.

Berta had explained to me that Jamie lost both his parents to the ticks when he was seventeen. His dad was a woodworker, and apparently Jamie had learned quite a bit from him. Thus his expertise at arrow-making. More than likely, it was also the explanation for the wonderful trim on the cottage.

A couple of cats looked up questioningly when Jayne and I walked onto the porch. They hissed at Jayne, who remained aloof as I knocked on the door.

"Jamie?" I called out when there was no answer. I opened the door, which squeaked, and Jayne and I stepped inside.

The interior was just as adorable as the outside. It pained my heart to look. Jamie and Claudia must have been so happy here. So much in love.

Their tragedy wasn't any different than possibly millions of others that had occurred through the ages. Death didn't care who it took: mothers, fathers, sisters, brothers, sons, daughters, lovers, friends. But Jamie was more of a friend to me than anyone I could remember. My heart was breaking for him.

I continued through the house, calling out his name while trying not to disturb the peace of the cottage. Jayne stopped before a door that was slightly ajar, and I knocked before opening it.

It must have been their bedroom. An iron bed piled high with quilts sat against the far wall, enclosed by a canopy of gossamer. Jayne went to the foot of the bed and meowed. I pulled the canopy back to reveal Claudia lying upon the quilts. Her hair was neatly brushed and she was dressed in a cream-colored gown of satin and lace. It looked like a wedding dress.

With a heavy sigh, I moved out of the room with Jayne on my heels. I went into the kitchen and saw a light in the yard out back.

"Jamie?" I called as I went through the door.

He was in the backyard, in front of an open-ended shed. Torches lit the four corners of an area that held two sawhorses. Upon the sawhorses sat a coffin. The ends were arched, and Jamie's bare torso and arms made great sweeping motions down the top as he planed the wood. His back was covered with a sheen of sweat, and sawdust covered the ground around him.

I watched him work for a moment. Watched the muscles of his back flex, and his hands, firm on the planer, guide the tool over the wood. When he was finished with his planing, he'd run his hand over it to feel the smooth texture.

I didn't speak until he stopped to wipe the sweat from his eyes with an old towel.

"Jamie?"

He turned and tossed the towel toward a table that held his tools. When he saw me he leaned on the coffin, placed both his palms flat on the wood.

"I was too late, Abbey," he said. "Too late to save her."

"Jamie, it wasn't your fault."

He smirked. "Using my own line on me, Abbey? Let me help you. 'It was her time. This is how it is. It's a risk we take every day. We all know it's bound to happen sooner or later. When it's your time to go it's your time to go. It happens, that's all.' " He went through all the platitudes he'd fed me since I'd arrived. " 'It's a part of life. Just a twist of fate.' " His voice broke as he added, "Some people refuse to let go." His head slumped forward against his chest and I touched his shoulder.

He turned to me with a sob. He wrapped his arms around my waist and I settled to the ground with him holding on. Sobs racked his body. I patted his head and made soothing noises until the sobs subsided. He sat up, rubbed his eyes and turned away as if embarrassed.

"Jamie." I rubbed a hand across his shoulders. His muscles jumped and then he sighed. "I'm so sorry."

"It's not your fault," he said. He looked sideways at me, and a slight mile chased across his face.

We sat for a moment in silence. Jayne, conspicuously absent during Jamie's tears, appeared beneath the coffin and walked around the sawhorses. Occasionally he'd lift his nose and smell the wood.

"It's beautiful, Jamie," I said.

"I've got some stain saved back to put on it," he said. "And I want to carve a rose on top."

"Is there anything I can do to help?" I asked, already knowing the answer.

"No," he said as he stood. He reached out a hand and helped me to my feet. "But you can hang around if you want."

I found a stool in the shed and perched myself on it as he went back to work. I figured he wanted to talk, and soon he did. He told me about meeting Claudia, about falling in love, about convincing her to leave her family and come live with him. About their life together, about their hopes for the future. About how Claudia woke up dizzy and nauseous the last morning coming home from the gathering and thought she might be pregnant.

"Abbey," he said after he described her death. "The time-twister. Can you go back in time?"

"According to Lucinda," I said. "She explained a lot of it to me while we were waiting around."

"You should go," he said. "Go back."

"Go back where?" I asked. "Do you want me to try and go back and save Claudia? Keep her from going to the gathering?" Was that even possible? What if I ran into me? What were the repercussions? There was still so much I didn't know. Could I be in the same place as myself? I felt another one of my headaches coming on.

Jamie looked toward the house. His eyes were upon

the window where Claudia's body was visible, lying on the bed, waiting for him to place her inside her coffin.

"No," he said finally. "No." He shook his head. "Go back to *your* time. To the place it all started. Put a stop to all this."

"What? How?"

"Didn't Shane tell you when and where he was changed?"

"Yes . . . but . . ."

"You could be there. You could stop it." Jamie looked out into the darkness. "You could stop Lucinda."

"He's right," Shane said as he stepped into the light. "You could stop her. Before all this happens."

"Even if I could go back, I don't know if I can get back to the exact time—and even if I do, how do I know I'd get to the alley in time? And how do I know I can best Lucinda in a fight?" I looked at the two male faces, lit by the torches. One man was my friend, the other my lover. The two were dearer to me than anyone I'd ever known, except my father. "And . . . what will happen to you?" I asked Jamie. "And Trent and Berta and Owen? If I change the past, what will happen to the future?" That was my real fear: losing everything I'd built here.

I felt Shane's eyes upon me but he did not speak. Jamie flung the plane toward the shed and spread his arms wide. Jayne jumped at the noise and went back to investigate.

"Any future you make has got to be better than this."

THIRTY-FIVE

Leaving Jamie's, I was surprised when Shane took my hand and led me in the opposite direction from his house. We walked silently through the darkness with Jayne alternating between galloping ahead and trailing behind. I did not question Shane. I figured he had a purpose, and his mind was probably on what Jamie had said, just as mine was.

A sliver of the moon hung in the sky like a smile. What did it have to be so happy about? Did it enjoy the fact that the human race was in a desperate struggle for survival? Or maybe it was just happy because there was no more pollution clouding up its view. Whatever the case, the sight of it did not help my mood. I was worried.

What was I supposed to do? There was no way I could even get close to the time-twister; Lucinda and her gang were parked right in front of it. And if I could get to it without Lucinda knowing, how did I make certain I went where I wanted to go? There were no guarantees that the things Lucinda told me were true. They could all be a trick on her part, nothing more.

Then there was the entire problem of activating it. How was I supposed to do that? And once it was activated, wouldn't Lucinda be able to use it again?

Of course, all the problems I created in my mind were nothing but an excuse for the real issue twirling through my brain and crushing my heart. What about Shane?

I looked at his profile as we moved through the darkness. His features were nothing but shadow, but I knew by the set of his jaw that he was purposely taking me somewhere. I was relieved to see that the red glow was still missing from his eyes. I also knew that they would change with the phases of the moon. How long did we have before the red glow and the unstoppable hunger returned?

Was it too much for me to hope that maybe I could somehow temper his cravings? Could I make the difference and somehow calm the demon inside him? He'd said things were worse since I arrived. But couldn't things be better now that we were together?

That was the root of my problem. Shane and I were together, and I didn't want to leave him. I loved him. That was my destiny. *Our* destiny. I welcomed it. I wanted to be with him, no matter what. How could I leave him for an uncertain future in the past?

The houses gave way to a dark emptiness, and I realized we were at the cemetery. Shane led me through the gate and guided me through the tombstones without missing a step. Jayne stuck close on our heels, as if he was spooked, and I couldn't help but share the sentiment. This was an eerie place, with the trees making weird shadows across the different slabs of marble and granite, and the rows of crosses from the newer graves. A huge mound of dirt blocked the view of the newest graves, and I knew this was where they were waiting to place Claudia.

We stopped finally, and Shane knelt on the ground

before a headstone. He touched the inscription and spoke.

"This is my brother," he said. "Sean."

I knelt down beside him. I had not told him that I already knew about Sean. I knew he was about to tell me in his own words; so I said nothing. Instead, I rubbed Jayne's head as he bumped it against my knee.

"He was ten when he died. I was twelve."

He stopped, and I knew he was waiting so I asked the question that had been on my mind since I found out he had a brother.

"How did he die?"

Shane smiled slightly and shook his head. "He died playing pirate."

I settled back on the ground and Jayne climbed into my lap. "How?"

"Sean thought being a pirate was really cool. Ever since he read *Treasure Island*, he was always playing at it. He had all these pirate toys—Legos and this giant Playmobil ship, and every year for Halloween he had the costume . . ." Shane sat back and wrapped his arms around his knees. "We figured he'd outgrow it eventually. He didn't, and I didn't help matters. He was still infatuated with it when he was about to start middle school. I picked on him a lot. I was into Ninja Turtles when I was little, so I was always telling him that ninjas were way cooler than pirates."

I smiled and nodded. So *that's* what that meant.

"Anyway, we had this treehouse in the woods behind our house, and Sean decided he would turn it into a pirate ship. He dragged a bunch of wood back there and was nailing boards on it so that it kind of arced out into a point, like a ship. He even had a pirate flag hanging on the tree trunk, which he called his mast. . . ."

Shane stopped and rubbed his forehead. I remained silent, my hand on Jayne, who rumbled contentedly in my lap.

"Mom sent me out to get him one evening and bring him in for dinner. I found him up the tree and called him a big baby. Sean got mad at me and was yelling, and the boards he was standing on gave way. He fell and . . . there was this broken tree branch . . ."

Shane rubbed his forehead again. "He bled to death." His voice was hollow, disembodied in the darkness. "I couldn't move him, and I didn't know how to stop it."

"That's why you became a doctor," I said after a long moment. "Because you didn't know how to save Sean."

Shane nodded.

"Do you want me to go back and save him?" I asked. It was the same question I'd asked Jamie.

"I don't think you should," he said after a long moment of silence. "What about you? Do you think there's anyone you should go back and save?"

My dad. Could I save him? Should I? Could I stop there? And if I did save him, would it keep me from finding the time-twister?

"If you start messing with the past like that, Abbey, then you can seriously affect the future," he said. "And we don't know what kind of effect their lives would have on the future."

I knew. I wouldn't be so alone. But then again, if Sean had lived would Shane still be a doctor? It was that never-ending circle again. The one that always resulted in my head pounding.

"But you *can* go back and stop Lucinda," Shane said. "You can stop the future she made. You know where she'll be and when she'll be there. She won't be expecting you. You can kill her and put a stop to this."

"I can save you, too," I said. "I can stop her from changing you."

Shane shook his head. "You've got to stop Lucinda. That's the first priority. If you can do it before she changes me, then great, but if not . . ." He pushed his hair back. "I'll tell you where she took me. So you know where to find us."

"Shane . . ." I didn't know which bothered me more: the thought of killing him or the thought of seeing him in bed with Lucinda.

"Now, we've got to figure out a way to get you to the twister," he said, ignoring my protest. "We need to draw Lucinda away so you can get in."

"What makes you think I can control this thing?" I asked. "What makes you think I can show up at the right place in the right time?" Jayne meowed in protest and stalked away. He sat next to Shane and licked the fur of his chest.

"Because you're the Time Guardian," Shane said simply.

"I don't want to lose you," I said, my eyes on the his shadowed face.

"Abbey, I've been lost for a hundred years." I saw a glint of red in the darkness, a flash from his eyes. The beast inside was stirring. His voice cracked. "I don't want to live this life anymore."

I moved without thinking. I did not hesitate; I crossed the distance between us, wrapped my arms around him and kissed him as if I was drowning and he was the only source of air.

He *was* my air. And I, his. I knew it by the way he held on. By the way he groaned low in his throat. By the way he moved against me, rolling me over onto the grass and pressing his body against mine.

He was urgent, demanding. His hands were everywhere: throwing aside my weapons, pulling my coat off, pushing my shirt up. His hands on me were rough, almost painful, but at the moment I didn't care—I just wanted him.

His mouth moved over me and I needed an anchor so I threw my arm backwards and grabbed onto the marble slab behind me. The thought that we were making love on someone's grave gave me a twinge of guilt, but it was soon chased away by Shane's hands on my body. I looked up at the night sky and arched my back against his mouth on my stomach.

Countless stars pinpointed the sky, and I saw one shoot across the velvety darkness and knew exactly how it felt. I burned also.

How could I leave him? How could I go?

He kissed me. Long, hard, a kiss that left me gasping for breath.

His hands moved to the top of my jeans and he jerked on them.

"Wait," I said. I tried to move. I wanted to help, but he didn't seem to be listening. He turned his head and I saw the red light in his eyes. "Shane," I said, a bit louder this time. I pushed up on my arms and he shoved me back down. My head hit the tombstone and I gasped in pain. Red haze filled my mind as I felt him pull my jeans down.

"Wait," I gasped. I felt like I was going to puke as nausea rolled across my stomach from the pain in my head. Shane pushed into me. What was he doing? I shoved against his shoulders. I couldn't see, from the dizziness, the pain, the darkness. "Shane. Stop."

He pounded against me so hard that I hit the tombstone again. His legs were pinned against mine. Couldn't he tell that I wasn't ready, that I couldn't . . . He hands grabbed my thighs and pulled them up.

"No!" I leveraged a thigh as he pulled back for his next assault and shoved against his shoulders.

He growled low in his throat, like an animal, and Jayne responded with a yowl that echoed eerily through the cemetery. Shane jerked at the noise. It was the opening I needed. I punched him.

He looked at me, his eyes glowing dangerously red. He was going to kill me. God, I loved him and he would kill me.

He swung his fist. I braced for the blow. I threw my arms up to block it but it didn't even come close. He was aiming for something else. I heard the impact of his fist hitting the granite behind me. He slid off my body and cradled his fist in his hand.

I lay there for a minute, willing my heart to regain its normal rhythm. If he wanted to kill me, he had the opportunity to do it. Finally I pulled my shirt down and found my jeans and boots thrown off to the side. I wasn't even conscious of him taking them off.

Shane sat huddled on the ground, his hand still cradled. I looked around for my katana, which was lying close at hand. Could I use it on him? Would I have to?

"Shane?" I said, kneeling down before him.

He shoved his hair back from his eyes and blinked. The red glow was gone. "I'm sorry," he said in a hoarse voice. "I couldn't, I wouldn't," he shoved his hair back again. "I love you, Abbey."

THIRTY-SIX

"Did I hurt you?"

"No," I lied because I did not want the demon Shane to come between us. "How's your hand?"

He shook it, clenched it into a fist, then stretched the fingers out. "Fine," he said.

I looked around once more. "I think you put a crack in the tombstone," I said, hoping maybe I could lighten the moment. I mean, it's not like I wanted things to get more depressing.

"It's my tombstone," he said.

I looked doubtfully at the tombstone in question. Talk about creepy. I didn't want to go there. So I changed the subject. "Can you see in the dark?" I asked, looking at his eyes. They were thankfully once again dark blue.

"It's one of the benefits, if you can call them that," he said.

"No wonder the ticks were able to find Jamie and me last night." Was it just last night? Once again, I felt like a lifetime had passed in a day. "Where's Jayne?" I asked when I realized I didn't see the cat anywhere.

"Over there." Shane motioned. "On a tombstone."

I yawned. I could not remember the last time I'd slept, and my head still felt woozy. I didn't dare rub it; I didn't want Shane to feel any more guilt. I also knew the day to come would hold Claudia's funeral. I wondered how Jamie would get through it. Just like everything and everyone else, I supposed: one minute at a time.

"We should get back," Shane said.

"Only if you promise I can sleep," I mumbled.

"You can sleep," he said quietly.

He was already pulling away from me. Already fearing what would come when his hunger struck again and the moon swelled each night. Already shutting off the good Shane that would be trapped inside when the demon Shane came out.

He was ready for me to go, but I still wasn't ready to leave. I didn't think I could ever leave.

Shane handed me my coat and weapons; then he stepped off to the side as I yanked on my socks and boots and strapped on the katana. I realized he was kneeling in front of his parents' graves.

I gave him the moment. I figured if he wanted to share it with me he would, and considering what he'd already shared with me tonight I felt he was done. He finally stood and without a word we began the long walk back to his house.

I felt so alone. It had happened so fast. I knew it scared him when he lost control. That he was afraid of hurting me.

Then he took my hand and our fingers locked together. It was his left hand that I held, the one that was his weapon. The one that gave him sustenance. I wondered if he clasped my hand so tightly to hold it in because he was afraid of what could happen.

I decided not to worry about it. For now I would just let things be. Let us be. We were together for now. That was enough.

"Do you really think I can do this?" I asked when we once again saw the light from the bonfire.

"You have to," was all he said as we walked into the house.

Because I'm the Guardian. . . .

The morning came, and with it a miserable drizzling rain. It matched my mood. I'd fallen into a restless sleep next to Shane, who seemed to be having his own problems relaxing. He crept upstairs shortly before dawn to check on his patients before finally crawling back in beside me.

Jayne meowed in protest when Shane left and when he came back, since the cat now thought it was his job to protect my feet while I slept. But truly sleeping was impossible. Every time I closed my eyes I saw myself lost in time, away from everything and everyone I cared for. My first trip had resulted in Charlie's horrendous death; there was no way I wanted to show up a hundred years from now and have Lucinda taunt me with the mummified remains of Shane, Jamie, Trent, or even Jayne.

I was scared. Terrified, even. I didn't want to be the Guardian. I just wanted to go back to my simple little life with Charlie and flipping houses, and the possibility that someday the hot doctor on the El would ask me out—the hot doctor who was now lying stiff as a board beside me, afraid to touch me.

I knew Shane was afraid to touch me. He was afraid that he would lose the control that he'd struggled for one hundred years to maintain. Like he'd said, things were different now, harder. My coming along wasn't exactly a blessing.

The thing I had to decide: Was I willing to risk every-thing on a gamble? Or was the life I was living at the moment better than any that could be?

If only I could know.

One thing I was sure of was that things, as good as they had been with Shane when they started, could not continue on this same track. Not with Shane withdraw-ing and getting moody. He was afraid of hurting me, and I was afraid I'd let him.

And maybe I was afraid that someday in the future I would have to kill him.

I was so tired. Tired of thinking, tired in body, tired of choices.

I gave up on sleep. I heard Berta's footsteps on the creaking floorboards above, and kicked away the blan-kets. Jayne complained as he hit the floor with a thud, but he followed me up the stairs.

I didn't turn to look at Shane as I left. I knew he needed to be alone.

I took a shower, put my jeans on and pulled out the last remaining T-shirt in my drawer. It was a black one with big red letters that said *Veni,vidi,volo in domum redire*. Beneath it in small white print it said *I came, I saw, I want to go home*.

If I was looking for a sign, this had to be it.

I wandered down to the kitchen, where Berta and Owen were sitting at the table. If ever there was a morn-ing for coffee, this was it. That's why I wasn't surprised to find Berta and Owen with their hands wrapped around thick steaming mugs.

"Would you like some tea, dear?" Berta asked.

"Please," I said, not even caring what flavor it was. I needed the comfort. I needed the camaraderie of sitting around the table and sharing the misery of the day and the coming funeral with people who actually cared.

"Have you seen Jamie this morning?" I asked Owen as I pulled out a chair and sat down. Jayne jumped onto an empty stool and curled his paws beneath his chest to settle in.

Owen nodded. "Boy's taking it hard."

"Poor thing," Berta added. "I've tried to get him to sleep a bit, but he wouldn't stop until he had that coffin finished. I took some food over and got him to eat a bite." She looked out at the rain beating against the windowpane. "I was hoping this would stop before the funeral, but I believe it's going to stay with us all day."

"It's fitting," I said, and we all took sips of our tea.

"Trent was asking for you earlier," Berta remarked.

"I'll go in and see him," I said. Once again, my mind imagined repercussions if I went back and changed the past. Would Trent even be born? Maybe he would. Maybe he'd have a wonderful life, grow up to be a movie star or president.

This was too much responsibility. I didn't want it.

"How long until the funeral?" I asked.

"We're gathering in about an hour or so," Berta said. "At Jamie's." She looked out at the rain again. "At least Shane can go."

I didn't say anything. I was pretty sure that Shane would not go, but it was up to him to tell Berta.

I felt Owen's eyes upon me as I took another sip of tea. "What?" I asked.

He yanked on the tail of my T-shirt. "Going somewhere?" he asked.

"I guess Shane told you what he has in mind," I said.

"He did," Owen said.

I looked at the Sheriff and Berta sitting there. They seemed happy in their life. Content. They'd obviously been together a long time.

The thought suddenly occurred to me that they'd never mentioned any children. Did they have any? Or had they birthed a child who died or was taken by ticks?

"Do you know what could possibly happen to you if I go back and manage to take out Lucinda?" I asked.

Berta reached across the table and squeezed Owen's hand. "We know."

"We'd never know the difference," Owen said. "So it shouldn't bother you what becomes of us."

"But it *does* matter," I said. "All of you, everyone here could cease to exist."

Owen laughed. "Sounds like a normal day to me," he said.

Berta patted my arm. "You do what you've got to do," she said. "For you and for Shane. If anyone deserves happiness, it's him."

I shook my head. Had they not heard that they could cease to exist? Didn't they care?

Owen pointed a finger at me and looked down his nose as he talked. I felt like I'd been called into the principal's office. "You get back there, and you take out that bitch. While you're at it, you keep her from turning Shane. Then forget about us. Don't come back here looking for us, either. You don't even need to tell Shane we existed."

"Owen," I began, but he kept on going, talking right over me.

"The future is what you make it, Abbey. You and nobody else. You can make things better for everyone. Everyone in the entire world. You don't think we'd make a sacrifice for that? So, quit your whining and worrying and go for it."

He shoved his chair back and stalked from the room. I watched him go with my jaw still hanging open.

Berta patted my arm again. "It's just his way, dear," she said.

"And here I was beginning to think he cared," I replied.

THIRTY-SEVEN

It was to happen that night. Shane insisted upon it. The rain would help cover us, and the ticks wouldn't be expecting something so soon—or so he said. The plan was simple. Owen was to send a message saying he'd changed his mind and wanted to trade me, that he wanted to negotiate terms. While Lucinda was occupied, Shane, Jamie and I would sneak into my house and send me through the time-twister.

Yeah. Simple.Not a problem. I didn't have a thing to worry about.

Except, I felt as if I was murdering the people I loved most in the world. They were acceptable losses, or so they kept telling me.

As soon as Claudia's service was over, Jamie was ready for revenge. He shrugged off the well-wishers as the rain poured over his bare head, and made his way back to Shane's with purpose.

I didn't know what to tell Trent. I hated saying goodbye; I hated thinking he might not exist if I succeeded. I just hated it.

So I lied to him and promised him lots more ninja lessons after I kicked Lucinda's ass to kingdom come and made the world a perfect place to live in. I hated it.

Shane was grim at best. He was back to the Shane who didn't care, the Shane who thought it best if I left, the Shane who was breaking my heart. I hated that, too.

"Is this it?" I asked him as we stood in the back hallway, strapping on our weapons. I added a long slim rapier to my left hip and tied it down with several quick jerks. "Don't I even get a 'It's been nice knowing you, have a great life, thanks for the memories'?"

Shane's movements mirrored mine—jerky, forced, with frustration simmering below his impassive expression. He strapped on a sword and stuck a pair of sais into a sling that went under his arms. He pulled on his long coat and stuck several throwing stars in the deep pockets. He pushed back the long hair that constantly fell across his eyes.

Then he looked at me, and my gut lurched. The pain I saw in his eyes hit me like a fist.

"I can't let it out," he said.

"Let what out?"

Before I could blink I was slammed against the wall, Shane pressed up against me. His hands roamed my body, pushing my clothes aside, seeking skin until he stopped with a sharp intake of breath, his left hand pressed over my breast. Jayne let out a low warbling growl.

"When I let out the good," he whispered harshly against my ear, "the bad comes, too." He ground his hand against my breast, and I felt the scratch of the thing in his palm. "I can't control it anymore," he continued. "I don't want to control it anymore."

"Shane . . ." I grabbed his head between my hands and pulled so that I could look into his face. His eyes glowed red, and I felt a moment of terror. Would he kill me? Would he suck the life from me because he needed to feed? My fear must have shown on my face, because he shut his eyes tight.

"I thought I could be with you, Abbey," he said. "But I can't. It won't let me." I saw a glimmer of moisture on his lashes.

He fought for control. Shane flexed his palm and moved his hand away, lowered his forehead until it touched mine. I felt a shudder run through his body, and a sob caught in my throat. He blinked and I saw nothing but blue in his eyes. He'd won the battle . . . for the moment.

"I've got to end it," he said quietly. "I don't want to fight it anymore."

"You're planning on dying tonight." I choked back the tears. I wasn't going to cry. Not now, when I had to be strong.

"I'm planning on taking as many with me as I can," Shane said. He stepped back and pulled my shirt down, and carefully, gently, tucked it into the waist of my jeans.

"But what if I can't get through? What then? What about us?"

"The only possibility for us is in the past," he said. "There's no future for us here."

"Because you're going to die. But Shane, don't you see that—"

He shook his head as if I were a recalcitrant child. "It has to end now."

I turned away and picked up my coat. "Were you always this stubborn?" I asked as I jerked it on.

"What do you think has kept me going all these years?" he said with a wry smile. "I couldn't let Lucinda win."

"Say I do get through. Say I kill Lucinda, and keep her from changing you. What then? Am I supposed to pretend like none of this happened between us and hope you ask me out for coffee again?"

Shane leaned his arm against the wall and rested his head against it. Was he still calming the demon inside? The set of his shoulders was tense, yet his posture was one of exhaustion, as if he'd fought a great battle and still had miles to go before he could rest. This was true, I suppose.

"I was always attracted to you. Since the first time I saw you on the El," he said, his back still to me. "But I felt as if I didn't have time to get involved with anyone, no matter how much I thought about it." He let out a sigh. "We wasted so much time."

"What if you see me kill Lucinda? Won't you think I'm some kind of homicidal maniac and call the cops?" I touched his back. I wanted to look at him. I wasn't sure how much time we had left, and I never wanted to forget him. *This* him. The one I'd fallen in love with.

As if I could.

Shane turned and looked at me once more. His eyes were sad, but they were also clear and deep and blue.

"Tell me about Sean," he said. "No one else knows. Tell me about the ninjas and the pirates.

"Ninjas are way cooler than pirates?" I said.

He nodded and smiled wistfully. "That should do it." He slowly reached out a hand and touched my cheek. "I love you, Abbey. It was worth hanging around a hundred years to have that."

I wanted to throw myself into his arms and never let go, but I knew his control was hard-won at the moment. I wouldn't take that away. I couldn't do that do him. Instead, I smiled and nodded. "It was worth it," I agreed. "Every bit of it."

"Let's go," he said. We took a few steps; then he stopped me. "The pandemic," he began. "It started March 25, 2043. They traced it to a cruise ship called the *Neptune* that docked in Miami. Three thousand passengers were infected and didn't know it. Their symptoms didn't show up until a week later. Then it spread so fast that the government couldn't keep up. It was like the Black Plague. Can you remember that?"

"I can," I said. "Save you, kill Lucinda, save the world," I counted off my tasks. "I can do it."

"If anyone can, it's you," Shane agreed.

It seemed as if the entire community was there to see us off. Did they know what was about to happen? Or did they just think it was another showdown between us and the ticks? They must have sensed something important was about to happen. They stood gathered under the trees and porches without even the benefit of the usual bonfire to warm them, not in the steady rain.

Owen was already gone with a dozen fighters to a place at the wall where they would signal the ticks. I didn't hold out much hope that Lucinda would believe his ruse, but if they could take out some ticks then so much the better for us.

Shane, Jamie and I faded into the darkness. Jayne followed, and I wasn't in the mood to tell him otherwise. His presence was comforting against the aloneness I felt. He kept close to my ankles and whatever shelter he could find in the tail of my coat. A few more cats trailed behind, and it reminded me of my first night here when I realized exactly what kind of world I had come to. It was raining that night also. The night Radar died.

Neither Shane nor Jamie spoke. They were both wrapped in their own thoughts, both fighting their own internal battles. I knew what they both planned tonight.

They were both hoping to die. They were tired of the fighting, but more important they were tired of never winning. All they'd done for years was just break even. But I didn't want to see them give up.

The rain hid us well. We kept close to the buildings, stayed in the shadows and quietly made our way around to the alley that ran behind my house. My feeling of déjà vu was strange, considering how much had happened since the last time we'd come this way. I stared through the wrought-iron gate at the back of my house and hoped beyond all hope that Lucinda had fallen for our ruse, that she was at this exact moment talking to Owen, that we could simply waltz in and activate the time-twister, and that somehow, some way, everything would turn out okay in the end.

The house was dark except for one dim candle in the parlor. It couldn't be this easy, could it?

Shane did his uber-hop and lay down flat on the house's surrounding brick wall. He extended his arm, and I used it to leverage myself up the side. Jamie handed us his bow before Shane and I pulled him, while Jayne scampered through the gate. The other cats remained in the alley.

As we dropped down behind the dogwood tree and made our way up to the house, I put my finger to my lips and stared at Jayne, willing him with my mind to stay quiet. He looked at me and snapped his tail before slinking up to the edge of the house and taking shelter under the eaves from the rain.

We crept to the window, and Shane peered in. He ducked back down with Jamie and me, and mouthed "Clear." I looked at Jayne, who now crouched beneath my knees. Surely if there were ticks about, he would let us know.

Shane erred on the side of caution. With hand signals we decided that he would go around front, and Jamie and I would enter through the back. He disappeared into the darkness and rain, and Jamie and I remained crouched where we were. Jamie took advantage of the time to notch an arrow in his bow. I saw from the bulges in his coat and pants pockets that he was a walking arsenal. One with a death wish.

I heard a creak, and was surprised to see Jayne disappear through Charlie's pet door. I held my breath as I waited for his yowl to sound, but all remained quiet. Jamie grinned and shrugged.

"I almost forgot," he said. "I got you a present." I couldn't see what he stuffed in my pocket and didn't have time to look as we went to the back door. I nodded when I was ready. Jamie kicked the door in at the same time that Shane crashed through the front. We saw no one.

I ran on the balls of my feet down the back hall, katana held ready. I met Shane at the bottom of the staircase. He looked upstairs with his sword in hand. Nothing.

Jayne sniffed around the doorjamb, and looked into the parlor. Shane grinned and swept his arm forward to usher me in.

I didn't like it. Something didn't feel right. Jayne should be pitching a fit, but instead he just looked around. It was as if there was nothing for him to smell. Like all smells had been erased.

Which meant, they knew we were coming here?

I looked toward the kitchen and saw buckets and rags lying on the countertops. The thought of Lucinda's minions down on their hands and knees with scrub brushes and rags would have been funny, except for what I now realized.

"It's a trap," I said.

Jayne looked toward the front door and arched his back. His tail flew straight up and he hissed.

Shane pulled me into the parlor, and Jamie followed. Shane pushed a large curio cabinet across the opening just as the front door crashed open. Jamie joined Shane in piling up furniture, but I stood like an idiot in front of the time-twister, trying to figure out how they knew we were coming.

Of course they knew we were coming! How stupid was I? It was all about the time-twister—whoever controlled it controlled the world. We'd thought we were playing Lucinda; instead she had played us. She needed me and the time-twister together, and here I was. As soon as I went through, Lucinda would have free rein again.

Unless I killed her.

"What are you waiting on?" Shane yelled. "Get out of here!"

Bodies beat against the barricade of furniture, which Shane and Jamie stood pressed against with their shoulders to keep from falling. I turned to look at the time-twister.

It stood, just as I remembered it, on the pedestal in front of the fireplace. Jayne sniffed around the base and hissed as the machine whirred and clicked. Was that because I was near?

How did this thing work? I didn't know how to activate it. I didn't know anything about it. I'd accidentally fallen through, nothing more. What was I supposed to do?

The windows in the front and back of the room crashed open, and ticks crawled through. Jamie turned and shot his bow. His arrow caught a tick in the throat and blood spurted everywhere.

"We've got to take her alive," one of the ticks said as they came at me.

"Good luck with that," I said as I flipped my katana into my hand. This, I knew how to do. As they attacked, I fought.

There was not much room to maneuver with three of us fighting, and furniture flipped and shoved into a mound around the door. Jamie's bow was useless in such close quarters, so he used a sword, but he did not have the skill with it that Shane and I possessed. These ticks were armed with knives and an odd assortment of martial arts supplies. I guess they'd been practicing.

I noticed the ticks that we killed were all exploding into dust, which meant that they were older. Lucinda's reserves were dwindling.

Yet, there were still too many to count. For every one we killed, two more came through the window.

"Get through the gate," Shane yelled.

"I can't!" It was now surrounded. Every time I got close, more ticks came. And even if I could get close, I still didn't know how to activate the thing.

I heard a screeching sound as the barricade of furniture started to topple.

"Jamie," I yelled. "Watch out!"

A chair hit his shoulder as the furniture pile crashed to the floor. It struck his sword arm, and he was trying to block a thrust from the male tick he was fighting. I saw the tick's blade slide into his gut, saw the look of surprise on Jamie's face as it was shoved in to the hilt. Jamie tried to pull away, but the tick grabbed his neck.

"*No!*" I screamed as the tick released his knife and slammed his left palm into Jamie's chest. I saw Jamie jerk, and his eyes widened in surprise and shock. I moved toward him, trying to shove furniture out of my way and fight off the two females who were currently trying to take me down.

"Abbey!" Shane yelled, as I kicked one of the ticks away. I swung my katana and decapitated the one feeding on Jamie. An explosion of dust surrounded me, but Jamie slid to the floor.

I felt another maelstrom of dust behind me, and I was jerked away from Jamie, who lay still at my feet. Shane shoved me toward the time-twister.

"Do it," he yelled. "You can't save him."

"You can't save anyone," Lucinda called out. She stood in the doorway as her minions shoved furniture out of the way.

Shane and I thrust and cut at the ticks in front of the twister. They scattered as two of their number fell.

"Leave it!" Lucinda commanded. They all fell back, and Shane and I stood panting in front of the pedestal.

"Do it," Shane repeated.

"But if I activate it, she can come through," I said. "She'll control it again." And I really, really didn't want to leave him.

"I'll stop her," Shane promised.

I looked at the group standing around. There were ten including Lucinda—seven men and three women, all holding weapons. He couldn't fight them all.

"Do it, Abbey," Shane said. He stood with his back to me, a sword in each hand.

"Yes, Abbey, do it," Lucinda echoed.

"Shane . . ."

He looked over his shoulder, and I saw his eyes glow red. His face was feral, changed. He welcomed this fight. He'd been anticipating it for one hundred years.

"You know what you've got to do," he repeated.

I knew. I saw Lucinda grin. She picked up Jamie's sword.

"This has been a long time coming, Shane," she said. "I'm going to enjoy this."

"Not as much as me," Shane replied. "You're going down tonight, Lucinda. One way or another."

"Oh, I'm going somewhere," she agreed. "But down is not it."

I knew she planned to kill me as soon as I activated the twister, and only Shane could stop her. But Lucinda didn't know I had no clue how to start the thing.

Think. Think! What did I do before?

I heard the crash of swords as Shane and Lucinda met in battle. Shane was a wall behind me. My mind screamed, *Turn around, help him. Kill her. Take Shane and run.* But I knew he wouldn't accept that fate. He would die here tonight. I had to get back. I had to save him. I had to save everyone, no matter the cost.

Think.

I touched the hourglass. It moved a fraction of an inch.

Before, I'd touched it and spun it clockwise. Time moved ahead. So, shouldn't I spin it counterclockwise to go back? That made sense, didn't it?

I touched the hourglass on the opposite side and heard a click. I pushed harder. *Click. Click. Click. Click. Click.*

I had to concentrate, concentrate on the exact moment I left.

Charlie . . .

A bright light burst from the pedestal. I turned away from it.

"Shane . . ." I stretched out my hand. "I can't leave you."

Lucinda laughed as she parried a blow from him. The motion spun him toward me. He looked at me. The red glow faded from his eyes, and he raised his sword to his forehead in a salute. Then he pushed me toward the pedestal, dropping his guard.

Lucinda swung her sword.

As I felt my body begin to dissolve, molecule by molecule, Lucinda's sword sliced through Shane's undefended neck. His body turned to dust as I was sucked into the darkness. I screamed but made no sound.

Then I landed in a puddle on the floor.

THIRTY-EIGHT

Charlie!

I threw my arms around my dog's neck and hugged him as he licked the tears that streamed down my face. The plan must have succeeded, because I was sitting in peroxide in a room that looked exactly like the one I'd left so many weeks ago.

I heard a meow and a hiss. Charlie stopped his licking, and he started barking.

"Jayne?"

It was Jayne! The cat arched his back and hissed, and then he jumped onto the ladder that stood off to my side.

"I love you, Charlie," I said as I hugged my dog again. "But you two have got to work this out. I've got to go."

Charlie gave me an obligatory sniff before looking up at Jayne, who twitched his tail threateningly on the ladder. Charlie didn't know I'd been gone for days. As far as he was concerned, I'd been here all along.

I picked up my katana, which had miraculously landed on the floor next to me. I don't know if I'd dropped it when I arrived or if it had somehow made the trip on its own; all I knew was it was there and I needed it.

How much time did I have? I turned to go, but noticed the pedestal was glowing. Was someone coming through?

Shane . . .

The Shane I knew was dead. No, this had to be Lucinda. I tightened my grip on the sword and watched as a form materialized in front of me. It was weird watching the shimmering mass, as I knew that my own body had just gone through the same process. Only, this time there would be a different traveler.

"What, you're surprised I waited around for you?" I said as I swung my katana at Lucinda's elegant neck.

She was surprised. Maybe she'd thought I'd take off as soon as I arrived. The look on her lovely face said it all as her head separated from her body and she slid to the ground.

"Too bad you didn't follow your own advice," I growled at the corpse. "You shouldn't occupy the same time as your other self. It could lead to disaster."

I charged out of the house and down the sidewalk, katana in hand. Would I make it?

My feet pounded on the pavement, splashing through the puddles that remained from last night's rain.

Was it just last night that it rained? It seemed as if years had passed.

They *had* passed. Still, the things they held were yet to occur.

Think about it later. Just run.

I had to get there on time. I just had to. I refused to think about what I'd do if I didn't.

My hand tightened on the hilt of my katana as I ran. The scabbard was laced against my thigh. I didn't even feel it; it had become so much a part of me in the time just past.

When I'd started martial arts training, I'd never even considered the thought that I would use the weapons I worked with to actually kill anyone. It turned out to be one of those funny twists of fate. It was just something that happened. Or it was something I was going to make happen.

One more block. One more block until Shane. One more block until the final showdown.

Don't think about it.

I saw the lights from Java Joe's up ahead.

He'd told me it happened when he left, when he got tired of waiting for me. How long had Shane waited?

The door opened, and my heart skipped a beat as light bounced off golden blond hair and Shane stuck his hands in his pockets and moved down the sidewalk.

"Shane!" I yelled as I tried to run faster.

She would be waiting for him just past the shop in the alleyway.

He didn't hear me. He kept walking, and then he disappeared. He was in the alley.

Shane had told me it happened in the alley. I gripped my katana in both hands as I reached Joe's and flew on by. When I reached the alley I skidded to a stop.

"Hey, Lucy," I called. My heart pounded wildly in my chest. I took a deep breath and willed it into submission. If I made a wrong move, Shane would be lost to me forever.

Lucinda turned. Her bright red hair fell beautifully around her shoulders, and she looked down her aristocratic nose at me. Behind her, Shane stood as if hypnotized, his bright blue eyes staring off into the night as if he were waiting for something. If only he knew what fate had planned for him.

"How do you . . . ?" Lucinda stopped suddenly and

looked me over appraisingly. "You know," she said. "You did it. You opened the gate."

"I did," I agreed. I held my katana firmly in my right hand and stood balanced on the soles of my feet, my legs slightly apart. Ready . . . waiting . . . willing to do whatever I needed to do to stop her.

"I think I'll keep him anyway," she said with a flip of her hair. "It will be fun to watch him fight against his nature."

"He's mine," I snarled. "He will always be mine, no matter what you do to him."

"How about if I kill him?" she said.

I twisted the blade of my katana so that it caught the streetlight and bounced its rays off Lucy's face. That also must have awakened Shane from whatever trance she'd put him in. He blinked and looked over Lucinda's shoulder at me.

"What's going on?" he asked. "What are you doing?" He looked in shock at my katana, which was now so much a part of me that I barely noticed I was holding it.

"Lucy and I have some unfinished business," I said.

"You told me you didn't know her," he said accusingly. My heart lurched at his tone, at the strangeness he clearly felt around me. I would fix that. I had to fix that, or I might as well have stayed where I was. Shane would be dead to me here, too.

But first I had to take care of something else. Or all the moments just past were meaningless.

"Oh, Lucy and I go way back," I said. "Don't we?"

"Do we?" she asked.

"About a hundred years, give or take a few."

"I'm out of here," Shane said.

He took a step, but Lucinda slammed him against the wall. With one hand closed around his throat she lifted him in the air so that his feet dangled over the ground.

She kept her eyes on me; even when Shane grabbed her wrists and kicked her in the side, she barely flinched.

"Put him down, Lucy," I said.

"Make me," she replied.

I looked back at Shane, who was desperately gasping for breath, his face full of confusion. I had to make sure he stayed. If he ran, then I might lose him forever. So I said the only thing that made any sense at all in the current madness that my life had become.

"Ninjas are way cooler than pirates."

I swung my katana then, and Lucinda dropped Shane and jumped out of the way. She flipped back the sides of her long coat and pulled out two slim blades from her tall boots. She crossed the blades and thrust them toward me so that sparks flew in the darkened alley.

I stepped between her and Shane, who knelt gasping against the wall with his hand to his throat. "You two are crazy," he said hoarsely.

"Just hear me out," I said, keeping a close eye on Lucinda. "No matter what you see here, keep an open mind."

"Oh, how sweet," Lucinda said. "Did you know your girlfriend was psychotic?"

"At least I'm not a murderer," I said. "And by the way, this will be the second time tonight that I've killed you."

"Thanks for the warning," she laughed. "I'll remember when I get to that place in time."

"Psychotic," I heard Shane repeat. "That doesn't even start to explain this."

"Tell me about it," I said.

Lucinda now knew that the time-twister was activated. All she had to do was kill me, and she would have control over it for eternity. Her eternity. There was nothing to stop her from attacking me. She had everything she wanted right before her. It was just a matter of victory.

I saw her eyes change from pale blue to a bright red glow, and met her two blades with my own. There was a flurry of exchanged blows and then I made her lock her thin blades against the greater width of mine. We pushed against each other, our steel singing as we tried to will each other back with greater strength. She was taller than me, lithe, and limber, but I was stronger and she stumbled back.

She flipped her blades around, showing her skill, and I was impressed. But if she was so good, then why hadn't she just come after me that first night when I didn't have a clue as to what I was doing?

Because she feared me. I could see it in her eyes. Even though they glowed with her craving, there was fear there.

I was the Guardian, and she feared me. I felt a power surge through my body. I was the Guardian. I was the good to counteract her evil. I was the balance against everything that she wanted to change. I would not fail.

My sword became a blur as I beat her toward the street. Shane was trapped behind me; the alley was a dead end, and there was no place for him to go.

Lucy's blades and my own flew and crashed like cymbals as we dodged and ducked and parried and attacked. Back and forth we moved like dancers, and I felt Shane's eyes upon us. I willed him to stay put, even though I could not take my eyes off Lucinda for an instant.

She tried to move his way, but I did not let her get by. She would use him against me.

The movement of our long coats served as protection. It was hard to see where a body ended and fabric began as we advanced and retreated. Finally, I scored a hit across Lucinda's thigh, and she countered with a slash across my cheek while my arm was down. My head whipped back and to the side, and she slashed my right arm. She followed that with a high kick that knocked the katana from my hand. I watched the sword fly loose and dove toward it, but Lucinda was right on me, anticipating my move. She kicked it away and raised one of her weapons to stab me in the heart.

"No!" I heard Shane yell.

She looked his way. For an instant. Enough to let me know that he was next.

That was all I needed. I pulled the extra sword I'd worn loose from its scabbard and drove it into her abdomen.

Lucinda looked down at me in shock. I didn't have time to mess around. I pushed with all my strength, rising to shove her against the wall. She gasped and reached for the sword in her. As soon as she pulled it out, she would heal. But I picked up my katana and swung at her neck.

Her bright red hair flew everywhere as it was sliced away. Her head followed, toppling over her shoulders and to the ground. Her body slid down the wall.

"What did you do?" Shane asked as he came up beside me.

"Wait," I said quietly.

We stood there, me holding my breath, knowing that the next instant would make all the difference regarding whether or not he would listen to me.

I'd been told the ancients died with dignity and beauty. That was true. Lucinda's body slowly dissolved until there was nothing left but a pile of what looked like glitter lying in the street. Then a swirl of wind

caught it and blew it away, and there was nothing left
but three swords—mine and hers—lying on the ground.

I let out my breath in a deep sigh, and looked at
Shane. It took me a second to realize his hair was short-
cropped again. I was so used to it being long and falling
over his eyes. His beautiful blue eyes.

"You're hurt," he said. He touched my cheek, then his
eyes widened as I felt the gash close. He looked at the
blood on his hand and then back at me. "Do you mind
explaining to me what just happened?" he said.
"Who . . . *what* was that?"

I looked at my katana. Blood and hair covered it,
both bright red. For some strange reason I stuck my
hand in my coat pocket and realized there was a rag inside. *Jamie.* He'd made sure I had something to clean
my weapons with. I wiped the katana clean and stuck it
back in its sheath.

"You want to get some coffee?" I asked.

"Coffee?" He shoved his hand through his hair in a
movement that was so familiar it hurt. I wanted to grab
him and kiss him. I wanted to hold him and never let go.

But that would have to wait.

"Sure," he said, and he looked around the alley as if
to make sure he hadn't missed anything. "Why not?"

I reached out my hand, hoping, praying, and wishing
that he would take it.

He did.

"You are going to tell me about all this, aren't you?"
he said.

"Yes," I said as we started towards Joe's. "I will tell you
everything."

"Wait a minute," he said. "How . . . how did you know
about ninjas being way cooler than pirates? Where did
you hear that?"

"You told me," I said.

"I did? I don't remember."

"That's because it hasn't happened yet. For you."

He opened the door to Joe's. "I might need something stronger than coffee for this," he said.

Coffee. How I craved it. But the memory of my caffeine withdrawal was still fresh, and there was no time like the present to make a change. "Not me," I replied as I looked up and saw Joe's familiar face. "From here on out I'm drinking decaf."

THIRTY-NINE

"What happened to snowboarding?" I asked the shop owner as he fixed our coffee.

"What a waste of time," Joe said. "I traveled all that way and no snow. So I just turned around and came back." He looked pointedly at the katana strapped to my thigh. "That's a nice look for you," he said. "Kind of a cross between *The Matrix* and *Alias*."

"Yeah," I said. "Thanks. I've been thinking about changing my image."

"Looks can be deceiving," Shane remarked. I cast a sideways look at him. I'd figured he'd be in shock; instead, he just seemed kind of amused. Pretty cool for a guy who had almost become immortal.

Or dead.

"I always thought you two should meet," Joe whispered as Shane turned to find us a table. "I guess last night was great timing."

"Yeah," I said. "Timing is everything."

I joined Shane at a quiet table in the corner and took a sip of my decaf. I felt a pang of guilt about leaving Charlie so quickly after I'd returned, but then I remembered. For Charlie, I'd never been gone.

Plus, now he had Jayne to keep him company. I wondered how that was working out.

"What's so funny?" Shane asked.

I looked up at him in surprise.

"You've got this look on your face," he began.

"I was just thinking about Charlie," I said.

"Your dog."

"Yes." I grinned. "Did I mention I have a cat, too?"

"At this point you could say you have a pet unicorn and I wouldn't find it strange," Shane said. "Now, do you mind telling me what just happened?"

"What do you remember?" I asked. "From the alley?"

He took a sip of his coffee and got a strange look on his face. "It's funny," he said. "I don't remember how I got there. I just suddenly remember seeing you there, with that sword in your hand."

"I was running a bit late," I said.

"I thought you said last night that you didn't know that woman."

"Last night I didn't know her," I said.

"She wasn't . . . human . . . was she?"

"No," I said. "It's a long story, Shane. A lot has happened since the last time I saw you."

"What happened to your bandage?" he asked and pointed to my arm.

"I don't need it anymore. It's healed."

Shane took my arm and pushed up the sleeve of my coat. "How?" he asked.

"Like I said, a lot has happened since the last time I saw you."

"Does any of it involve ninjas and pirates?" he asked.

"As a matter of fact, it does. And there are some ticks involved, too."

"Ticks?" he said. "It sounds interesting." He sat back in

his chair. "Go ahead," he said. "I'm listening. I've got all the time in the world."

Lucky for me, now he did.

Even better, he seemed to believe me. Of course, I had to show him the time-twister and there was no other explanation for the things that I knew. Things about him and his brother that he'd never told anyone.

We didn't mention any of these things when he took me to meet his parents several weeks later. We weren't sure how they'd feel about their future daughter-in-law being a Time Guardian, so we left the introduction to "She's an architectural student who flips houses."

By that time, Shane and I were living together, since my house was so convenient to the hospital. We also figured we'd wasted enough time pretending we weren't interested in each other while riding the El.

The house turned out beautiful. Shane was a big help. The last job we tackled was refinishing the wood floors downstairs.

"So, I guess we just work around this thing?" Shane asked, motioning to the time-twister as he brought in the sander I'd rented.

"I'm afraid to move it," I said. "I don't know what repercussions there'd be."

Shane knelt down to examine the floor nearby. "You mean, things like the earth changing its axis and continents disappearing and such?" He shoved Charlie's head away as the dog sniffed around the pedestal.

I came over beside him, and Jayne followed. "I don't want to take any chances until I know more about it," I said. "I watched you die once . . ."

He put his arm around me and kissed me. "It's going to be a long time before I turn to dust," he said.

"I hope so," I replied.

Shane laughed and glanced behind me. "What is that crazy cat doing now?" Jayne was standing on his hind legs and batting at the carving on the pedestal with his paws. We heard a strange click, and we both shot backward in case any light suddenly appeared.

Instead, a panel opened and Jayne stuck his head inside.

Shane and I cautiously looked into the open panel. Inside was a thick book. I pulled it out. It appeared to be ancient.

"What is it?" Shane asked, as I gently flipped the pages.

I shook my head in wonder. "I think it's my family history," I said.

Shane grinned. "Check and see if there're any operating instructions in there. Maybe there's something about making time stand still."

"Why do you want to make time stand still?" I asked.

Shane wrapped his arms around my waist and gently kissed me. "So we can stay like this forever."

"That's fine with me," I said and closed the book. Time was precious. I could read later. "This is where I want to stay."

I've decided my fate. No more twists for me.

WIN
A PUBLISHING CONTRACT!

Ever dream of publishing your own novel?

Here's your chance!

Dorchester Publishing is offering fans of **SHOMI** a chance to win a guaranteed publishing contract with distribution throughout the US and Canada!

For complete submission guidelines and contest rules & regulations, please visit:

www.shomifiction.com/contests.html

ALL ENTRIES MUST BE RECEIVED BY APRIL 30, 2008.

The future of romance where anything is possible.